THE POOL

THE POOL

HANNAH TUNNICLIFFE

ultimo press

ultimo press

Published in 2025 by Ultimo Press,
an imprint of Hardie Grant Publishing

Ultimo Press
Gadigal Country
7, 45 Jones Street
Ultimo, NSW 2007
ultimopress.com.au

⌾ 𝕏 ⓕ ultimopress

All rights reserved. No part of this publication may be reproduced, stored in a retrieval system or transmitted in any form by any means, electronic, mechanical, photocopying, recording or otherwise, without the prior written permission of the publishers and copyright holders.

The moral rights of the author have been asserted.

Copyright © Hannah Tunnicliffe 2025

A catalogue record for this book is available from the National Library of Australia

The Pool
ISBN 978 1 76115 365 5 (paperback)

Cover design Andy Warren Design
Cover image by Stanley Dai / Unsplash
Author photo Courtesy of Michelle Sokolich
Text design Simon Paterson, Bookhouse
Typesetting Bookhouse, Sydney | 12.75/16.5 pt Adobe Garamond Pro
Copyeditor Dianne Blacklock
Proofreader Pamela Dunne

10 9 8 7 6 5 4 3 2 1

Printed in Australia by Opus Group Pty Ltd, an Accredited ISO AS/NZS 14001 Environmental Management System printer.

MIX
Paper | Supporting responsible forestry
FSC® C018684

The paper this book is printed on is certified against the Forest Stewardship Council® Standards. Griffin Press – a member of the Opus Group – holds chain of custody certification SCS-COC-001185. FSC® promotes environmentally responsible, socially beneficial and economically viable management of the world's forests.

Ultimo Press acknowledges the Traditional Owners of the Country on which we work, the Gadigal People of the Eora Nation and the Wurundjeri People of the Kulin Nation, and recognises their continuing connection to the land, waters and culture. We pay our respects to their Elders past and present.

THIS ONE IS FOR YOU, LIZZIE.

MY SHARONA, DEEP AND MEANINGFULS,
CUPS OF TEA AND SISTERLY LOVE FOREVER X

'My stars shine darkly over me; the malignancy of my fate might, perhaps, distemper yours; therefore I shall crave of you your leave that I may bear my evils alone.'

WILLIAM SHAKESPEARE – SEBASTIAN IN *TWELFTH NIGHT*

PROLOGUE
BAZ

There is a moment before my body lies in a pool of its own dark blood – black as the moonless night, black as the crow with its death caw, black as the road I left behind – when time is a single thing. The future is now, the past is now. A thunder clap. Everything, all at once.

It is a murmuration of moments – swelling, expanding and moving.

I am at my wedding and Jemima's wedding and Joe's birth and my own funeral. I am singing, I am weeping, I am pretending not to care.

I have sand between my toddler toes on St Kilda beach. I watch Birdie with our grandchild doing the very same thing, her mouth open and laughing.

I am holding Joe's small warm hand and I am also holding it, cold, to my lips before I say goodbye. Both true, both at once.

I am twelve and twenty-three and forty-five. I have skin as soft as milk and knees that don't work and I am lying, all the time lying. Small deceits that become larger deceits, that become easier and easier to tell.

I am kissing for the first time and the last time.

I am betraying the people I love the most.

I am smashing my mother's favourite vase just to see what it feels like, the pieces scattering across the kitchen floor. I am falling off the monkey bars in Year 3 and fracturing my arm. I am splintering Birdie's heart.

And I am flying off the side of a cliff and breaking.

All of me breaking.

NINE YEARS BEFORE

THE BARBECUE

Joe hangs off Birdie's side as she presses her forefinger against Tamsin Turner's doorbell. It's a cracking day in Hawthorn with only one week left in the school term. Clear and baking, the sunshine is good enough to bottle. Parakeets flirt in the wattle trees, the cloudless sky opens its arms wide. The breeze is Goldilocks-perfect. The kind of day that convinces you that nothing can go wrong.

'I'm sure we can borrow some goggles, Jem,' Baz is saying to their daughter. 'Wyatt's mum probably has loads of goggles.'

Jemima's lips thin as she presses them together hard. Her red hair, exactly like her mother's, looks electrified. Birdie shifts Joe to her other hip; he's getting too big for lugging but she doesn't put him down.

'I'll have a look in the swimming bag when we get inside,' she soothes. 'They might be in there.'

Baz tugs at the collar of his work shirt; he's come straight from the office. 'I already looked.'

'Won't hurt to check again.'

'I have eyes, Birdie. I'm not an idiot,' he snaps.

'I wasn't trying to—'

'I told her to pack her goggles this morning so if she doesn't have them she doesn't have them. She needs to learn.'

'She's six, Baz.'

'You baby them.'

Birdie sighs and rolls her eyes.

'Look, I know you don't want to be here,' Baz mutters, 'but it's good for business and the kids will see their friends.'

'I never said I didn't want to be here.'

'You didn't have to.'

The sleek black door swings open and Tamsin Turner appears, small, white and fragrant as a frangipani flower. The pale linen she is wearing makes Birdie think of potential stains. She captures Joe's fat fist in one hand, as though he might reach out and taint her.

'Hey!' Baz greets her with a glittering smile.

The air conditioning from inside the house reaches out and strokes the small hairs on the back of Birdie's neck. Tamsin's scent travels on its fingertips; it's the same perfume that Abigail Meyer wears. Birdie squares her shoulders and longs for a cold glass of wine.

'The Kings!' Tamsin declares, smile wide and teeth to match her blouse. 'Come in, come in!' She squints at Joe and ruffles his hair as though it's the first time she's seen it. 'I just can't get over this hair!'

Joe and Birdie both flinch. Baz throws an arm around Jem, drawing her towards him. 'Bluey Adamses, the lot of them!'

Only Tamsin and Baz laugh. Tamsin lifts herself onto the balls of her feet to reach Baz's cheek. She's short and slight, the kind of woman he'd pop on his shoulders at a concert.

'I want *my* goggles,' Jem mumbles again, now glaring at Tamsin, who beckons them all inside.

The Turners have done renovations. It's the real reason for the invite. Light pours in, accompanied by splashing and laughing, through the large glass sliding doors added to the back of the house. Tamsin bounces into the kitchen, which faces the pool.

'Thirsty?' she asks. 'Bubbles? Rosé? Prosecco?'

Baz drops the swimming bag by the kitchen counter. It's a big blue IKEA shopping bag with yellow handles and he can't stand it. Birdie keeps it for that reason. 'You have any beer?'

'Corona?'

'Perfect. Thanks, Tam.'

Tamsin's husband, Alex, strides in from outside. He's shorter than Baz. Birdie watches him lift his chest as he approaches, trying to get a few more inches. He reaches out to pump Baz's hand. 'Mate!'

'You're dripping all over the floor!' Tamsin scolds.

Alex throws back his shaved head and laughs like the neighbours need to hear it. He's wearing board shorts and a white linen shirt to match his wife's. It looks brand new.

'I paid for it so I reckon I can drip on it. Am I right?'

Baz grips his shoulder. 'You're the drip, mate.'

Alex Turner greets Birdie then, leaving a thick, wet kiss on her cheek. Joe tucks his head into his mother's chest as though he might be next. Tamsin passes Baz a bottle of beer, a wedge of lime stuffed in the neck.

'Come out to the barbie,' Alex insists, gesturing outside.

Birdie knows he doesn't mean her. Baz looks where Alex is pointing and they both see Jess Dhillon, tucking her hair behind her ear. She moves her fingers slowly in a coy wave.

Jem tugs on the hem of Birdie's t-shirt. 'I wanna go for a swim.'

'Okay darling, we'll just—'

Baz heads outside with Alex, whose wide palm is pressed against the back of Baz's work shirt. Jess, the mother of three boys, is wearing a short floral dress. She has golden skin and smooth long limbs and wears a quartz pendant on a silver necklace. She has an easy smile like nothing bothers her.

'Go for it, Jem, honey!' Tamsin encourages. 'Rose and Queenie are in the pool with their mummy. My lot too . . . Wyatt? Wyatt!'

Birdie's gaze swivels to the Turners' new swimming pool and surrounding garden. When she was last in Tamsin's house, the backyard was mostly grass, burned brown, and a Hill's hoist in the centre like a dead Christmas tree. Now it's lined with hydrangeas and neatly snipped buxus, the corners marked by magnolia trees. Creamy, saucer-sized flowers bloom among the dark green and copper-coloured leaves.

Wyatt Turner, the same age and in the same class as Jemima, thumps into the room with a wet faux hawk. His confidence is unshakeable. He looks at Tamsin like he's got places to be. 'What, Mum?'

Tamsin's voice is tender. 'Show Jemima and Joe the bathroom so they can get changed into their swimmers?'

Wyatt rolls his eyes.

'What can I get you to drink, Birdie?'

Birdie puts Joe down. He holds his favourite toy rabbit by one ear. She and Baz hadn't agreed who would drive home.

'Bubbles?'

'Sure.'

Tamsin's new fridge has French doors and her dishwasher drawers are hidden behind custom cabinetry. Tamsin cheerfully explains the built-in ice machine, the temperature-controlled wine cupboard and the induction cooktop. Then she reaches for a large bottle of Veuve Clicquot and pours some into a tall flute.

Once upon a time, Birdie would have been interested or able to pretend that she was interested, but Tamsin has barely spoken to her in months since she became friends with Abigail Meyer. Birdie was surprised to get the invitation to the end-of-year barbecue.

She accepts the glass Tamsin offers her. 'Are the Meyers coming?'

Tamsin's smile tightens. 'No, can you believe it? Abi's got a migraine. Poor thing.'

'Poor thing,' Birdie repeats.

'Disaster,' Tamsin says, looking like she means it too. 'She gets them really bad.'

The champagne sizzles on Birdie's tongue.

'Madison is here though.' Tamsin nods towards the backyard, her voice aiming for insouciance but falling short. 'With Indi and Camilla.'

Birdie turns back to the garden, now seeing Abigail's nanny, Madison, on the new lawn. The young woman has a small tribe of children with her – Jess's boys and Abigail's girls combined – all trampling the pure, golf-green turf.

Birdie rolls the champagne around in her mouth, grateful for the way it numbs as it slides down her throat. 'Garden looks amazing,' she says.

'Thank you. Cost a fortune . . .' Tamsin laughs. 'But what are you going to do?'

'I like the magnolias.'

'Leaves drop everywhere, I've been warned, but the flowers are beautiful.'

Birdie can see the bees diving in and out of the waxy bowls of blooms where nectar has pooled. They'll be working themselves to death storing up for winter. Birdie has always liked the coppery suede secret underside of magnolia leaves.

'Alex says Baz might have some work for him?'

Birdie drinks more champagne. 'Oh?'

'A property developer. Frank somebody. Sounds like a big shot.'

'I don't know him.'

'Well, it's nice of Baz. The mortgage is crazy.' Tamsin glances at Birdie and quickly adds, 'We're fine obviously.'

'Of course,' Birdie reassures. 'But who couldn't use extra?'

'Exactly.' Tamsin smiles, relieved.

In the pool, Paloma Albertini is throwing one of her girls into the air. Birdie can usually tell the twin girls apart but not when they're wet and wearing matching swimsuits.

Tamsin says, 'I invited Mr Lee, did I tell you?' She studies Birdie's face.

'Did he say yes?'

'Said he'd come after he gets the classroom tidied up. Sweet of him, don't you think?'

Birdie shrugs. 'Doesn't he want a break from our kids?'

Tamsin laughs. 'Well, end-of-year barbecue . . . I figured I should. And, you know, I think he was grateful for the invite. Don't think he has much of a life outside of teaching.' Tamsin leaves a pause. 'Poor guy.'

Birdie says nothing.

'He could do with getting out more,' Tamsin adds.

'He's been a great teacher,' Birdie says carefully.

'Yes!' Tamsin's eyes light up. 'I wasn't sure to start with. A *male* teacher? You know . . .'

'Jem loved him,' Birdie says.

Tamsin scrunches up her nose. It's a playful look Birdie imagines some men find adorable. She lowers her voice. 'He's kinda cute, right?'

'Mr Lee?'

Tamsin titters. 'Birdie! When you call him "Mr Lee" it makes him sound like a pensioner! He's not *not* cute, right?'

'I hadn't thought about it,' Birdie says, not sure if she can trust Tamsin with her opinion. 'Not *not* cute, I suppose.'

Chin raised, Jemima prances into the lounge. She is wearing her swimsuit, printed to look like a mermaid with purple, green and blue metallic scales. Shimmering, she pushes her goggles into her mother's free hand.

'You found them,' Birdie remarks.

'They were in the bag.' Jemima manages to sound accusing.

'You do the eyes,' Birdie instructs. Jemima presses the goggles to her face so Birdie can pull the strap up and over her head. 'There you go.'

Jemima heads to the pool, hair wild and mermaid scales winking. The swimsuit is already a bit small even though Birdie only bought it a few months ago. It gives her a catch in her chest. She glances down at Joe, who is clinging to his rabbit and is pressed against her leg. His soft pink cheek is warm against her skin and Birdie feels relieved he's still small. Still hers.

Tamsin is staring out at the pool. Her head is propped on her hands.

Outside, Paloma's girls are sitting on the edge of the pool, playing Humpty Dumpty. Rose and Queenie take turns to drop in with a splash. Their happy shrieks scatter through the air like handfuls of shiny coins. The three of them are carbon copies: dark-haired and dark-eyed with thick wilful eyebrows and expressive mouths. Paloma Albertini is younger than the rest of them, a single mum still in her twenties. Birdie likes her – Paloma is perceptive and funny. But she usually keeps to herself, so Birdie is surprised that Tamsin invited her and that Paloma said yes. In the water she's like a Renaissance painting, a version of *Venus* by Botticelli. Plump, soft and luminous, the water beads on her skin and shines in her hair.

With a delicate sigh, Tamsin murmurs, 'Shame. She could be really pretty.'

•

Birdie sits next to Richard Dhillon at the side of the pool. He offers her a silver bowl. 'Chips? They're the expensive kind.'

She takes a handful before he turns to Joe.

'Want some, buddy?'

Joe shakes his head. He's chewing the ear of his toy.

'Rabbit is tastier? Fair enough. But I'm going to take your share home in my pockets, okay, Joe? Deal?'

Richard looks like a parrot. The pattern on his bright shirt clashes with his orange and blue board shorts. His build is ropey and restless. He slips his feet out of worn thongs. 'How are you going, Birdie?'

'I'm okay. How are you?'

Their eyes slide towards the barbecue – Jess, Alex and Baz are cooking sausages. The three of them laugh and shove each other's shoulders.

'I'm glad to be almost at the finish line. Taking the summer off to be with the boys.'

Richard is a builder. He does a lot of house renovations in Hawthorn and the occasional new build. He has a small crew – a couple of older guys and one young scrawny apprentice who looks like he's about to be eaten by wolves as an appetiser. Richard gets roped into helping at the school, building stage sets, fixing fences, digging a sandpit, making trestle tables for the annual bake sale.

When they're in a group and the dads split off, Richard always stays with the mothers. He's kind and makes bad jokes. Birdie knows more about Richard than she knows about Jess – that he makes a great kedgeree, is allergic to mangoes and has a tattoo of Donald Duck on his shoulder blade, a mistake explained by too many Bundy and Cokes during a night at Chasers on Chapel Street.

'You wrap up next Friday too?'

'Yup. I'm almost done. Aside from soul-crushing amounts of paperwork and invoicing.'

On the lawn, Madison is holding Richard's son Monty under his armpits. She's twirling him round and round, Monty yowling with delight.

'How are the boys?'

Richard laughs. 'Three under six? What were we thinking?'

'I don't know how you do it.'

'Well, Jess does most of it,' Richard says quickly.

Birdie knows that Baz would never give credit that easily, but Richard is generous and loyal. Loyal to Jess, his boys and the Richmond Tigers, in that order. Standing by the barbecue, Jess is listening to something Baz is saying. Her face is upturned and reflective, a girl with a buttercup under her chin. Her eyes are transfixed on Baz's mouth, like she wants to kiss it and everything that falls from it.

'Frank somebody,' Birdie says.

'Sorry?'

'Tamsin mentioned that Baz is working with a property developer called Frank somebody. Says he might throw some work Alex's way.'

Richard's eyes narrow slightly. 'Frank Agosti?'

'Do you know him?'

He shrugs. 'Not personally. But by reputation, yeah. Why?'

Birdie doesn't look back towards her husband but feels her cheeks redden. 'No reason. Showing an interest, I guess.'

Richard throws some chips into his mouth and waits till he's finished chewing before answering. 'Frank has the contract for the apartments where the old Belwood Community Centre used to be.'

'Oh, right. Okay.'

She turns now towards Alex, Baz and Jess. There's something about how close they're standing that makes her feel a bit sick in her gut. 'It's nice if they can work together. Alex and Baz, I mean.'

Richard glances towards his wife. 'Yeah, I suppose.'

He changes the subject. 'Did you see this photograph she took of the boys at the beach a couple of months ago?'

He scrolls through his phone and holds up the snap. Jack, Monty and Harrison are mid-yahoo as the foam of a wave swirls around their middles. Harrison looks up at his big brothers while

Jack's and Monty's eyes are squeezed shut in delight. Their bodies shine in the summer afternoon light.

'It's great, right? I keep telling her she should be a photographer.'

'It's really good,' Birdie replies, trying not to sound bitter.

Tamsin is walking towards the barbecue and Birdie watches as Jess turns and smiles, her lips lightly glossed and her golden hair catching the sunlight. Tamsin is carrying a plate of raw steaks in one hand and a champagne bottle in the other. Blood slips from the plate and hits Tamsin's new tiles.

'She's so talented,' Richard continues.

'Talented . . . yeah,' Birdie murmurs, picking at the hem of her t-shirt, envious of Richard's easy praise for his wife, the affection in his voice.

Jemima stands on the edge of the pool with her hands pressed high above her head, lips tightly closed. 'Eiffel Tower' is what her swimming teacher calls it. She dives into the pool lopsided, almost crashing into Paloma.

Birdie turns away from Richard. 'Sorry!' she calls out, hand to her cheek.

Paloma laughs. Water rolls down her face.

•

'What are we talking about?' Tamsin appears suddenly and takes a seat. She declines Richard's offer of chips. Birdie swallows another mouthful of her drink. It scorches on the way down.

'The kids finishing their first year of school,' he says. 'It went so quickly. And Albert was great with them, wasn't he? Such a good start for them.'

'Birdie and I were just saying that!' Tamsin nudges Richard's arm happily. 'Weren't we, Birdie?'

Tamsin leans in. 'You know, Abi and I were thinking . . . him and . . .' She tips her head towards the pool and Paloma bobbing in the water. Richard laughs awkwardly.

'You can see it, right?'

In the pool, Wyatt does a bomb and water sloshes over the edge. Tamsin's daughter Charlotte, who everyone calls Charlie, shouts, 'Mum! Wyatt!'

Tamsin waves it away. 'Just ignore him, Charlie!' Then, turning towards Richard and rolling her eyes, 'Boys.' Tamsin tops up Birdie's glass as Jack Dhillon, wearing pink swimming shorts with red lobsters, sidles up to his father. He leans against his shins.

'Going in again, buddy?' Richard asks.

Joe pulls at his mother's t-shirt, his eyes on Jack. 'I wanna swim.'

Birdie looks at her freshly poured champagne. 'I don't think so, darling. Wait till Daddy gets in.'

Jack opens the pool gate and stands by the edge. Wyatt shouts for him to get in.

'I hot too,' Joe complains.

Birdie cups his small face with the hand that was holding her glass. 'Is that better?'

'I wanna swim too.'

Birdie smooths Joe's hair away from his wide eyes.

'Please?' Joe has a slight lisp.

Before the kids came along, Birdie had almost finished a masters in speech therapy. She knows the lisp will go eventually. Joe's voice will become clearer and firmer as he grows and Birdie will miss this version of him.

'I don't know if I brought your floaties, mate.'

'Bugger,' Tamsin interjects. 'I just gave Wyatt's away to a neighbour.' She turns to Richard. 'Does Monty have some?'

Richard shakes his head. 'Grommets. Just put in. Has to stay out of the water for a week.'

'Oh, what a shame! Poor Monty! Jess didn't say.'

'Mama?' Joe pleads.

'It is very hot,' Tamsin says. 'Could he stay on the steps?'

Birdie looks over at her husband. Jess's hand, light as a bird, has landed on Baz's shoulder. He's leaning towards her, ear close to her mouth.

'Wait just a little bit longer, Joe-Joe,' Birdie says. 'Daddy said he'd get in with you.'

•

Birdie watches Baz heading back inside the house and follows him, Joe trailing close behind. Joe goes to the lounge to annoy the Turner's aging cat and Birdie slips into the bathroom behind her husband.

'Listen,' she appeals, 'Joe wants to go in the pool, and you said—'

'Alex burned the steaks,' he says, shaking his head.

'We can probably go without,' Birdie suggests. She knows that fetching new steaks and cooking them will drag the afternoon out even longer.

Baz sniffs. 'A barbecue without steaks?'

When Baz met Birdie she was a vegetarian. It took four months of needling and teasing to get her to eat a cheeseburger while sitting in his lap at a booth in McDonald's on Lonsdale Street. She'd been drunk on vodka and orange juice. Birdie still remembers the taste of it coming back up later. But she'd eaten meat ever since because it was easier than dealing with Baz's constant persuasion. He was sly and relentless. Born to be a lobbyist.

'He's nipped out to get more,' Baz says.

Birdie looks in the bathroom mirror and tucks her t-shirt into the waistband of her shorts. They're a few years old and the elastic is starting to give up.

'Joe wants to go swimming.'

'Sure.'

'You said you'd go in with him.'

Baz unzips his pants. The cufflinks she bought for his birthday glint. Baz loves a shirt that requires cufflinks; these ones are silver discs with prints of Jem's hand and Joe's tiny foot. The cufflinks are the only sentimental thing she's bought him that he actually likes.

Baz ignores her. He snorts, 'Jess didn't know Mandela had died.'

'Sorry?'

'Nelson Mandela. Jess didn't even know he'd died.'

Surprising even herself, Birdie feels defensive. 'She's got young kids, Baz.'

'You'd have to be living under a rock.'

Baz is building the narrative that Jess is stupid to convince her that someone like him would never have an affair with someone like her. It's so transparent it's an insult to Birdie's intelligence. She bites down on nothing, molars meeting molars.

'Joe,' she says again, more firmly and resisting the urge to slap him. 'Joe wants to swim.'

'I'm helping with the barbecue, Birdie.'

'He's hot,' she insists.

Baz's urine hits the bowl in a loud stream. 'Then why don't you go in with him?'

'You said you would.'

'Well, I didn't know Alex was such a dickhead with a barbie, did I?'

'I didn't bring my rashie, Baz.'

Baz shakes and zips himself back into his pants. Birdie looks down at her feet, the black and white geometric floor tiles making her eyes hurt. By the sink there's a basket piled high with handtowels formed into sushi rolls. Baz reaches for one after washing his hands.

'Why don't you see if Richard's going in?'

Baz leans in close to the bathroom mirror. His contacts have been playing up lately. As a kid he wore glasses. Braces too. He hates photos from his childhood.

Birdie tries hard not to be petulant. Baz hates a sulker.

'Richard?' she echoes. 'He's already been in and you said—'

Baz turns to her and sighs. 'I'm just being practical, Birdie. Joe can wait till after the steaks are done *or* you can go in with him *or* he can go in with someone else. Three good options, right?'

Practical. The icy burn of it. Birdie grinds her teeth again. 'I guess.'

Baz pats her shoulder as he leaves.

•

Joe's face is brighter than Christmas lights.

Birdie pulls up his tiny swimmers covered in rainbow-coloured budgies. She got them for his birthday, and adult ones for Baz that matched. Birdie's mother-in-law, Patricia, had been horrified.

'Aren't they a bit . . . you know?' she'd whispered over a sherry.

Joe always asked for them – 'the birdy ones'. It made Birdie so happy. Her father had nicknamed her 'Birdie' on account of her red hair, said it reminded him of a parakeet. Her given name, Martina, was a tribute to her mother's father, Martin. He was the grandfather Birdie had never warmed to.

'Baby,' she says, crouching down. Her legs feel wobbly and she tries to count up how many drinks she's had. 'You have to promise me that you'll stay on the steps.'

Joe nods. Though he's only four, he is a responsible kid. He likes to be good.

'I know you think you can swim but that's with your floaties on,' Birdie warns. 'We don't have your floaties here so you can't go in the deep end.'

'I know,' he says.

'Yeah, you know.' Birdie kisses his head and lifts herself up. 'Okay then, bud.'

He's skip-walking, excited, as they head to the pool, his hand in hers. She opens the gate and watches him step down one stair and then two.

'No more than that!'

Joe rests his chin on the top of the water. His lips curl back in a huge smile; he looks like a baby crocodile.

'Did you hear me?'

Joe splashes in reply.

'Jemima?' Birdie calls. Her daughter is down the end of the pool with Paloma and her twins. 'Make sure your brother stays on the steps, please?'

Jemima ignores her. Birdie unclips the pool gate and lets herself out. Richard leans over the glass fence. 'Who wants to do a swimming race?'

Rose and Queenie, Wyatt and Charlie and Jemima all holler 'Yes!'

Birdie rolls her eyes. 'They listen to *you*.'

Richard shrugs.

Birdie sits on the couch closest to the pool steps and watches Charlie win the first swimming race and Wyatt beg for more. Richard comes up with various competitions – backstroke after freestyle, swim 'like a dolphin' after that. Joe remains on the second step, watching, splashing and grinning at the big kids. Alex walks past with a shopping bag and Jess and Baz cheer from the barbecue. Madison is still on the lawn with Monty and Harrison and Camilla and Indigo. She's rubbing sunscreen into Camilla's shoulders, her fingers reaching under the straps of the lacy white dress. The girl, who looks so much like her mother, is pulling away as Madison tries to keep a grip on her wrist. Madison looks weary. Birdie checks Joe again – he's still on the steps, dipping his head under the surface every now and then to blow bubbles.

'All right, Joe-Joe?'

'All right,' he says, smiling.

'Nice and cool?'

He nods in reply.

'Okay to stay there for just a minute?'

He nods again.

•

Birdie grabs two glass Coke bottles out of a bucket of ice and heads towards Madison. She walks past the barbecue as Baz says to Alex, 'You don't have to keep turning them!'

'Don't need a lesson, mate,' Alex mutters.

'I'd say you do. Wouldn't have given your last attempts to a dog.'

Jess laughs like Baz is filling stadiums with his stand-up comedy performances. Birdie gets her husband's attention by calling out in a tone more affectionate than usual, 'Babe?'

Baz turns, slightly startled. 'Hey! Yeah?'

'Keep an eye on Joe for a minute?'

'Hi Birdie,' Jess says. Birdie smiles and turns back to Baz.

'I'm cooking,' he replies.

Birdie glances at the beer in his hand. Alex, wearing an apron with a silicon mould of a woman's naked figure on it, chuckles and waves an egg slice. 'Yeah, he's a real help, Birdie. Don't know what I'd do without him.'

'He needs me,' Baz counters with mock earnestness. Jess laughs again.

'Just a minute, yeah? He's on the steps,' Birdie asks.

Baz reaches over to one of Alex's apron's breasts and squeezes. Birdie looks back at Joe, who's trying to keep water in the cupped palms of his hands. She walks past Alex, Baz and Jess – still giggling breathlessly – to the lawn where Camilla has escaped Madison's grasp. She's sticking her pink tongue out and running around the lawn in circles. She's closely followed by Harrison, his chubby legs pumping and cheeks working at a dummy held between his lips.

Madison looks worn out. She's only young, maybe early to mid-twenties – Birdie has never asked. She's wearing denim shorts with a tight t-shirt tucked in. It stretches over her high round breasts and soft stomach. Fine blonde hair hangs limply down her back.

Birdie passes the Coke to her. 'Thought you might like a drink.'

'Thank you,' Madison replies, her grey eyes impassive. 'I can't get sunscreen on Camilla.'

'Mine hate it too,' Birdie says.

'If she comes home burned, Abigail will be mad.'

Birdie doesn't doubt it. Abigail Meyer is particular and demanding. The coolest, prettiest mother at St Bernard's school gate. Birdie imagines Abigail would be an icy boss.

'They hate the feeling of it, don't they? Can't blame them, I do too.'

Madison nods, putting the soda to her lips. She's quiet and observant, Birdie has noticed, as though she's taking mental notes. Abigail talks about her as though she practically hauled her off the streets. Madison was her hairdresser's assistant – the poor, downtrodden girl who swept hair from the floor and fetched cups of coffee and tea. Abigail had bestowed the nannying job upon her like she was Gabriel in a budget nativity play. 'I don't think she had a very good upbringing,' Abigail could be heard saying in whispers that were too loud to go unheard.

'The sun is fierce these days,' Birdie continues. She looks down at her forearms, the skin peppered with light brown freckles. She tucks a strand of hair behind her ear. Baz once said her hair was the colour of Australia itself, the red of Uluru in picture postcards. 'Mind you, I got burned so much as a kid. Maybe I'm made for the cold.' She smiles.

Madison frowns into the bright sunlight. She tips her head back and swallows the rest of the Coke in one go.

Birdie searches for another topic. 'Friday the thirteenth. Are you superstitious?'

'Sorry?'

Madison's inexpressive face can be unnerving. But Birdie knows what it's like to be on the outer so she tries again. 'It's Friday the thirteenth, 2013. Lots of thirteens?'

Harrison falls over; the hollow percussion of the ground meeting his rib cage makes both women turn. Camilla stands next to him, looking guilty. Like a wind-up toy, it takes Harrison a couple of seconds to start crying.

'Oh baby!' Birdie says, reaching for him.

'He fell!' Camilla protests.

Madison clicks her tongue and smooths his hair.

Harrison's palms pummel at Birdie's arms. 'Mummy! I want Mummy!'

But when Madison and Birdie turn to the barbecue, only Alex is there now, his novelty apron removed, beads of sweat sequinning his bare head. Birdie swivels to the poolside.

Jemima, Wyatt, Charlie. Rose, Queenie, Paloma. Birdie notes them all and keeps searching. Richard is there, his back against the pool fence. He's talking to Tamsin who's sitting on one of the new poolside couches.

Just a minute, she hears inside her head.

The air leaves her lungs. Her son's name fills her mouth.

She looks at the second step of the pool stairs.

It's empty.

FOUR WEEKS BEFORE BAZ IS MISSING

JESS

The day Tamsin's invitation arrives, Jess takes a man to bed. It's the same man she has taken to bed for years now, mostly memory and a fraction fantasy. She imagines him kissing her roughly. He slips his hand down the front of her jeans and when he laughs, Jess longs to make him laugh for the rest of her life. He is pushy and fast and fun like wrestling a dog on the carpet with a chew-toy, unlike Richard, who is slow and careful and doesn't assume permission. The man smells like money. Like leather upholstery in a new car or shirts freshly full of chemicals from the drycleaner. He takes opportunities and risks and isn't always safe or steady. The man likes to bite Jess's neck.

The man doesn't talk about work. He doesn't talk about the kids. He doesn't worry about the mortgage or ask if she knows where the anti-fungal cream has gone. They never argue about who used the last of the milk or the right way to raise a child. In fact, they don't talk at all.

The man is hers. All hers. When she closes her eyes tight he is suddenly there, biting her neck and tossing her onto her front. While Richard asks, 'Is that okay?' the man says, 'You like that, don't you.' and his is not a question. Perhaps they are on a beach late at night, the sand scraping against her bare back, or a city hotel where Jess grips the thick sheets until her knuckles are white. Sometimes they're in the toilet cubicle by the St Bernard's school hall and the cold of the tiles meeting her skin makes her gasp. The man never apologises. He never waits for her approval. He barely seems to care about Jess at all, and that might be the most intoxicating part.

The man is fiction. A fabrication. A mirage. Like this, Jess doesn't have to share him; she can pretend there is no one else but her. But the man has a name, even if Jess tries her best to excise it from her mind. Sometimes she has to bite down to stop herself from saying it out loud.

•

The next morning, Jess's phone rings as she's driving to work through an avenue of eucalyptus trees, bark sagging and hanging in strips.

'I'm in the car,' she says, putting it on speaker.

She can't remember if she packed her 50-millimetre lens. She'd taken it out of her work bag to get some photos of Jack dressed for a date. He'd asked her to edit out the acne on his chin. The clarity you get with a 50-mil lens is sometimes unbearable.

She checks the name on the screen. 'Richard?'

Her husband sounds like he's far away. 'Did you see it?'

'I can't hear you. Are the kids okay?'

'The boys are fine. Tamsin Turner's invite. Did you see it?'

Jess tries to keep her thoughts in the present. The car smells like her sons' footy uniforms – pungent and hormonal. She could pull the car over and check for the lens but she wants to be at the wedding venue early.

She stalls, 'I don't know.'

'How does she even have our address?'

Jess pictures the Turner family Christmas cards. A few years back there was one with a photograph of them all in the snow.

Tamsin, Alex, Wyatt and Charlie among a picket fence of skis and poles, all wearing bright snowsuits with a crown of white-tipped mountains behind them. Jess puts the cards in the bin before Richard sees them.

She starts to feel a bit strange, her foot coming off the accelerator.

Richard is incredulous. 'Celebrating our sweet sixteens, it says. Is it a reunion?'

Jess is dizzy. 'I should get going. I'm sure it's nothing. A mistake.'

'She's written on the back,' Richard continues. '"Getting the old gang back together".'

A ute blares its horn; Jess hadn't noticed it getting closer. She's only going sixty k's an hour. On a motorway. She raises her hand in apology and then flicks the indicator and pulls over. She's suddenly hot and sweating. Her hands grip tight to the wheel.

'Are you still there? Have you seen this?'

Jess laughs. It comes out awkward and slightly strangled. 'I don't think I read it properly, love; probably thought it was advertising.'

'Jess, it says it's a pool party.'

The ute thunders past and Jess feels sweat on the back of her neck. She can't quite get a firm grip on herself. The edges of her body suddenly feel obliterated.

Richard's voice is worried. 'Are you all right?'

'Yes,' Jess says again. The lie is a fishbone in her throat.

•

Jess's bride has dark purple–red nails, deep and shiny as the skins of ripe plums. Her white satin dress falls as though it's made of liquid. Her shoes have square heels covered in rhinestones, which scatter the summer light like mirror balls. Jess takes ten quick photos in a row as she laughs with an open mouth at nothing. The groom, hair thick as fur and sporting a tastefully trimmed beard, squints hopefully beyond Jess's left shoulder at the marquee, humming with guests all having their first champagne of the day.

Jess's thoughts are in the past. Memories of that day, nine years ago, keep rising up like sick. She remembers putting all the boys in shirts rather than t-shirts – even though Harrison had thrown a huge tantrum – to make them look fancy. Because Abigail Meyer was fancy and Tamsin Turner was fancy and Baz King was fancy and Jess wanted to be fancy too. The golden highlights in her hair had been fresh and she'd had a manicure they couldn't afford. The whole day there was a restlessness fizzing in her stomach. A terrific and terrible tingling of being bad in secret. She had loved it, and hated herself for loving it at the same time. When Richard had decided to come with them to the barbecue that day, Baz wasn't upset. If anything it seemed to encourage him.

The bride comes to stand beside her now, looking at the images on the screen of Jess's camera. 'You're so good at this!'

'Thank you.'

'How long have you had your business for?'

'Eight years, give or take.'

Jess swallows. It had all gone wrong. All those years ago she'd thought about getting caught. She'd even thought about running away with Baz somewhere. But she could never have imagined what actually happened, the very worst thing. She could never have guessed how it would actually fall apart.

'Oh, that's right, I asked before. Look at my husband.' The bride gestures towards him with her bouquet. 'Dying to have a drink.'

Jess wracks her brain to recall the groom's name. Polly, the bride, is a beautician who lives in Northcote and is about to buy her own salon. Jess knows Polly's favourite colour, the names of her future children, even that her eyelashes are naturally white-blonde like her hair.

Matthew? Mark? She's been forgetting things like this a lot lately: names, keys, lenses, bills to be paid.

Marcus.

'Facing me, Marcus?' she says, finally, taking more photos. 'That's it. Just a bit more . . . perfect.'

She remembers that Marcus is an electrician who likes to surf and wonders if Polly's ambition and Marcus's lack of it will be the unravelling of them. Jess used to be a romantic. She used to believe in happy endings and good conquering evil. Now she has ungenerous thoughts like this often. She knows that good marriages disintegrate all the time.

It was a miracle that hers and Richard's hadn't. After what happened with Joe in the pool, Tamsin had put the television on. They were all a mess. Jess remembers Jack and his brothers sitting in front of the screen with his classmates, Camilla Meyer and Wyatt Turner. Faces like ghosts, deadly still and illuminated by the greenish light. The paramedic had given them all stickers. One each. He'd been sweet, but stickers weren't going to solve anything. Out of pity, he gave Jemima King a whole sheet.

Her eye on the viewfinder, Jess frames Polly and Marcus holding hands and looking earnest, with tall hedges on either side. She tries not to think of Joe King's sweet and pensive face. But he comes to her anyway. Turning to her from beneath a pink umbrella, smiling at the sound of her calling his name. She rubs her eyes.

With the sunlight gracing them, Polly and Marcus are beautiful, no one would deny it. He's strong and capable, you can tell from the way he holds himself, and she's got a fire inside that glows right through her skin. She wants things and he wants her. Youth, hope and love are better than any cream or injection you can buy. Their foreheads are uncreased, their eyes bright. Jess suddenly feels ancient and sad. Stupid. Earlier in the day she had presumed the bride's mother was Polly's sister. She looked to be Jess's age and was wearing almost identical sandals.

'Family shots?' Jess suggests, lowering the camera.

•

Hi Jess, Hope you and Richard and the boys can make it, would be so great to see you and get the old gang back together. Hope Kyneton is treating you well! Tamsin & Co x

Jess and Lizzie are in the pharmacy where Lizzie works but not very hard. Jess once heard her shout across the store to a woman picking up kids' bath bombs, 'You can get them at the two dollar store!' Lizzie is nothing like the women of Hawthorn. They were all lawyers, chief financial officers, personal trainers and stay-at-home alpha mums. No one there does anything by halves.

Lizzie was the first friend Jess made when they moved to Kyneton. Jack had been invited to Lizzie's daughter Jasmin's birthday party. Jess prepared as she usually did – buying several thoughtful presents from the local bookstore and wrapping them in pretty pink paper covered in mermaids and a turquoise grosgrain ribbon to match the mermaids' tails. The Hawthorn kids' parties Jess had been to featured colour-coordinated bunting, hired entertainers, sugar and gluten-free food options and rows of neat party bags. At Jasmin's party, the cake was from Coles and piled high with lollies. Balloons of all colours bobbed about the floor and kids hurtled through them squealing and laughing. There were no hired fairies or platters of raw vegetables. Lizzie had taken Jess's tower of presents and pressed a thin can into her hand. 'It's wine,' she'd explained. 'Don't let it get warm.'

Apart from loyalty, Lizzie did everything by halves.

She is restocking multi-vitamins, making imperfect lines of white bottles.

'I don't know what's wrong with me,' Jess says. 'I keep crying. I cry at everything and Richard makes me furious even when he's being nice. Maybe *more* when he's being nice.'

The bottles rattle in Lizzie's hands. Jess continues. 'There was a woman at the wedding this weekend who I thought was the sister of the bride but turned out to be the mum. I felt so old.'

'We *are* old, Jess.'

'I forget things. People's names . . .'

'Yup. And it'll only get worse.'

Jack was only six when they moved. Now he's growing hair on his top lip – fine, soft and black. It makes him look like a brainless thief from an old kids' movie. Jess longs for him to be small again. She wants to wrap her arms around the younger version of him and kiss the top of his head like she used to. To hold and protect him and to have his youth somehow protect her.

She asks Lizzie, 'You don't care?'

Lizzie laughs. 'What am I going to do about it? You're either getting old or you're dying.'

Jess flinches. She'd never told Lizzie about Joe King. She'd never told anyone in Kyneton. She wanted a fresh start; she wanted erasure. It was better for everyone.

'We got an invite from some people . . . in our old neighbourhood . . .'

Lizzie looks suspicious. 'From Melbourne?'

'Yeah. It's nothing, I guess. I just—'

'I didn't know you still had friends from there. You don't talk about them. You went down a couple of months ago, right?' She tries to sound nonchalant. 'Did you catch up with anyone?'

Jess dismisses the question. 'Not really.'

But she sees him again, as though he's right in front of her. Older now, hair shot through with grey strands, lines around his mouth. He had stood – his frame still lean and muscular, maybe more stooped in the shoulders but not much – and pulled out a chair for her. The gesture was both gallant and irritating, as though she couldn't manage it herself. Her heart had betrayed her by racing, hands shaking like leaves. After they'd left Melbourne, she had told herself to hate him. Everything had fallen apart and he was to blame. She'd tried to hate him and forget him but neither pursuit worked. When he said her name – 'Jess?' – it felt like sliding into a hot bath. It felt like the old days – his breath on her neck and fingers in her hair. The scent of never having been on a building site, of not sweating for a living. Good cologne and expensive hair product, skin that felt cool and silky without the rough of salt and labour. She had felt that old urge to make him hers; to possess him between her thighs and not let go.

'Jess?' Liz looks over from the shelf, 'Are you okay?'

Though she tries to smile, the corners of Jess's mouth tug downwards. She lifts her hands. 'This is what I mean! I hate getting old. I'm losing it.'

Lizzie darts around the front of the counter. 'You're not! I'm sorry, I was being a dick. Getting old could be okay . . . what do I know?'

Jess sighs. 'Getting old is terrible.'

Lizzie reaches for a travel pack of tissues for sale by the till and rips it open. 'You weren't wrong about the crying.'

Jess blows her nose and lies, 'I don't know what's up with me.'

Since Jasmin's birthday party, Jess had rarely gone a week without seeing Lizzie. Lizzie had looked after the boys when they went back to Melbourne for Jess's mother's breast cancer operation. She left a bottle of Bundaberg rum in her letterbox the time her sister Astrid took her whole family to Europe and Jess quietly simmered with envy. Lizzie had drunkenly declared, 'You're my very best friend' only six months after they had met and Jess had thought she was joking. But she wasn't – she meant it. It was both hugely comforting and claustrophobic to have a friend like Lizzie.

'Crying is normal,' she offers, trying to sound convinced.

'I don't know about that,' Jess replies. 'I cried during a Medibank commercial the other day.'

Lizzie groans. 'How do you not have Netflix?'

'Richard reckons we don't need all the streaming things.'

'Richard, god love the guy, is dead wrong.'

Lizzie did love Richard. She was always telling Jess that decent men were hard to find and she should know – she'd sampled a fair chunk of the state of Victoria's population and found it to be sorely lacking. She admired that Richard's business employed locals, especially the young blokes who became his apprentices. Lizzie's aunt's stepdaughter had a break-up and moved from Melbourne to Kyneton so Richard had just taken her on as a personal assistant. It was admirable, Jess quietly agreed, his employing locals and not wanting contracts with big developers. But it meant money was an issue. They couldn't always buy new things, they couldn't take overseas vacations. Richard's lack of ambition was a turn-off, not that she would ever admit that to Lizzie. Jess also hadn't told Lizzie about Baz King because Baz King was not a decent man.

'Don't go to whatever dumb thing you've been invited to,' Lizzie says. 'I bet they're all stuck-up.'

Jess thinks of Tamsin Turner's family Christmas cards, always featuring a photograph of the family in an exotic location. Europe, in the snow. Bali, with cocktails.

Lizzie doesn't wait for her to answer, 'You could try evening primrose oil. I think it's total bullshit but there's a lady who comes in every single month. Swears by it.' She reaches over and pulls evening primrose oil capsules from the shelf. 'If you want to flush fifty bucks down the toilet, be my guest.'

Jess reads the back of the bottle: *When taken regularly can assist skin health, circulation, and provide support during premenstrual period and menopause.*

'Menopause?' Jess asks, glancing up at Lizzie.

'I could get you something stronger,' Lizzie suggests, nodding towards the pharmacist at the back of the store. His name is Walter and he often naps behind the tall shelves when the shop is quiet.

Jess tries to remember her last period. She's wearing period underpants these days. She likes washing them out in the shower, watching the swirl in the drain turn from red to clear. On that day at Tamsin's there had been blood on the tiles by the barbecue; it had come from the steaks. It felt dangerous, like her and Baz together. The dark red against the light tiles almost the colour of skin; a reminder of being animal and of death. A mess on Tamsin's curated perfection.

'Yuh,' Lizzie says flatly. 'Menopause.'

There is a tightness in Jess's throat.

Menopause.

Lizzie shoves three vitamin bottles onto a crowded shelf. 'That's where we're at. I told you. End of the line.'

MADISON

'Mrs King?' The receptionist is dressed in lilac, looking up from the computer at the glass desk. 'Zaina wasn't expecting you for another hour.'

Everything in the waiting area, apart from her, is black or white or silver. The floor tiles are gleaming, all the reflective surfaces are polished. It's already giving Madison a headache.

She attempts a smile. 'I know. I'm early.' Madison leans closer to the desk. 'My son is being looked after so I wanted to get here. I brought my computer.' She lifts up a leather laptop case, a Christmas gift from Baz.

'I don't have a meeting room available for you to work in but—'

'That's okay,' Madison interjects. 'I can sit out here. If it doesn't bother you too much?'

'Of course not, Mrs King.'

'Madison.'

'I've got a wi-fi password you're welcome to use. I'll write it down for you.'

Madison takes the slip of paper she offers and sits on a long couch. It's black leather and mercifully cool in the air conditioning. She unzips her case and props the laptop on her knees. She rubs the back of her neck. A man at the opposite end glances up from his phone and smiles a little too hopefully. Madison tries not to make eye contact.

Baz had been right about agreeing to finally get Archie christened. It had made Madison's long-campaigning mother-in-law, Patti – or Mrs Joseph E King as her mail announced – now extend her support at every turn. She'd been offering to babysit for the past week almost incessantly, suggesting Madison have her nails done, get a haircut, a massage or do some shopping. 'What about your friend Tamsin?' she encouraged, 'You could do a girls' lunch together . . . with some champagne!'

Madison hated champagne and didn't rank Tamsin much higher. She had never been good at making friends with other women. Nonetheless, she'd taken Patti up on her offer and lied about getting a facial. Patti was pleased she'd actioned one of her ideas; it clearly made her feel useful.

Madison finds the wi-fi account on her laptop and types in the password that was given to her. It takes a few seconds to connect and the receptionist asks in a sweet voice, 'Did you log in okay, honey?'

Madison nods. She types in the name of the university and the course she's been looking at. There's no timetable available yet so she scans the entry requirements once more while the cursor hovers over the 'Apply Now' button.

'Sorry,' the man with the hopeful smile says, 'I couldn't help noticing you're looking at RMIT.'

Madison swivels around, half-closing the laptop. The man is in the tidy kitchenette behind the long couch. He is making himself a coffee from the reception espresso machine.

He points at her screen. 'I work there.'

Madison says nothing.

'Is there anything I can help you with?'

She gives a small smile – pleasant but dismissive. 'I'm fine.'

'Do you work in fashion?'

'No.' She glances down at her screen, which reads, 'Associate Degree in Fashion and Textile Merchandising' in large letters, and mumbles, 'Not yet anyway.'

'Do I detect an accent?' He looks pleased with himself.

Madison shrinks. 'No.'

She's worked hard to make herself sound like the mothers in Hawthorn, to change the way she used to speak. To change herself in general.

'My mistake,' the man says, his eyes finding her chest then quickly returning to her face. 'You have a look, I guess. German? Nordic?'

She doesn't reply.

The receptionist lifts her head and calls out, 'Mr Kildare? Zaina will see you now.'

The man gathers his things and Madison notices a pallid line of skin on his ring finger. He hesitates and adds, 'I'm Derek, by the way. Maybe I'll see you later. At RMIT.'

Madison murmurs, 'Maybe.'

As soon as Derek is gone, she opens her laptop again and waits for the screen to refresh. She clicks on a tab that says, 'I am an Applicant with Work and Life Experience' before worrying a fingernail and leaning back against the couch. Her phone rings.

'Patti? Is everything okay?'

'Everything is absolutely fine!' her mother-in-law sings. 'Archie just wanted to tell you something. Is it a good time?'

'Well, no, I'm about to go—'

The receptionist glances over at her.

Archie's voice floods her ear, 'Mama!'

'Hey, baby bear. How are you?'

'I made a hat.'

'A hat?'

'Out of paper.'

Madison hears Patti in the background. 'Newspaper!'

'Newspaper,' Archie repeats.

'That's really cool, buddy.'

'Grandma says it can't go in the rain.'

'Oh. If it's paper it can't.'

'Or the pool?'

Madison swallows. 'No. Not in the water.'

She glances at her watch, wishing she hadn't arrived so early. The watch is white and rose gold. Baz gave it to her after she had Archie. He had seemed so ready for their baby son. So in love with her. Madison's heart, scaffolded with oxytocin, had swelled with joy and pride. She saw herself as a kind of captain, steering Baz's ship out of the storm, erasing the hurt of Joe's passing, patching his broken soul and flagging spirit. On the reverse side of the watch Baz had engraved: *From your boys x*.

Archie yells, 'It can't go in the water, Grandma!'

'Archie, mate,' Madison whispers, 'Mummy's got to go.'

'What about the sea, Grandma?' Archie is still yelling. 'The *sea*!'

'Arch?' Madison begs. 'Can I speak to Grandma?'

Madison can hear Patti speaking, then Archie and the phone bumping against something.

'Madison?'

'Sorry, Patti. I have to go into . . . the room . . . in a minute.' Madison avoids eye contact with Zaina's receptionist.

'Sure, sure.' Patti laughs. 'We made paper hats.'

'I heard.'

'Jemima came around before and the two of them . . . you should have seen . . . they were playing pirates. So sweet! Birdie came to pick up Jemima and remembered a story about a little pirate woman. Do you know it? Something about living on a jetty over the water . . .'

Madison's stomach clenches. 'I don't know it.'

Before she had Archie, Madison thought about Birdie King every day. She compared her body to Birdie's, her skin, her face; she wondered if Birdie had been better in bed. She studied the way Birdie was with Jem and resolved to be a better mother. She congratulated herself on being younger than Birdie, less worn out. She cut her long hair into a sharp bob, which made her feel like someone smart and important – a newsreader or a real estate agent. Madison dressed nicely these days too – cashmere, leather, blazers that fit well on the shoulders and white sneakers she kept white. Madison kept their lives clean, smooth, calm and easy. Secretly, importantly – Madison would never let a child of theirs drown.

'A pirate woman,' Madison says coolly. 'Cute.'

When they first started seeing one another, Baz happily pointed out all Birdie's inadequacies and Madison allowed it, secretly enjoyed it. When Madison and Baz were newly married, Birdie had turned up late one night so blind-drunk she'd screamed down the neighbourhood. It had given Madison a quiet thrill. Baz had wrapped his arms around her. It was the two of them against her. He'd said, 'She's nuts.'

'I have to go, Patti. I'll see you later,' Madison says. She didn't sleep well thinking of today's meeting and the exhaustion is catching up with her. She hangs up without waiting for a goodbye. She stares at the black screen of her laptop.

Everything is different now. That old version of herself feels like another person. When Baz had bullied her into christening Archie, the way Baz always did – with the unruffled certainty of a person used to getting his way – Madison stood in the church feeling hollow as an old bone. She had shaped herself in the service of someone else again. She could see that it would be this way forever – her playing the supporting actress, always proving herself, always auditioning. She had found herself in another family she didn't belong in. As Patti wiped away a tear and a poorly sung hymn washed over her, Madison saw that the castle she was the queen of was really just a house of cards. Built upon fear and envy, made of hope and heartache. She'd looked across the aisle towards Corey and noticed the sway of his body, like he was being blown by a light breeze. Realised that her brother had been hollowed out too. She'd been responsible for that as well.

•

Madison had been to see Corey earlier in the week. The door to his flat was wide open like there was nothing inside worth taking anyway. The smell of the insides came out to greet her. She stepped over a wet towel abandoned in the entranceway and called his name. There was a radio on somewhere, the sound of shock jocks trying to out-shock one another.

She tried again, 'Corey?'

In the kitchen, flies gathered on the rims of dirty mugs; a full and defeated rubbish sack wept brown liquid onto the lino floor.

The door at the back of the kitchen opened and her brother stepped through it, exhaling the last of a cigarette and tossing the butt outside. He was barefoot and bare-chested, dark jeans bunching on his thin legs.

'Mads!'

She nodded towards the cigarette butt. 'You'll start a fire.'

Corey laughed. 'Probably needs it.' He followed her eyes taking in more of the room – desiccated noodles spilling out of takeaway containers, once-silver spoons and a large ball of used tin foil.

'You should have told me you were coming,' he accused, guiding her towards the lounge.

'I tried. You didn't answer your phone.'

Corey sank into a couch and rubbed his face. 'Shit. Sorry. Yeah. My phone got nabbed. Or I lost it.'

Madison moved a plate out of the way before sitting. 'When?'

Corey stared. 'What?'

'When did you lose it?'

The skin on his belly gathered in small neat pleats, like a fancy Japanese lightshade in Tamsin Turner's house. 'Do you want a coffee? I've got instant,' Corey asked. He sprang to his feet again.

'No,' Madison replied.

Corey left her perched among second-hand furniture reeking of second-hand smoke. Every choice Madison had made since she got to make her own choices was to keep her from lounge rooms like this one.

Corey returned with a steaming mug. 'You sure?'

'Yeah, I'm sure,' Madison replied.

He was restless, even with the coffee now in hand. His leg jiggled as he faced her. 'Everything all right, sis?'

'With me?' Madison answered. 'Yeah. I was worried about you.'

'Me?' Corey pulled a face. 'I'm right as rain.'

'Except you don't have a phone and you look like shit.'

Corey giggled like he used to when he was a boy. Madison was supposed to be the one who needed looking after. She was younger after all, although not by much. Eighteen months and barely enough time for their mother to realise what a bad idea the first child was, let alone a second.

'Aw, I look okay, sis.' He leaned back and let his legs fall apart. There was a hole in the seam halfway up his thigh. 'No complaints.'

'You look like that guy Tony used to listen to all the time.'

'Iggy Pop?'

'And this place is a fucking dump. I don't know how you bear waking up in it every morning.'

Corey's voice was hard-edged. 'We can't all live in Hawthorn, Mads.'

Madison had bristled at the nickname. He was the last to still be using it.

'Yeah, well, you don't have to live like this.'

Corey drank from his mug. 'It's temporary.'

'You've been saying that for years.'

'Christ, is this what you came over for? To dump on me?'

Madison inhaled. 'No. I wanted to make sure you were okay.'

'Well, here I am. Okay. You can go now if you want.' Then he muttered, 'You're like that woman the Wiz always has over.'

Corey put his mug down on some junk mail and dug into his back pocket, pulling out a packet of smokes. Madison watched him light one. She resisted the urge to point out that he'd just finished one. He watched her watching him.

'Vaping is supposed to help you cut down,' she said.

Corey blew a smoke ring. It was an old trick. One that helped him lose his virginity at fourteen.

'Do you want it?' he asked, holding out the cigarette.

Madison hesitated and he leaned towards her. She took it and dragged. She blew the smoke as far away from her clothes as she could but it scarcely mattered, she'd smell like garbage from being in Corey's flat anyway. She would have to wash everything.

The smoke racing down her body brought back memories. The smell of their stepfather, Tony, and his yellowed nails. The taste and feeling of Johnny Bernard's tongue pressing into her mouth, his rigid penis trying to do the same through their jeans. Bummed ciggies outside of nightclubs, out the back of the hairdressers she used to work in and in the back of cars. Her life before working for the Meyers. Before meeting Baz. She passed it back to her brother.

'You can keep it, I can light another one,' he said.

She shook her head, soft hair swinging. 'Nah.'

They sat together in the comfortable silence that siblings afford one another. Madison realised that the stench of the flat was lessening; she was growing used to it.

Madison and Baz argued about Corey. Madison wanted to give him more help but Baz felt he'd done enough for Corey and now he needed to, as he put it, pull himself up by his bootstraps. Baz had helped him get work, he'd given Corey tips about how to dress and what to say in polite company. For the first few years of their relationship Baz enjoyed Corey's company, it gave him an opportunity to deliver encouraging sermons about work ethic, pride and self-confidence. But over time Corey's inability to execute Baz's advice grated on him. Madison noticed Baz's judgement; she caught the eye rolls and exasperated sighs. She didn't disagree exactly, of course she wished more for and from Corey. She resented the way her brother repeatedly fell into trouble so easily, never learning from his past mistakes. She was bitter about having to constantly rescue him. The difference was that Madison knew, intimately, the kind of childhood that had led Corey directly to the kind of man he was now. The same childhood that had turned Madison into a chameleon had shaped Corey into who he was. He was surviving in the ways he knew how, just like she was.

Baz made mean, underhanded comments – about the way Corey spoke, dressed and walked, the condition of his teeth, his ability to lose money or get in with the wrong crowd – and passed them off as jokes. Madison hated him for it, this thoughtless superiority. Madison was too sensitive, he prodded, surely she could see the humour in it? The cliché that was Corey Leck? Her husband was a lazy playground bully.

Madison stood and brushed lint that wasn't there off her pants.

'I should go.'

Corey stood too. He took a last long drag of the smoke before dropping it into the half-drunk coffee.

'Sorry I don't have anything to give you. Need to do a shop. I'm going to fix out the back soon. You, Baz and Archie could come over. We could do a barbie.'

Madison nodded. She knows that will never happen. Corey wouldn't manage to make it happen and Baz wouldn't want to go.

Corey walked Madison to the front door. He leaned heavily on the handle, waspish body twisted to one side.

'Wizard's going to sort me out. He's got a big job coming. You'll see.'

Madison grimaced. 'I wish you wouldn't call him that.' She hated it when Baz called him that too. She shifted her foot on the dirty carpet. 'Maybe you should get some other work, different work.'

'Why? I'm doing good.'

Madison chewed the inside of her cheek. 'I don't know. Mix it up? So you don't have to be waiting for big projects to start. What do you do for him anyway?'

Corey scratched his head. 'All sorts. Whatever he needs doing really.' Then Corey said, 'Hey, sorry about the Hawthorn thing.'

Madison shrugged. 'Yeah, well, sorry about being a stuck-up bitch.'

Corey smiled. 'You wear it well.'

Madison did a small fake curtsy and they both laughed. 'Damn right I do.'

As a man, Madison's brother was a mess. But she still remembered the boy who held her hand under the bed as Tony called their mother names and the scrape-kneed kid who shared every bag of chips he stole and dropped packets of gum into her school bag so she'd have something to chew on at lunch. She didn't feel so different from Corey, tiny bits of luck had kept one sibling from turning out like the other. She had been poor, dirty, vulnerable and needy too. If Baz was so disgusted by Corey, Madison wondered how he could really, truly love her.

•

'Mrs King?'

Madison jerks awake then slams her hand over her mouth. A woman with tight black curls pulled into a ponytail stands above her.

'You're not the first,' the woman says warmly. 'Zaina Thomas.'

'Madison . . . King.'

'Young children?'

Madison's cheeks burn as she snaps her laptop shut. 'What? I mean – pardon?'

'You have young kids, I bet.'

Madison says. 'Just the one.'

'One is plenty,' Zaina says, smiling. She gestures towards a frosted glass door. 'We're through here.'

Madison follows Zaina into her office. Her tongue is slow, still asleep. 'I love him though,' she mumbles. 'My son.'

Zaina stands behind her desk. The two women stare at one another.

'Of course you do,' Zaina says. She motions towards a chair. 'Please take a seat, Madison, and we can get started.' She opens a lined yellow pad to a fresh page. 'My receptionist said you were referred?'

'A mum at day care,' Madison explains, sitting. 'Amy Decker.'

'Amy, right. And Simon,' Zaina says. 'I remember now. Are we waiting for your husband today or is it just you?'

Madison straightens. Sometimes she feels herself tighten inside at 'your husband'. It still feels fraudulent. The names 'Baz and Birdie' had been like salt and pepper shakers, always paired. When Madison sat a few rows back from them at Joe's funeral she had stared at their backs. Birdie wore purple and Baz was in an expensive black suit with a white shirt and silver cufflinks. Madison had wanted Baz then, not that she would ever admit it. He was the handsome centre of pity and admiration. Wealthy, successful and in need of healing. The star of the show. Madison had wanted him because others did – Jess Dhillon especially, who clung, wan, shivering and guilty, to her husband, Richard, both towards the back. Madison didn't know her own desires because she'd learned not to desire. It wasn't Baz she wanted to win, but the winning itself. Life had taught her that what she wanted didn't count, wasn't important. Better to follow someone else's choices and desires. Madison hadn't ever learned how to choose, only how to work to be chosen.

'Just me,' Madison replies.

'Okay. Why don't you start by telling me what you're hoping for, Madison, and we'll go from there.' Zaina pauses. 'I might interrupt with a few questions, just to clarify how I can best be of service. Then we can talk about the process and any recommendations I can offer you.'

Madison inhales raggedly. What *is* she hoping for? Isn't her life now exactly what she had hoped for? What she had planned?

She was Baz King's wife. When they got married in Bali the air was hot, sweet and damp and she had stood in front of him, in that atmospheric fever, wearing a light dress and staring into his eyes, believing he would take care of her for the rest of her days. Believing that his certainty and money would cancel out not fitting in. As Baz King's wife, Madison would have a legitimate place in the world; she would be a legitimate person. She'd have crawled into him in that moment if she could. Madison was willing to dissolve for Baz. To evaporate her name, obliterate her past, vanish and never come back.

Madison feels the light breeze from the air-conditioning duct above her, a whisper on her skin. She had been so sure of everything back then. Sure of Baz, sure of the perfect life she was putting all her chips on. She doesn't trust anything anymore, especially not Baz.

'What I want . . .' she says, voice soft then growing in confidence, 'is to leave my husband.'

Zaina nods.

'And I want the house,' Madison adds.

She's already pictured it. Corey can move in. She'll buy him new clothes and burn the old ones. He'd look great with a fresh haircut. He doesn't need rehab, she can do that for him. Shut him in a room and let him sweat it out; he'd thank her in time. He could get a job at a cafe, nothing too taxing. He'd be a good barista, good at talking to people. He'd probably find a girlfriend soon enough. Madison imagines her and Corey and Archie at the playground at Central Gardens and the girlfriend coming by, someone with nice skin and clean hair, planting a kiss on her brother's filled-out cheek. They're great friends, Madison and Corey's girlfriend. They get on like a house on fire. Madison's never had close female friends but Corey's girlfriend will change all that. His girlfriend will be forever grateful and in awe of Madison turning Corey's life around, getting him away from the Wizard and the drugs and all the roads that led him to that miserable, rotten flat and his skin barely hanging on to his bones.

In all of Madison's imaginings, Baz simply vanishes. It makes her feel pleased, erasing him completely like a scuff mark on an otherwise pristine wall, a spill on a countertop.

She adds, 'And Archie. I want Archie.'

'Archie is . . .?'

'My son.'

Zaina nods, making notes on her yellow paper.

'Our son,' Madison corrects herself.

PALOMA

Stefano greets Paloma with a lift of his chin as she slides onto one of Pellegrini's red stools. She nods in reply, knowing she'll soon have a granita in front of her. Her shoulder is pressed to her ear, her phone sandwiched between.

The voice at the other end says, 'Paloma! How are you?'

'Busy.'

She drops her bags by her feet and sits tall, stretching out her sore back. The voice belongs to Gordon Tuttle, the political reporter for *The Age*. Years ago, his job was Paloma's.

Gordon laughs generously. 'Don't be like that,' he cajoles. 'I just wanted to know if the prem had any additional comments—'

Paloma cuts him off. 'Regarding?'

'Peter Bol? The doping scandal?'

'The athlete? Why would the premier—'

'He trains here, he went to University of Melbourne.'

'No, Gordon, the premier does not.' Paloma presses her lips together, glancing up at the menu hanging above the bar. Stefano places a granita in front of her and mouths, 'Lasagne?' It's past 10.30 pm. Too late for dinner and Paloma should be at home with the girls, but she nods quickly, pressing a palm to her heart in thanks.

'His lawyers are saying he's been "publicly besmirched",' Gordon persists.

'Are they? Good for them. The premier tends not to involve himself in doping allegations. Especially ones that lead to nothing.'

'Is that on the record?'

Paloma snorts. 'Scraping the bottom of the barrel, Gordie?'

Gordon pleads. 'Come on, Paloma, I need something that isn't the Australian bloody Open.'

'You'd better watch yourself,' she warns in jest. 'Calling it the Australian bloody Open is very un-Australian. It's a cultural institution.'

'I need something—'

'I hope you've written about free entry to the zoo these holidays.'

'Christ, Paloma.'

She can't help smiling. It's amusing making Gordon work as hard as she had to. Paloma had to do his job with two kids at home. She thinks it's important for Gordon to be hungry and desperate and earn every single story he files so he'll build the kind of shellac coating required for the work.

'There are *three* baby elephants, Gordon,' she teases.

He groans.

'I'm going now,' Paloma says and then adds, 'Good luck.'

She puts the phone down in front of her and takes a long, slow drink of the granita, watermelon-flavoured like summer trapped in crushed ice. She tastes her childhood in it, all the times her father brought her to Pellegrini's because it made him feel at home. The cafe has been a constant in all the stages of Paloma's life – as a kid, when she would spin around on the stools until her father put his hand firmly on her knee, or when she was at university and it was one of the few restaurants she could afford in the CBD and sometimes only for strudel and a coffee. She's brought the twins to Pellegrini's over the years and some dates too, though not recently. Paloma is too busy for men who disappoint.

Stefano is at the other end of the bar, serving a couple of tourists who are taking photos of everything from the black and white tiled floor to the red and green printed paper napkins. Paloma turns her back to them so she won't feature on their Tripadvisor review. She picks up her phone again and sends a message to Rose, because Rose is the daughter who will check her phone and reply.

Sorry love. Quick dinner at Pellegrini's. Home in thirty.

Sure enough, seconds later Rose replies with a love-heart emoji. Paloma decisively drops the phone into the abyss of her handbag as Stefano places a plate of lasagne in front of her. It's so hot and fresh it steams her face.

The door swings open in a rush and four middle-aged women tumble through it, laughing. They're wearing high-heeled sandals and mini dresses. All blonde. One protests loudly, 'I can't do carbs, I told you I can't do carbs. Mike will kill me.' Another groans in reply, 'Screw Mike.'

They stagger towards the line of stools. The tourist couple nearby scowl like they own the place and are suspicious of interlopers. The women cackle and grab one another like they need steadying. Paloma leans over her lasagne, fork stabbing deep in the mince and sliding through silky layers of pasta.

There's a shriek. 'Paloma?'

She lifts her head.

'Paloma . . . *Albertini*?'

One of the flock totters towards Paloma on thin legs with a deep fake tan. Paloma forces a smile. 'Tamsin.'

'My god, it *is* you!' Tamsin turns back to the rest of the group, who are arguing over pizza versus pasta, while pointing at Paloma's left breast. 'I know her! Her girls went to St Bernard's!' She slides onto the stool beside Paloma, grips her knee and says, slightly out of breath, 'I *knew* it was you. You look exactly the same! How are you?'

'I'm good, yeah, thanks. You?'

Tamsin's smile is loose and drunken. Her diamond studs twinkle in the light. '*So* good. So good!'

Paloma glances at her lasagne, the red mince sauce glistening. Having good food so hot and close without eating it gives her an ache in her gut that feels a bit like loss.

'New house! It's a dream, honestly,' Tamsin says. 'Butler's pantry, extra bathrooms . . . it's the little things, isn't it? You just don't realise how great they are until you have them.'

'Yeah, I'm sure,' Paloma says, her smile fake.

Tamsin leans in. 'Alex is really killing it.' Her eyes widen. 'Kill. Ing. It. Couldn't be prouder, honestly. On fire.'

'And Wyatt?' Paloma hears herself ask, though she doesn't really care. 'Charlie? All good?'

Tamsin nods. 'Great. They're both *really* great. Yours?'

Paloma shrugs. 'Big. Loud.'

Tamsin chuckles with her mouth wide open and sneaks a look at her friends. 'You're so funny!' She leans forward. 'Hey honey, did you get my invite the other day?'

Paloma has the urge to look behind her. 'Me?'

'Yes *you*!'

'I didn't see anything in my emails—'

'No!' Tamsin objects. 'Not digital. I posted it.'

'You *posted* an invitation?'

The only mail Paloma can recall being interesting this week was a plain, light brown A4-sized envelope containing several old newspaper clippings. There hadn't been a note with it. She'd flicked through the clippings but they were all from well before her time in the premier's office and well before the current premier. The premier's office got their well-meaning obsessives – a woman who thought the Russians were listening to her phone calls, a man who thought of himself as the personal saviour of the growling grass frog – it was probably from one of their ilk.

Paloma had pushed the papers back into the envelope and held it over her trash bin. But something had kept her from dropping it in. Instead she'd opened the middle drawer of her desk and slid it underneath a pile of hardback notebooks.

Tamsin pats Paloma's wrist. 'Check your mailbox. It's an invite to the new place, next month. Saturday eighteenth. You *have to* see it. Just up the road from the old one!'

'Oh, I don't think—' Paloma is startled. An invite to Tamsin's place feels like a poor-taste joke. Déjà vu but with added dread.

Tamsin stands. 'Don't forget to bring the girls!'

'That's really kind,' Paloma says quickly, 'but I don't think we can. We're really busy and we've . . .' She wants to say 'moved on' but it dies in her mouth. Seeing Tamsin Turner swaying in front of her makes Paloma's heart race, like waking from a terrible dream. She still remembers Tamsin cornering her in the school playground almost a decade ago, convincing her to come to the end-of-year party. The weird hints she'd made about Mr Lee and how cute they'd look as a couple. The insistence that she and Abigail's nanny, Madison, would 'get on like a house on fire' despite having nothing in common except their age. The way Tamsin looked Paloma up and down whenever she saw her as if editing her with her eyes, deciding what to keep and what to delete.

Paloma had agreed to go to the barbecue that afternoon because her mother had worried she wasn't making friends. *Mum friends*, she'd clarified with a meaningful expression. Paloma hadn't wanted any 'mum friends' from St Bernard's. The mums all looked down on her, not knowing that Paloma couldn't stand any of them. Especially Abigail Meyer. Abigail and Tamsin together reminded Paloma of characters from *The Crucible*. But she'd figured accepting Tamsin's unexpected invite might keep her mother off her back. After all that had happened, it did shut her mother up, but the price was far greater than Paloma could have ever imagined.

Tamsin wags her finger and closes one eye as she steps backward to her friends. 'Don't bring anything, we've got it covered. Apart from swimmers. Remember to bring swimmers.'

Paloma's voice is much louder than she expects. 'What? No.'

She slows her breathing and tries to soften, tries to use the sweet but firm tone she sometimes has to use with the premier. 'Tamsin, no. We won't be coming.'

Tamsin chortles before turning around. 'So funny.'

The pack of women leave as quickly as they arrived, with loud disagreement about sushi and pho noodle soup. One is chanting 'Screw Mike! Screw Mike!' and the rest of them are falling apart with laughter and walking sideways into one another across the black and white floor.

The door closes and the women's voices snap and billow in their wake like bright windsocks. The negative space they leave behind is a relief. Paloma sighs and swears into her pasta.

•

It is best to get to Queen Victoria market early – that's what Paloma tells her sixteen-year-old daughter. Queenie doesn't agree. She's mutinous about it, wearing dark Ray-Bans, a cropped t-shirt and thick brows brushed into a fury. Her twin, Rose, is allowed to stay the night at her boyfriend's while she suffers the unbearable injustice of getting up in the brittle morning, conversing with her own mother and being bipedal.

Queenie's real name is Beatrice. When she was small, Paloma called her 'Queen Bee'. It quickly became 'Queen' and eventually 'Queenie'. Rose, whose full name is Rosita, says her sister's nickname should have been 'Despot'. Rose – the crowd favourite – is thoughtful, compliant, kind and pliable. Queenie, on the other hand, is competitive, stubborn, contrary and moody. She is the daughter that reminds Paloma most of herself. The truest version, the one beneath all the layers of social etiquette.

They head into the covered fruit and vegetable market, vendors chatting to one another and still unpacking boxes. Tables are piled with papayas, dirt-covered potatoes and glossy, almost-black eggplants. Paloma chats to the sellers she knows. The woman with one gold tooth who has the best herbs. The man who proclaims 'This one works for the premier!' and tells her she has to pay double now she is 'famous'. Her strategy is always to buy the heaviest things first – potatoes for gnocchi, carrots, a melon. She arranges and rearranges her wheeled bag expertly and zigzags through the aisles, making her own sense of the place. Boxes of berries go in next, tomatoes that smell of sun and earth, then herbs. Finally, leafy greens like rocket and spinach, which last twice as long as any she's bought from Coles.

The leafy-greens seller, Shirley, opens her arms wide when she sees the two of them together. 'Who is this beauty?'

'Morning, Shirley. You know Queenie.'

Shirley is a small woman with hair that forms a cloud around her face. She wears glasses on a chain around her neck and brash bright polyester shirts. Her adult son is sorting through a box of spinach leaves, taking out any yellowing ones. He looks depleted.

'Your sister?' Shirley asks, squinting. She forgets to lift the glasses to her face.

'Daughter, Shirley. I've got twins, remember?'

'Daughter!' Shirley exclaims, like she's never been informed. 'Beautiful!'

Queenie glares like she'd rather pull out her own molars than shop with her mother. Paloma doesn't take it personally, she remembers being sixteen and constantly infuriated or bored. She had five sisters who fought over everything back then: their father's attention, the telephone, the TV remote, the best tube of lipstick, a pair of jeans with perfectly placed rips. At Queenie's age, Paloma was going to WeightWatchers at the suggestion of the Albertinis' kindly family doctor. She was at least a decade younger than everyone else and felt like a spectacle. At Queenie's age, Paloma had felt wrong through and through to her 'big bones'. When the twins started at St Bernard's and the other mums assessed her size and age, thinking Paloma wouldn't notice, she had felt that familiar, gnawing otherness again.

The thought reminds her of Tamsin Turner. She had found the invite buried deep in a pile of junk mail on the bench seat by her front door. She'd torn it in half, right through the words 'Pool Party' and dropped it, revolted, into the recycling bin.

'Maybe you'll have grandchildren soon,' Shirley says with a wink.

'Ew,' Queenie replies.

Shirley is encouraging. 'Never know!'

Paloma shakes her head. 'No one is ready for that.'

'I'm not having children ever,' Queenie says emphatically. 'I'm going to be an actor.'

Sounding too much like her own mother for her liking, Paloma hears herself say, 'You could be a mum *and* an actor.'

'Not if I want to be any good,' Queenie replies with unshakeable conviction. She folds her arms and says with authority, 'Kids ruin your life.'

Paloma rolls her eyes. 'You're telling me.'

She buys half-priced spinach and a bag of sorrel before wheeling her trolley away with Shirley waving as they go.

•

After the market they head down Queen Street towards the city centre. Queenie strides with her arms swinging, making her look like she's ready for a fight. Under her skirt, Paloma's thighs swish together in their chafe shorts as she matches her daughter's pace. A tram thunders by like a huge canister of bolts when they reach Bourke Street Mall and Queenie complains as they turn into Royal Arcade. She is dragging the shopping trolley like a reluctant pet.

Paloma's mother, wearing flat shoes and matching soft pink top and trousers, waiting by the pastries counter in Caffé e Torta, turns and waves to them. When they reach her, Queenie kisses her cheek.

'Queenie! Your clothes!' Connie Albertini exclaims, pointing at the exposed flesh of her granddaughter's stomach.

Queenie shrugs. 'It's hot out there, Nonna.'

Connie touches the necklace at her throat.

'Why don't we take a seat?' Paloma suggests. 'I'll get coffees.'

'Hot chocolate and a vanilla slice,' Queenie replies smoothly.

'*Please*,' Connie says with a hard stare.

Paloma points at a small empty table. 'Everyone sit.'

The two women do as they are told but glare at one another across the table. Connie and Paloma's father had looked after the twins while Paloma went to university and then before and after school when Paloma was working. When Paloma returns with a table number, they're huddled over Queenie's phone.

'See this?' Queenie is explaining. 'It's purple and has a dip in the back . . .'

'It looks cheap.'

'It costs five thousand dollars, Nonna!'

'I could make that myself.'

Queenie brightens. 'Would you?'

'Not that! You'd look like a . . . worm.'

Queenie holds up her phone to Paloma. There's a photograph of a woman on the screen wearing a tight metallic purple dress. 'Mum! Nonna says I'll look like a *worm* if I wear this dress to the formal.'

'Formal dresses? In February?' Paloma murmurs.

'A worm! She said a worm!'

'I got that part.'

Queenie scowls and slumps in her chair.

'How was church, Mama?' Paloma asks.

'Good,' Connie replies. 'The service was lovely. I saw your friends there – Baz and his family.'

Paloma winces. 'Baz King?'

'Yes, Patti's boy. His wife—'

'Madison.'

'Ah yes, I always forget. Their boy was christened recently.' Connie lowers her voice and looks around as though members of the congregation might be listening in. 'Bit *old* for it but . . . never mind. He was wearing funny clothes. Do you know his name?'

'Archie, I think,' Paloma replies slowly. 'How old is he now?'

'Four, I think.'

Joe King had been four. Paloma thinks of his flame hair, his tiny body. A waiter delivers their coffees and food.

Queenie mutters, 'I still can't believe that arsehole married the nanny.'

Connie gulps. 'Queenie!'

'Madison's a person, Queenie,' Paloma says, 'not just "the nanny".'

Paloma and Madison were supposed to become friends. It seemed obvious to Tamsin and Abigail and their pals – they were both young! Paloma had felt sorry for Madison both then and now. She'd been liberated from the Meyers only to end up with Baz King without much of a breath in between. Baz King had been one of Paloma's least favourite fathers at St Bernard's. She'd had the displeasure of bumping into him through her work in journalism and state government, and always felt torn between pity because of what had happened to Joe, and her natural instinct: loathing. She'd watched on as Baz King had manipulated his way to success.

'If you say so, Mum.' Queenie screws up her face. 'Birdie is a person too. He just goes and leaves her after all she went through? And Jemima?'

Paloma reaches for her espresso. Birdie King was one of the few St Bernard's mothers who spoke to Paloma as an equal.

They'd kept in touch for several years but not much lately. She feels a squeeze of guilt in her gut. 'What else happened at mass this morning, Ma?'

Connie wrenches her gaze away from the speciality teas and cheeses. 'We prayed for Pope Benedict, God rest his soul.'

She looks at Queenie again as though she momentarily forgot the girl was there, gaze moving down her body and back up to her face. She rests a hand on Paloma's arm as she tells her granddaughter, 'Darling, your mama will agree with me . . . you can't go walking around like that. It'll invite trouble.'

Paloma raises her eyebrows. 'I'm not sure I do agree, actually.'

'Of course you can wear what you like,' Connie continues. 'You can drink and smoke and . . . do whatever girls do these days . . . but people will *think things*.'

'Where is this going?' Paloma asks.

Connie turns to her. 'You have to admit, sweetheart, nice girls don't wear tops like that.'

Paloma sighs. 'Here we go.'

Queenie grins. 'I'm *not* a nice girl, Nonna.'

'Paloma!' Connie implores, looking for support.

'I can wear whatever I like,' Queenie replies. 'Whenever I like.'

Connie beseeches Paloma again, 'Tell her! Trouble will find her!'

'Oh, Mama,' Paloma says, laughing. 'She *is* the trouble.'

Connie throws up her hands before looking out towards the cafe counter. Her face suddenly brightens. A tall, thickset man is picking up a tin of green tea. 'Oh, there he is! George! George! Over here!'

The man turns and offers a wan smile.

'So good to see you! So glad you came!' she cries. 'Come! Sit!'

Paloma stares at her mother and then back at the man suddenly in front of her.

'Hi,' George says, lifting a large square palm. His face is apologetic.

Queenie has put her phone down and is looking up at the sudden new character to their familial drama.

There are only three chairs at the table so Connie jumps up to fetch another from the neighbouring table. 'Sit, sit, sit,' she insists happily.

George lowers himself into the chair as directed. His fingers and hands are so large it looks awkward when he presses them together on his knees, folding himself up as though apologising for the amount of room his body takes up. Above a woolly beard, his eyes are clear, sad and green.

'You seem familiar. Let me guess . . .' Paloma says slowly, 'your mother attends St Paul's.'

'Be nice,' Connie scolds. 'This is George; George, this is Paloma, my daughter. My *sixth* daughter.'

'Wow,' George says. 'Six. Hi Paloma.'

Queenie watches the exchange like she's going to be quizzed on it later.

Paloma gestures to her. 'And this is my daughter Queenie.'

Queenie thrusts out a hand. 'Hi George. I'm a twin. There are two of us.'

They shake hands for a few moments too long. Paloma realises that Queenie is clinging to make George unnerved.

'Twins . . .' George says with polite interest.

'Are you Italian?' Queenie interrupts. 'You look Italian.'

'Greek. And some other stuff. Mongrel?'

'We're Italian.'

'Ah, yes I—'

'Do you have children?'

'No.'

'Why not?'

George looks to Connie for guidance. She has a mortified expression on her face and says nothing to help. 'I didn't get around to it, I guess.'

'How old are you?'

'I'm thirty-seven.'

'You could still have kids.'

'Well—'

'Mum is thirty-five.' Queenie nods towards Paloma. 'She had us *really* young. Does that bother you? She could probably have more kids, but she doesn't want to and, like, ew, gross. You know?'

George laughs. It's a nice laugh, Paloma notes. Deep and warm.

'I feel like we've met before,' she mutters.

'What do you do for a job?' Queenie asks.

'I'm a cop.'

She baulks. 'A cop?!' She looks at her mother. 'A cop.'

'Yes, darling, I heard him. I'm right here. When would we have met—'

Queenie leans in. 'Mum hates cops.'

'No!' Connie objects.

'That's not an accurate assessment, Queenie,' Paloma says.

George isn't the first man Paloma's mother has tried to set her up with this year so far. 'Relentless' is how Paloma describes Connie's obsession with finding Paloma a partner. Her mother tells others 'she's still single' the way a person might whisper 'haemorrhoid cream' to the pharmacist.

Connie and Queenie squabble while George leans towards Paloma and says softly, 'Sorry about this. My mother spoke to your mother and—'

'No need to explain.'

'I'm not looking for—'

'Who is?' Paloma interrupts. 'I've told my mother a thousand times I don't want to date.' Then adds quickly, 'Nothing personal.'

'No.' George is visibly relieved 'That's fine. That's better than fine. Me too.'

They sit in silence for a moment as Connie and Queenie continue arguing and Paloma sips her coffee. The premier is visiting a new playground tomorrow that was built in consultation with neurodiversity education specialists, but he'll need a quick debrief with the education minister beforehand so he doesn't say anything that will get him cancelled. Paloma makes a mental note to talk to Linda, the prem's diary person, to make it work.

'My girlfriend broke up with me,' George says suddenly, breaking through her thoughts. 'Last year.'

Paloma focuses on him. 'Oh?'

'Too much information?'

'It's okay.'

'Actually, she broke up with me on my birthday.'

'Wow.'

'Not the best gift I ever got.'

Paloma laughs then says, 'I don't suppose that's very funny.'

George shrugs. Paloma clears her head of work and debriefs and the needs of the premier. She peers at George with greater interest. 'So . . . you're a cop.'

'Eight years now.'

'What do you do? If you don't mind me asking.'

George scratches the back of his neck. 'Lots of things. Investigations of one kind or another. Homicides, missing persons, organised crime . . .'

Paloma picks up the Portuguese tart she ordered and studies his face carefully. George seems familiar from a moment in her memory that is just beyond her reach. She has an uncomfortable feeling that she's missing something. She tries to find it in his features. His dark beard is unruly, his lips thick and pink. He's got what her daughter Rose calls 'smiley eyes' – creased, honest and generous. He doesn't look away while she stares at him. He doesn't even flinch when Queenie bursts out of the argument she's having to declare, 'Look at that, Nonna – the cop is *still* here!'

George breaks eye contact with Paloma to explain. 'Well, I wasn't always a cop. A long time ago I worked in health.'

'Oh yeah?' Queenie drawls, pretending to be bored.

'Yeah,' George replies, 'I was a paramedic.'

The pastry slips out of Paloma's fingers as the memory she was searching for slips into sharp focus. George is clean-shaven. His briny-green eyes have no lines at the corners, no weariness. George is there, at Tamsin's, pulling sheets of stickers out of his pocket. Six-year-old Rose chooses a parrot and Queenie wants a mouse wearing a crown. Younger George is trying to make the horror bearable. Younger Paloma, wet, frozen and terrified, had watched him with all those kids.

'You were there,' Paloma whispers, her fingers and toes feeling fuzzy and her tongue suddenly thick in her mouth. 'That day.'

No one hears her.

George is shrugging, still talking to Queenie. 'But I gave it up.' After a loaded silence, he adds, 'It got too hard.'

BIRDIE

'It's open-heart surgery without the drugs,' says the young woman who introduced herself as Attica. She's new. Freshly bereaved.

Jeff, the octogenarian, reaches over with a quivering hand and pats Attica's back. Last month, he whispered cheerfully to Birdie, 'Can you believe I haven't had Covid yet? What a joke. I was looking forward to it knocking me off.'

Sheila, the facilitator, reaches out with a box of tissues but Attica is weeping too hard to notice. No one in the small group shushes her or tells her it's going to be okay. No one tells her that time heals or everything happens for a reason. There's no bullshit at Griefshare.

Attica's hair is dark at the roots and sea-green at the ends. She is wearing a tracksuit that's too big for her. A month ago her twin brother was hit by a car while out cycling. She is the youngest in the group by decades. Sheila is in her seventies, Geraldine her fifties, and then Birdie in her mid-forties. A few other regulars and their respective losses – Bob (husband), Radhika (daughter) and Cosimo (two brothers and one nephew) – are missing today.

Jeff takes the box of tissues from Sheila and gently waves a couple in front of Attica's face until she grabs at them.

Sheila says, 'Would you like to tell us more about him?'

Attica's face is grazed by tears. 'Can I?'

The group listens as Attica talks about her brother Blaze in the present tense. No one corrects her. Blaze is training for a triathlon. Blaze lives with two of his mates from high school. *God, he can't cook to save himself, you should see the kitchen.* Blaze once had three Tinder dates in a single day. He has a thing for blondes – men or women, he doesn't care. He also has a thing for space movies, always has, and Attica can't stand them. Some of the twin-stuff they tell you about is true, she says, like mind-reading and finishing each other's sentences. They smoke a lot of weed together. The twin-stuff is especially true when they've smoked a lot of weed together. As a kid Blaze collected AFL cards and he barracks for the Bombers and has never missed a game.

Attica doesn't have to say 'until now' because she goes silent and Jeff passes the tissues again. Sheila knows from years of facilitating that Attica is all out of words for today. She lets the silence swell like rising dough into something soft and warm, before asking if anyone else would like to share.

Jeff raises his hand. He reads a small section from a book by CS Lewis, which is so worn the cover is disintegrating. Jeff likes the sound of his reading voice; he used to be a librarian. It is a piece about the perfection of a marriage, so delightful that God has to intervene to halt it.

Halfway through, Jeff allows a small silence to bloom for appreciation and Attica shifts in her seat like she wants to leave. Birdie is no longer fidgety when Jeff or anyone – there was Gretel before him – talks about God. Her mother-in-law used to tell her about God's plans and God's wishes and how precious Joe was if God wanted Joe with him, until one day Birdie screamed in the IKEA car park and threw a Swedish hotdog at Patti's good winter coat, mustard and all. But in Griefshare, it's different. Jeff, and Gretel before him, just want to make sense of things for themselves. They don't expect Birdie to unearth some perverse, divine beauty in her pain.

After anaemic applause for Jeff's reading, Sheila passes round a small stuffed panda. She asks everyone to share how they are feeling right now and something they're going to do for self-care this week. The responses vary: tired, better, fine, get a haircut, go for more walks and book a trip to the Gold Coast to see my cousin.

When the session is complete, Birdie reaches into her handbag to check her phone. There's a message from Baz on the WhatsApp group they named 'Jem Admin' which reads *Thursday pick-up from my place, 8.30 pm, post writers' club* and a text from Jem which says *Get loo roll?*

Birdie goes into the community centre kitchenette where Attica is standing by the Zip filling a mug with boiling water. She startles when she hears Birdie's footfall. 'Were you waiting?'

Birdie shakes her head. 'No, go ahead.'

She reaches down into the small fridge and takes out a bottle of milk. She peers at the expiry date before passing it over to Attica.

'It pays to check.'

'Have you been coming here a long time?'

'Almost ten years.'

'Oh.'

'That's how I know about the milk,' Birdie confesses. 'Learned the hard way.'

Attica forces a tiny smile. 'Yuck.'

Birdie drops a teabag into a cup and fills it with hot water.

'My aunty told me about this group,' Attica explains. 'She comes to painting classes here. Said it could be good.'

'I think it's helpful,' Birdie replies. 'The people who come here . . . well, they get it.'

At times Birdie's grief has felt so big and burning bright, it's like walking around with the entire sun coming out of her chest. People simply cannot look at it, cannot look at her. They cross the street or look away when they see her coming. Inside, people seem to move towards the walls.

She sips her tea and wishes it was wine.

'What's the deal with asking people, you know, why they're here?' Attica asks.

Birdie presses out her teabag and lobs it into the bin.

'You can ask any of us.' She nods towards Jeff, Sheila and Geraldine, each holding a twosome of Scotch Fingers. 'Jeff lost his wife, Mary, like he said. Geraldine's daughter Kit died – brain cancer. Sheila's first husband, Peter, died ages ago. Decades even. Heart attack, I think? She's remarried since.'

Attica nods. 'And you?'

'My son,' Birdie says. 'His name was Joe.' Birdie touches her right earlobe, 'Jemima is my daughter. Jemima and Joe.' She takes a breath. 'Joe was four when he drowned.'

'Shit,' Attica replies.

'Shit,' Birdie agrees. She breathes slowly, like her therapist taught her.

Attica clinks a ring against the mug. 'Does it get easier?'

Birdie looks over Attica's face. She's so young there are lumps of acne forming a landscape beneath her foundation and the thick mascara she was wearing has mostly been cried off. She can't be too many years older than Jem – ten years, tops. She has the look of the newly bereaved: pink and raw.

Attica's question is one of Birdie's least favourite.

She's evasive. 'Easier? Not exactly. It changes.'

Attica looks crestfallen. 'I don't know how you bear it.'

Sheila looks over to them both with a question in her gaze. Sheila is gentle but direct, a natural leader for Griefshare, which she rules with barely perceptible territorialism. She thinks Birdie needs to go back to therapy. Birdie gives Sheila a little nod to let her know they're both okay and she hasn't put Attica off coming back to Griefshare.

She says, 'I dunno if it counts as getting easier, but I've stopped waking up forgetting what happened and then remembering again. I hated that. Thank god it fades. Not that you ever accept what happened, just that your brain catches up.'

Attica leans back against the kitchen sink. 'I never thought it would happen to him. To us. We were connected, you know?'

Birdie thinks of Paloma and Queenie and Rose. 'My friend has twins. I know what you mean.' Paloma's girls were chalk and cheese but there was still a tight, almost inexplicable bond between them. Seeing them together always left Birdie envious.

'I thought we were immune, you know?'

Birdie nods. Of all the sure things, death is the one everyone is convinced will dodge them. A kind of collective insanity. Sometimes Birdie feels as though that is at the root of all grieving: disbelief.

'Now I think everyone I love is going to die,' says Attica. 'Today or tomorrow. Soon. I can't get it out of my head.' She looks hopefully at Birdie. 'How do you get it out of your head?'

All Birdie can think of is booze. She doesn't tell Attica that. It's why she cannot let herself love Albert. It's too big a risk. She already feels like she's walking a knife's edge with Jem, every day an opportunity to lose her, to lose another child.

Before she can say anything, Attica is talking again, like a valve has burst. 'And I'm so angry. I'm pissed he's left me with this. Feeling shit, sorting through all his shit.' Her hands are shaking. 'I feel terrible that I'm angry at him.'

'Don't. You're allowed to be angry.'

'Yeah, but it's not *his* fault.'

'You're still allowed,' Birdie says firmly. 'I'm angry all the time. Furious.' Then mutters, 'Makes me want to kill someone sometimes.' As she says it, Birdie realises just how true this is, despite the time that has passed, despite all the therapy.

'Yeah, but did you feel *guilty*?'

Birdie squeezes the mug in her hands.

'Sorry,' Attica says hurriedly. 'Sorry I asked that.'

'It's okay,' Birdie lies, pointing to a plate. 'There's Scotch Fingers to go with your tea if you want some. They taste like wet sawdust to me but Sheila says they offer the best value of any biscuit.'

•

Birdie pays attention to the small things as she leaves Griefshare. Spider webs in some iron fretwork, the bittersweet resin scent of eucalyptus, an empty chip packet cartwheeling in the gutter and the intimate swish of lycra as runners bound past without a glance. Eventually her lungs fill and shoulders fall, her skin stops prickling and pulsing.

The air is hot and she is sweating now. The garden is full of grand old European trees. Heading back towards the old fire station on the curling concrete path, she's dwarfed by their summer finery, thousands of huge flapping leaves bigger than Birdie's own hands. But by winter they'll be bare. With great concern for their welfare, Jem had once asked Birdie, 'Why are they so bony, Mummy?'

She takes the path that veers away from the children's playground. She doesn't want to hear the kids begging for an audience and the mothers squinting back at them from under a tree, longing to be anywhere else. When the kids were young, Birdie had yearned for a time when she didn't need to constantly seek out playgrounds, McDonald's, toilets with nappy-changing tables, or beaches; when she wasn't stuck pushing a swing or wiping a bum. She had known every nearby park and where to find shade, a toilet, get water or dispose of a heavy nappy.

Despite herself and logic, Birdie still looks out for Joe. It's a habit. She searches him out as a teenager – shaggy-haired and loose-limbed. She imagines him lolloping, the way fourteen-year-old boys lollop, as though their arms and legs are barely stitched on.

Perhaps he'd be almost as tall as her, able to rest his forearms on the top of her head till she smacked him away. Or perhaps he'd be short and squat, getting ready for a growth spurt. He could be into boys or *Star Wars* or surfing or musical theatre. He could be one of those kids who dresses up as Japanese movie characters.

This is the trick Birdie's brain plays on her regularly – that Joe still exists somewhere, the age he would be now if he hadn't died, simply slipped through a crack in time. As though he might bound up to her, plant a kiss on her cheek and carry on like he'd been on some kind of long cosmic holiday. Birdie can never quite decide if these kinds of thoughts are masochistic or comforting.

Her phone rings, Albert's face flashing up on the screen. He is Birdie's boyfriend now but as a joke Jemima has loaded him into her mother's phone as 'Mr Lee'.

'Hey,' he says languidly, never in a rush. 'Where are you?'

'I've been at Griefshare.'

'How was Jeff?'

'He did a reading from *A Grief Observed*, CS Lewis.'

'Good old Jeff.'

Birdie smiles to herself. 'Good old Jeff.'

'Apparently CS Lewis and Tolkien were mates, did you know that?'

'No,' Birdie replies. 'But it seems like exactly the sort of thing you would know.'

Albert is Dr Lee now, having gained his PhD in pedagogy. He teaches others how to teach.

'I could handle a spot of Narnia right now though,' Birdie says. 'It's boiling. Roll me in some snow.'

'Huh. Makes me think of that quiz night at St Bern's? Do you remember?'

'I'm perimenopausal, Albert. I don't remember yesterday.'

'*Frozen* theme.'

'Ah, right. A Tamsin and Abigail special. I wanted to go to that like a hole in the head. Everyone in ball gowns—'

'Not you though.'

'Not me.'

It was a school fundraiser and Birdie had dressed as a snowman. She could barely sit down in a chair for all the stuffing. All the other women were versions of Elsa – long glittering dresses and blonde hair extensions.

'You were smoking out the back. Remember?'

Birdie doesn't say that she was too drunk to remember.

Albert says, 'Told me that the Meyers were dickheads. Spoke to me like I was a human.'

'You weren't though. You were a polar bear.'

'Touché. God, I was sweating in that thing. Okay, next question.'

'Is this a quiz?' Birdie asks.

'Our first kiss.'

'What do I win?'

'A Thermomix?' Albert suggests.

'Didn't you call that the best Christmas gift ever? Your mum will kill you if you give that away.'

'I'm willing to risk my life.'

'Readings book store,' Birdie answers. 'We went for a midnight walk. You smelled like mint.'

'It was my shampoo.'

Birdie nods to herself. Albert's hair is soft, downy almost, like she imagines a baby bird to feel. 'How did I do?'

'I'll have to check the scores.'

'Good, because I want that Thermomix.'

'It's all yours.'

A boy passes her, earbuds stuffed in, in a different world from this one. He looks through Birdie as though she's made of vapour.

Birdie's gaze follows him. The way he stares down at his phone, the way his hair curls on the back of his neck, the chewed cuffs of his hooded sweatshirt, the precise wear on the soles of his shoes and knowing his feet must pronate.

Albert says, 'I'm all yours.'

Birdie wonders if the boy's mother bought him fresh laces because they look new. She wonders if she scolds him for chewing his cuffs and tells him she needs to book him a haircut. Washes his clothes, buys him shampoo, mends the things he tears, puts away the things he leaves on the floor.

'Birdie?'

•

On Thursday night Birdie holds a piece of card by the corner, her thumb and forefinger barely touching, as though it might be poisoned.

'What is this?'

Baz ignores her. 'Red or white?'

'I'm not staying. I'll go when Jem gets here.'

Baz holds up two bottles.

'Red,' Birdie surrenders. 'Only one though.'

'She could be a while, you know. They chat.'

'I don't know about this group.'

'They're a writing club, Birdie,' Baz says. 'How bad can it be?'

'Have you met them?'

'I've seen them. I've dropped her off and picked her up. They seem all right.'

'Yeah, but have you *met* them? Have you met their parents? Do they have nice parents?'

Baz muses. 'I actually think she might like someone there.'

Birdie looks up sharply, her spine suddenly rod-straight, 'What?'

'Just something she said.'

'What did she say?'

Baz shrugs and smiles, the wine *glug-glug-glug*ging into the glass.

'I don't believe you.' Birdie's eyes narrow. 'She wouldn't tell you anything she doesn't tell me. You're so full of it.'

'Tetchy! You really do need a drink.' Baz slides the shiraz towards her and plucks the card. 'And this . . . it's an invitation.'

'I can see that.'

'From the Turners. She's sending one to you too, she told me. It's probably in your letterbox right now.'

'You can't seriously be thinking of going.'

'Why not? I thought Jem might like it.'

'Sure!' Birdie huffs with cynicism.

'To see some of the crew from early St Bernard's days. It'd be good for her. She's not a leper and neither are they. There's a nice note on the back from Tam. She wants to get the old gang back together.'

'That woman is delusional.'

Baz shrugs. 'She's probably invited Albert too. Has he said anything?'

'No, he hasn't,' Birdie says, voice hot and clipped. 'Hey honey! I got an invite from those arseholes whose pool killed your son. They want to host some kind of reunion. You know, with you and your ex and every woman he put his dick into?'

Baz sighs. 'Are you done?'

Birdie slugs back her wine and pushes it forward for a refill. 'If the shoe fits.'

Baz tops her up. 'They've got a new house.'

'Just up the road from the old house.'

'Well, I do some work with Alex so I'll probably go.'

'Alex Turner. That man is a snake.' Birdie rubs the bridge of her nose. 'You'd take work from Jack the bloody Ripper. And that house—'

Baz interrupts, 'It's *not* that house.' He sighs and points towards the lounge. 'Why don't we sit in there to argue. I can be more comfortable while you sling shit at me.'

Birdie shrugs. 'Wherever you prefer.'

•

Baz and Madison's house always feels staged to Birdie. The lounge chairs are stiff and spotless, the kind you might find in a medical centre reception, and most of the cabinetry is white. Baz only has one painting Birdie likes – it's colourful and abstract, the trunks of gum trees in a crowded cluster – but it's usually propped under the hallway table. She noticed it wasn't there when she came in. Madison probably banishes all items of more than two colours, Birdie thinks to herself.

There is a huge television taking up one wall.

'New telly?'

Baz looks away. 'It was a gift.'

'A gift? From who?'

'It doesn't matter. A client.'

'You take gifts from clients now? What does he do?'

'Wine good?'

'Sure.'

'And where's Madison?'

'She's got a mother's group thing.'

'Archie?'

'With Mum.'

'Why isn't he here with you?'

'I'm . . .' Baz gestures expansively, 'working from home.'

Birdie rolls her eyes. 'On a Thursday night. Of course you are.'

'I meant to ask if you could have Jem an extra night next week. Friday. I've got a work trip.'

'Aha.'

'Aha yes or aha that'd be right?'

'Both.'

'Don't be bitter, Birdie. Yes or no?'

'Yes of course and don't tell me how to be. Did you get her a new phone, by the way?'

'Yes.'

'And earbuds?'

Baz shrugs and nods.

'Could you please run that past me next time? You spoil her and then I look like the shit parent.'

'Okay,' Baz replies, unconcerned.

Birdie's gaze settles on the corner of the room where there is a neat pile of Archie's toys. Big colourful bricks, the kind that are perfect for small hands, trucks, cars and tractors and a wooden train track from IKEA, the exact same kind she'd bought for Joe.

'How is Mr Lee?' Baz asks, smiling down into his glass.

'Don't call him that.'

'Why not? I'm sure he calls me all kinds of names.'

Birdie's eyes narrow. 'Your charms don't work on him – bet you hate that. But no, he's too classy for name-calling.'

'Classy Mr Lee.'

Birdie's jaw clenches. 'There has to be meds for whatever you have. What *have* you got?'

Baz looks up, his voice turning to blades. 'A credit card? Trousers that reach the floor?'

'Dickhead,' Birdie mutters.

'Come on. What kind of man chooses to be a teacher? He's a bit of a sook, isn't he?'

'He's a lecturer now.'

'Ah yeah, a *lecturer*.' Baz's voice is silky and teasing.

'You're an arsehole.' Birdie stands too quickly and wobbles.

Baz reaches out and grabs her wrist. 'Stop.' He's suddenly breathing heavily.

'Let me go.'

'No, wait.' There's something pathetic about him that gives Birdie pause. 'Please?' His eyes are shining. 'You're right. I'm an arsehole.'

Birdie leans back to take him in. 'Did you just say "you're right"?'

A melancholy smile pulls the corners of his mouth. 'That's off the record. I'm really tired. And I like fighting with you these days, you make it interesting.'

Birdie lowers herself back into the chair. 'You have issues. Next you'll be apologising.' She hesitates. 'You know, I genuinely hate your guts, Baz. If you weren't the father of my children, I'd never want to have anything to do with you ever again.'

Baz lifts his palms and smiles. 'See? You make fighting fun.'

Birdie talks into her glass. 'You're messed up.'

They sit in silence for a few moments, Baz's leg twitching like it wants to be running or dancing. He drums the arm of his chair. 'How'd we get here, Bird? You and me, always at each other.'

Birdie glances at the toy train track in the corner. On the mantelpiece next to it is a black and white family photograph with Baz and Madison behind and Archie in front. Birdie swallows what's left in her glass and murmurs, 'Do we need to go over it?'

Baz's gaze drops to the floor. Then he turns to his phone for a few moments. Music is soon streaming out of a nearby speaker. He nods at it. 'So we don't have to talk.'

The song is soothing and orchestral. Birdie is drained from their fighting, the adrenaline now dissipating. She's tempted to close her eyes and float away with the music. She remembered how she used to sing Joe to sleep. He liked 'Annie's Song' by John Denver, which her own father had sung to her. Joe liked the part about the ocean being sleepy best. When the music pauses between tracks, Baz and Birdie look at one another as though they might be having the same recollections. Baz seems weary too.

Then 'Baby Shark' erupts out of the speaker at twice the volume.

Baz's arms fly out in surprise, his wrist catching the edge of his glass. Shiraz spatters over the pristine carpet and he leaps out of his chair. 'Shit!'

Now there's wine on his crotch too, darkening his trousers.

Birdie laughs till she gasps; it's unstoppable. Baz tries to brush the wine from his pants but he makes it worse, the stain spreading.

Birdie gestures with her empty wineglass towards the stain. 'Shall we get you a nappy?'

Baz smiles and shakes his head. 'Oh fuck you.'

'Doo doo de doo de doo,' Birdie replies cheerfully, in time with the song.

•

Three glasses in.

'Watching you try and clean wine out of a carpet is the best part of my day so far.'

Baz is on his hands and knees with a yellow cloth in his hand. 'I think it's getting worse.'

'Of course it's getting worse. You're smearing it everywhere.'

'I don't really know what I'm supposed to be doing.'

'That's pretty clear. It looks like a homicide.'

'Do *you* know how to deal with this?'

'I might,' Birdie says. 'But you couldn't pay me enough to help.'

Baz throws the cloth at the stain and lifts himself to his feet with a groan. He goes to the kitchen and returns with a new bottle of wine. He pours himself a glass and then leans towards Birdie.

'Can't. I've got to drive us home. When Jem finally gets here.'

'You're not driving home now. You're over the limit.'

'Am not.'

'You are!' Baz shakes his head. 'Honestly. Do you ever change?'

'More than you,' Birdie says, pointing at the floor. 'You're going to leave that mess for Madison to clean up?'

Baz shrugs. 'I'm in trouble anyway.'

Birdie's phone vibrates. 'Jem says she's forty minutes away. They went to Hungry Jack's.'

'See? She's fine. You should get an Uber home. You can pick the car up tomorrow.' Baz tops up Birdie's glass and she doesn't resist. 'Remember that time we took the kids to Dreamworld? I've been thinking about it lately.'

'Joe vomiting at the wildlife park?'

'Oh god.' Baz laughs. 'I'd forgotten that part. Right by the kangaroos, wasn't it? And then that other kid chundered too . . .'

'Contagious.'

Baz grimaces.

Birdie raises her glass. 'Fun times.'

'They weren't so bad,' Baz says with a nostalgic sigh. 'Remember how scared Jem was on those huge swings?'

'I think she worried she might get flung out of them.'

'Joe held her hand and said he'd go with her.'

Birdie looks down at her feet.

'He must have been scared,' Baz says. 'Do you think he was scared?'

'I don't know.'

'If he was, he didn't show it. You remember? He had that little red cap on? He was so small. He took her hand and off they went. I think I . . .' Baz rubs his eyes, 'underestimated the little guy.'

Birdie stares. 'What is this, Baz?'

'What do you mean?'

'I don't think I can deal with this tonight.' She's furious. 'You've just now realised how brave Joe was? You don't remember all the times I told you to give him a break?'

'I know you did—'

'He was *quiet*, Baz, he wasn't a coward.'

'I know, Birdie. I see that now.'

'Now?' Her voice quavers. '*Now*? He was four, Baz.' She puts her wine down on the side table with a clatter. 'I should have learned by now not to stay, not to give you any extra chances. I have to go.'

Baz stands up too quickly. He's unsteady on his feet. 'Don't, Birdie. Stay.'

'You've had enough time to figure out your regrets. Years.' Her voice is getting louder. 'I don't need to hear them now.'

Baz opens his mouth to speak and then closes it again.

Birdie jabs her finger at him. 'He was four and you acted like he needed to be a man.'

'I'm sorry.'

Birdie gazes up at the ceiling, throat constricting at his apology. She can't remember the last time Baz said sorry. It doesn't feel like she thought it might – vindicating and triumphant.

'Now?' she whispers. 'Really? Now? You were supposed to watch him, Baz. I asked.'

Baz suddenly seems small and scared. 'I thought we agreed with that therapist that we wouldn't go over it and blame one another.'

'Ha,' Birdie snorts. 'Like you don't blame me in your head all the time. At least I'm being honest about it.' Her vision blurs with her rapidly spilling tears. 'It's too late for all of this.' She presses her fingertips to her eyelids.

Baz steps towards her, placing his hands on her shoulders. 'I'm sorry, Birdie. I mean it. I'm really sorry.'

'Don't touch me!'

She doesn't move away.

'I know I got so many things wrong.'

'This is what you do, isn't it?' Her voice is strained, as though someone has their foot against her throat. 'Change the story, shift the blame, twist the truth.'

'I'm trying to tell you that I'm sorry.'

'No,' she says firmly. 'I don't believe that.'

'You don't trust me.'

'*Of course* I don't trust you.'

When Birdie opens her eyes she sees that Baz is crying too, his face wet and wretched.

Then he leans in and kisses her. The wine and emotion makes Birdie dizzy. She grabs hold of Baz's arms for balance, wanting to push him away, but he kisses her again, more deeply this time, and she clings on and lets him.

BAZ

*S*oon, I will be missing. When Madison calls the police to tell them I haven't come home from my work trip and she can't get in touch with me, they will ask a lot of questions: When did you last see him? When did you last speak to him? How was his frame of mind? Does he have any enemies?

That last one bugs me. The real question is – does anyone get to their mid-forties without having enemies? Maybe you only have a few. Good for you. But there will surely be some you don't even know about. This is the way I figure it – you're not for everyone. Thinking that everyone will or should like you isn't just stupidity, it's manipulation.

Yes, absolutely I have enemies. But I prefer the word Jem reminded me of the other day – it's from her writing club: antagonists. It sounds more elegant and complex than 'enemies'. Antagonists have their own free will, motivations and intentions. In any story, Jem reminds me, antagonists are necessary. A hero isn't a hero without one. Harry Potter is nothing without Voldemort. Superman needs Lex Luthor. Clarice and Hannibal. Robin Hood and Prince John. Donald Trump and The Media. Only people with antagonists make it into history books. Only people with antagonists are interesting enough to write about.

In my line of work, antagonists are par for the course. Let's say you're a salmon farmer. You want the government to make it easier to farm salmon. You want it to be cheap – less tax and tariffs – so you retain greater margin. You want predictability in the market but only if it favours you. You want your product to be highly valued. Prized. Like diamonds, gold and saffron. But you don't want a ton of competition. You want the latest quack doctor eating your salmon every single day and raving about how the oils in its flesh demolish cancer cells or some other bullshit. In fact, you want Gwyneth Paltrow bathing in a tub of salmon after sunning her perineum.

You might think my job – working on behalf of you, the salmon farmer – would be to out-nice the lobbyist for wild mackerel, flathead, sardines and pink snapper. To be the best goddamn fish spin doctor of all the fish spin doctors. Sure, there's some schmoozing and back-scratching, but it's not as simple as that. I can't out-nice the fact that Richard Flanagan wrote a book called Toxic: The Rotting Underbelly of the Tasmanian Salmon Industry. *What do I do? Try and reason with the guy? Counter with goodwill and manners? I'll tell you what actually works: discrediting, diverting, undermining and sidelining.*

Fact is, we don't trust people who are unfailingly kind to us. People who treat us a little mean, those we can believe. Because we know their voice already. It's the voice that lives inside our heads, niggling and nagging, sounding like our mother or our father; it's familiar. So you outsource judgement to these people because they must know better. You trust their guidance. You work to earn their admiration and you love it when you get it because it's not cheap.

Look, I'm not always a dirtbag. But I do think dirtbags have some undervalued skills. We get things done.

Do I feel rotten about a marriage that failed and another headed in the same direction? Sure. But it doesn't sink me. Getting divorced makes things complicated and custody is a bitch, but I'm realistic about whether a relationship is going to work or not, whether it's run its course. I'm pragmatic. If you argue that I'm transactional, I'll say, what's the problem with transactions?

But there's one snag. Loving your kids is different. You love your kids the way you love your own limbs, the way you love air or sunshine or water. You love them to the point of pain. Like an ache you cannot locate but which never gives up. The ache of foreboding doom. When you love a kid, your kid, it's like walking around with a 'kick me' sign on your back enticing God to snap you in two whenever the hell He feels like it. You'd think a love like that would stop you from fucking the whole thing up. But, as it turns out, it doesn't. Love like that is so foreign and rattling it leaves you perpetually terrified. Got self-sabotage tendencies? Don't have children. There's nothing like the love of a child to botch your brain. It strips you down to your worst and truest. Raw as steak. Freshly filleted and poised beneath a tenderiser.

Jemima was supposed to be a boy. All the superstitious tests with a ring on a string and all that nonsense said she was a boy. 'Boy,' Birdie's hippie friends said. 'Boy,' my mother said. 'Boy,' the online fortune-telling test said when Birdie typed in her last known period and age. Birdie wanted to call him 'Banjo' and I wanted 'Joseph'. Birdie figured both could be shortened to Joe.

But after thirty-eight hours of labour and Birdie refusing a caesarean (which I thought was stupid), Jemima slid into the world. She was covered in white paste and beneath all that, her skin was still the colour of cement. She was revolting. Plus, she was attached to a cord that looked like a gruesome rope of old calamari. On the blood-stained bed, Birdie's bits were so swollen and mutilated they reminded me of a gutted fish on the lid of an esky. I wanted to chunder. The whole thing was a sci-fi/dystopian horror show and yet everyone was grinning and cheering and dabbing their eyes, acting like it was the second coming. The obstetrician wrapped up the outcome, now a less awful shade of pink, and passed her over. I tell you, Jemima was *sobbing so hard and mutinously, she was angry from top to toe. Even her bare red gums were incensed.*

I joggled her a bit like a complete amateur, because it seemed like the kind of thing they did in the movies, and suddenly the kid's eyes sprung open. I swear she looked right at me. After that I could barely make sense of anything. The whole world shrunk to me and her. That baby was totally disgusting and perfect. Tiny, mad, pasty and slippery. A shitting factory with the cutest fingers and toes and lips you've ever seen. Mine to keep safe from all the world. I put her back in her mother's arms with zero grace or elegance, instantly terrified. I had no plan or strategy that would guarantee her safety or ensure I wasn't a dreadful parent, and in that moment, I was prepared to let her be named Banjo or SkyLark or Marmalade or Telephone or whatever the hell Birdie wanted. As for her being a girl – I didn't have a moment's disappointment.

I haven't been the best father and now I am gone for good. It's reasonable to say I've had my fair share of fuck-ups and absences. I changed nappies. Sometimes. But I didn't get up to Jem or Joe in the night. There was a lot I didn't do. Birdie bought their clothes, wrapped presents for kids' parties, shuttled them to ballet and swimming lessons, cooked, fixed buttons on shirts, vacuumed, made beds, cleaned sheets, kept dentist and doctor appointments, communicated with teachers, arranged playdates, packed snacks, contributed to school bake sales, remembered Book Week, called my mother, arranged babysitters, washed, bathed and shampooed, packed lunchboxes, wrote notes from the Easter Bunny and the Tooth Fairy, folded laundry, helped out on school trips, combed for nits, organised drawers, did the grocery shopping, took in spare clothes when the kids wet their pants, organised family holidays, made birthday cakes and hosted parties, made sure to be at home when tradies offered an unhelpful six-hour window, administered worm tablets, knew how to stack a dishwasher so it would actually clean the things in it, made friends with the neighbours so they would keep an eye on the house when we went on holidays, held Jem and then Joe in the small hours and all the times they got sick.

I haven't been perfect. But I never aimed to be. I got some things right. I got some things wrong. One thing, on one ordinary summer's afternoon, I got wrong in the worst way possible. You can judge me all you like but your judgement will never compare to my regret. Carried within me. Swallowed, like stones.

MISSING

BIRDIE

Birdie traces a nothing-shape on Albert's naked shoulder, in bed beside her. Outside, the cockies and kookaburras blare and shriek, the way a mother calls to her children in the shitshow of a long afternoon. Someone, somewhere close by, is making coffee. Birdie can smell the tang and punch of it drifting in through the ajar bedroom window. She had woken up too early, before it was day, and waited and watched until a fingernail of sunlight had appeared, painted neon orange.

Birdie hopes Albert will wake up as she lightly strokes his skin. He can sleep anywhere. Birdie has watched him fall asleep in the middle of dinner and once at Jem's birthday party, surrounded by hollering nine-year-olds. Through an electric storm, midway through a movie, and now, after an argument. He's sweet when he's sleeping – intellect and curiosity temporarily on pause, body soft and relieved. She presses herself to his back, head aching, and breathes him in. He still smells like the restaurant they were in last night – woodfire smoke and fresh sourdough.

Birdie listens out for Jem's radio, usually tuned to 3AW. She has it on even when she sleeps, says it makes her feel less alone. But Birdie can't hear it and she resists the pull to get up and check on Jem. Baz still thinks she's too cautious, too fussy, even after everything that happened. She leans back against her pillow, head pulsing, and watches reflections shimmying on the ceiling.

Like Baz said it would, the invite from Tamsin Turner arrived. Jemima put it on the fridge under an old souvenir magnet from Dreamworld, even though Birdie wanted to light it on fire. Baz and that invite were bad news and bad luck. They were drawing her back into the past like quicksand, back into thoughts and memories she doesn't want to keep company with. She's been retracing the moments on that day, something that Dr Patel told her to try and avoid. But it's an old habit now, one that's hard to break. Her brain is a toddler doing exactly what he wants, all desire and no reason – in the water when he shouldn't be, getting himself into trouble.

Birdie arranges the scene in her mind. The children are clusters of wet heads and little limbful bodies. They make a line on one side of the pool ready for Richard's next race. Jem quivers with determination like a baby sparrow. *Ready? Steady?* Paloma's twins – Queenie and Rose – are already in the water, bobbing like a couple of beach balls. Paloma is there too at the pool edge, always on the margins. Madison is on the lawn wrangling all those children, Tamsin sipping a drink and pining for Abigail. Alex is at the barbecue. Albert – only ever 'Mr Lee' back then – is on his way but not fast enough. And Joe is on the second step of the pool, where Birdie left him.

Birdie knows now that if a four-year-old makes a promise, you cannot trust it. Even if you and he have a connection, the same vivid hair and a bond so special and pure you would paint it silver like the tail of a shooting star. Even if you'd confess he is your favourite child, though only secretly, to the right person. Even if he has the dark eyes of an earnest man, an older man, probably a poet or maybe a priest, but one of the good ones. Because he is not wise, he is four.

So before everything happens, before things go wrong, Birdie rearranges things. She plucks Joe out of the pool and wraps him in a towel – *like a burrito, Mama!* – the way he likes. Her and Joe stay next to Richard because he's the one she despises the least out of the whole rotten lot. She doesn't take a bottle of Coke to Madison. She might never have to talk to Madison again if she fixes it right. Baz and Jess can do what they like, Birdie no longer cares. Albert arrives earlier. She can look forward to seeing him. And when Tamsin goes to top up her drink, Birdie does exactly what a good mother is supposed to.

Everything is in order.

The explosion stays in the bomb, the lightning in the dark cloud. There are no black cats, ladders to walk under or spilled salt. No invisible ledger with a price owed. There is no blame like a bow firing poisoned arrows and no burning, scarring guilt to atone for. No need for guilt at all. Joe is not gone. All of their lives – hers, Joe's, Jemima's, even Paloma's and Richard's – can take the course they were meant to take.

•

Birdie listens to Albert's teeth grinding together as he stretches his long feet. She doesn't tell him that she does these things – imagines it all differently and looks for Joe when she's out.

She kisses the divots of Albert's spine until he rolls towards her and opens his eyes. His lashes are long and dark, pretty like a girl's, and he kisses her, sleepy and slow, before sitting up. He tries to find his glasses with his hair falling into his eyes. His palm hits an old poetry book on the side table first. Birdie had found it in her bag after she last saw Baz. She feels a bolt of shame at that memory – his lips on hers, sinking in to his touch like old times.

Albert slides his glasses on. 'Is it early?'

'Seven,' Birdie says. 'Almost. I can't hear Jem.'

Albert yawns and gets out of the bed. 'You want me to check?'

Birdie looks him up and down – the bare legs and chest, his sleepy face and rumpled hair. 'Maybe not like that.'

Albert searches the floor for his clothes. He yanks up his trousers and buckles his belt as Birdie watches. She wants to curl her fingers through his belt loops, tug him back into bed and kiss him so hard the world around them turns to ether. Instead she gets up too and throws on a robe.

She pushes gently against Jem's bedroom door. 'Her room is empty.'

Albert whispers, 'She's not there?'

Birdie can't answer. She turns to Albert with fear skewering her heart.

'Baz and Madison?' he asks.

'No, she's staying with them tonight.'

Albert takes her shoulders in his hands. 'Where was she last night?'

'She went out with new friends,' Birdie says. 'People she met at a club.'

'A club?'

'Not like that. The writing club.'

Albert's hand slips down her arm to hers. He grips it. 'Let's go to the kitchen and think it through. Okay?'

'Okay.'

Birdie sits in the blue chair at the dining table. Last summer she and Jem had taken to their old wooden chairs with test paint pots. Birdie figured it was cheaper than buying new ones. The colour of the blue chair she's sitting on was called 'Havana Memories'. Albert takes two mugs out of the cupboard. He always uses the cup with a giant 'A' printed on it that Jem gave him for Christmas. He switches on the kettle.

'I think she said something about a gig.' Birdie presses her fingertips to her brow. 'Brunswick?'

Albert drops a teabag into each mug. 'Who can we call?'

Birdie's head hurts. 'I don't have any of their phone numbers. She's been . . . I don't know, she's been different lately – something on her mind. She's been so quiet the last few weeks. You noticed that, right? I think she might have met someone. A new girlfriend.'

Birdie stands and goes into the bedroom, returning with her phone pressed to her ear. 'She's not answering, Albert.'

'Give it a second.'

Birdie dials again.

'She's probably sleeping,' Albert says.

'Sleeping where?'

Albert brings the mugs to the table and sits down. 'Didn't you put that tracer thing on her phone?'

'She earned the right to take it off again.'

'How?'

Birdie sighs. Jem is a good negotiator, a trait she probably got from her father. On top of that she seems much older than she is; she had to grow up fast. Birdie can't even remember how she'd argued her way out of the tracing app.

'I'm sure she's okay,' Albert says. 'She probably stayed with a friend. Didn't you say she was hanging out with one of the Albertini girls lately?'

'Queenie. But I don't think she's seen her in a while.'

Albert sips his tea slowly. 'She'll probably call you back in a minute. Did you say she met someone? At this club?'

Birdie frowns. 'Maybe. I don't know.'

She calls Jem's number again, her eyes filling with tears. 'It went to voicemail.'

Birdie presses her hand to her mouth. She stands and goes to the sink.

'She's a responsible kid, Birdie.'

'Is she?' Her voice rises. There's been a distance between her and Jem lately. She can't put her finger on it but she knows it's there.

Albert pats the wooden table, worn with age and glitter stuck in its crevices from when Jem was younger. 'Sit down for a second.'

'She said something about someone in the club.' Birdie's throat feels choked. 'I can't remember the name. Where was she going?' She grips the edge of the sink. 'Was it a gig? Or someone's house? Maybe it was this kid's house . . .'

'I'm sure she'll call back.'

Birdie turns to him, hands clenched. 'How can you be sure?'

'Her phone probably ran out of charge.'

'I got her a mobile charger for Christmas.'

'She might have forgotten it?'

'She could be in a ditch!'

'She's not in a ditch.'

Birdie is shaking. 'You don't know that!'

Albert stands and moves towards her. He reaches out.

'Don't touch me.'

'I'm sure—'

Birdie points. 'Except you're *not* sure, Albert. No one can be sure. Not ever.'

Lightning in the storm cloud.

Black cats.

Open ladders.

Albert's hands fall to his sides. A key crunches in the lock and they both turn.

'Hey Mum. Hi Albert.'

•

The figure in the doorway is more woman than girl. She's small-framed, wearing denim shorts, heavy boots, a tiny backpack and snug crop top. She holds an oversized purple sweatshirt in one hand, almost big enough to be a doona. Her fox-orange hair is short at the front and longer at the back – she cut it herself before Christmas. Her eyelids have been painted with metallic silver eyeshadow and they look as though they're made of foil.

Her dark brown eyes slide towards her mother. 'You okay?'

'Where were you?'

She shrugs, 'Out.'

'I tried to call.'

Jem dumps her keys on the kitchen counter and glances at Birdie's untouched mug of tea. 'You drinking that?'

'I tried to call!' Birdie squeaks.

Jem takes her mum's tea. She shrugs. 'I had something to do. I went for a walk. My battery's dead.'

Albert avoids eye contact with Birdie as Jem looks him over. 'Where did you come from anyway, Albie? You stay here last night?'

'He came for breakfast,' Birdie says quickly.

'Yeah?' she says, unconvinced and amused. 'What are we having then?'

•

Birdie plucks a rogue blueberry off her plate and pops it into her mouth. Jemima has gone to her room after eating three big pancakes with maple syrup and sprinkles.

'She went for a walk,' Albert says. 'You buying that?'

'In Doc Martens,' Birdie adds. 'And full makeup.'

'Hmm.'

'I'm trying to pick my battles,' Birdie says.

He drums the tabletop with anxious fingers. 'I'm sorry about what I said. About her not being in a ditch.'

'You were right though. She wasn't.'

'I know. But I shouldn't have said it.' He lowers his voice. 'Are we going to talk about last night?'

'What about it?'

'We never finished our conversation. I want to be part of your life, Birdie. A proper part.'

'Lives,' she replies. 'There are two of us.'

'That's deflection and you know it.'

The Panadol tablets she swallowed haven't taken effect yet. 'I'm a mum, Albert. I have to think about Jem.'

'I can help. I can share bills, make it easier. Surely I can do a better job than . . .'

He stops himself short. Albert keeps whatever feelings he holds about Baz to himself. Classy indeed. Birdie is less gracious, especially after a few wines.

'We don't need looking after, Albie.'

'Everyone needs looking after, Birdie.' He shakes his head slowly. 'I want my life to move forward. If this – whatever this is – is going nowhere then I need to know. I need to change things.'

Birdie sighs. 'It's been a crazy morning.'

Albert reaches for her hands. 'I want to be here for crazy mornings, Birdie, that's the point. I don't want to pretend I've come for breakfast.' He rubs her knuckles. 'I don't want to be a tourist. I want to be a family.'

'I like how things are.'

'I know. I know you do, Birdie,' Albert looks crestfallen, 'but what about us? Me?'

'I had a family, Albie. I had things the way you want them and it wasn't any good.'

'I'm not him,' Albert mutters.

Birdie feels another pang of guilt. Albert doesn't ask for much, he's usually unruffled. Birdie's mind keeps pinballing back to her and Baz, twisted around one another, naked and slick with sweat. Her hair in her eyes, his breath in her ears. They had made love in such a rush, in such a frenzy, that they'd not used a condom. It was probably nothing to worry about but she did anyway. She didn't want to be pregnant or the proud new owner of a sexually transmitted disease, and she can't trust Baz or where his dick has been. She feels a bit nauseous.

'It would be different,' Albert pleads, 'with me. Us.'

Birdie doesn't have time to reply.

'Mum?' Jem thunders down the hallway, phone in hand. 'Did you get any calls from Madison?'

Birdie shakes her head.

'My phone just charged and I have a bunch of texts from her.'

'Maybe she's trying to work out plans for the day. You're staying there tonight, remember?'

'They're not like that. They sound . . . urgent.'

They all turn towards the door where there's the sound of feet shuffling and muffled voices.

•

'Mrs King?'

The two police officers in the doorway couldn't look more different. A young woman in uniform and a tall, middle-aged man in a suit.

'Sort of,' Birdie replies. In order to keep the same name as Jem and Joe she'd never changed her surname. 'Ms.' She corrects.

The man presents his badge. 'Sorry to bother you.' His voice is warm, 'I'm Detective Zavros, this is Officer Braithwaite.'

Birdie leads them through to the lounge where Jem, standing in the open kitchen, stares at her mother. 'You did *not* call them about me. I told you, I went for a walk.'

Birdie shakes her head. 'No, I didn't call them about you.'

The detective says to Birdie, 'We're looking for Sebastian King.'

'What?'

'Madison King reported him missing last night.'

'What?' Birdie glances at Jemima who has gone suddenly silent, her face wan. Albert clears his throat and Birdie looks towards him now, remembering the times she has said hateful things about Baz to Albert. Wishing him gone. Wishing he would die somewhere quietly, uneventfully, painlessly. Wishing she had made different choices, never walked down that aisle, never met him at that party.

Hitting rewind on the video and watching it extract him from her life. Pause, do it all again without him in it.

Birdie steps closer to the police officers. She senses Albert moving to stand beside her. Her voice has shrunk. 'How long has he been missing?'

'Approximately twenty-four hours.'

Jem is in the lounge now. She whispers, 'A whole day?'

Detective Zavros raises a palm. 'It's very likely he's with someone he knows; that's usually the case. Mr King went to Bendigo for work and forgot to take his phone with him, his wife says.' He pauses and checks their faces before continuing. 'Mr King called her from his hotel room when he arrived and should have been home yesterday. We were just wondering if he'd made contact with either of you.'

'He didn't take his phone with him?' Jem drops down onto a couch. Birdie rushes to her side.

'We didn't mean to upset anyone.' Detective Zavros takes a half-step backward. 'We have to ask,' he says. 'It's part of our missing persons protocol. As I said, it's likely he's with someone he knows.'

Birdie rubs her daughter's arm. 'In which case,' she says, her voice protective, 'you can both leave now.'

•

The police stay longer than Birdie wanted, asking more questions and checking messages on phones. When they return to their car, Officer Braithwaite flicks through her notes, muttering. George turns the engine over and indicates.

Braithwaite is young and new. She treats every case like a TV crime mystery, looking for hidden clues and angles. George tries to be patient with her enthusiasm but in his experience the answers are usually obvious.

'What are you saying?'

'Nothing,' she replies. 'Well, maybe something. Two things actually.'

'Go on then,' he says with some reluctance.

'Did you see the invite on the fridge?'

George shakes his head and concentrates on the traffic.

'Fancy-looking. Had the text stamped in – I don't know what that's called but it's expensive. The other Mrs King had one too.'

Letterpress, George thinks but doesn't say. 'And the other thing?'

'The last contact she had with Mr King was a bit weird. She showed me text messages on her phone and there was one from a couple of weeks ago. Mr King said, "I'll see you on the weekend. Late morning?" And she replied, "Okay".'

'Uh huh.'

'But before that Mr King had written, "Sorry about before. Didn't mean for that to happen".'

George squints into the sunlight. 'What happened before?'

'I don't know,' Officer Braithwaite replies. 'She said she couldn't remember. Said it was probably a misunderstanding.'

George hesitates. He hadn't expected to have the Kings back in his life so soon after meeting Paloma. He felt a bit dishonest seeing Birdie again and not saying who he was or, more accurately, who he'd been.

'I imagine it was probably a minor argument,' George says to Braithwaite, 'but worth noting. I want to know more about his work. Can you find out who he works with and for? Any conflicts or disagreements? Do a company search to see what else he is involved with.'

Braithwaite nods in reply.

Missing persons don't usually stay missing – they return home. It's likely that George won't see Birdie again, perhaps for another ten years. Most missing persons are depressed or having an affair, running to or away from something or someone.

But an uncomfortable feeling ricochets inside George. A gut instinct, an uneasiness. It reminds him of biting into the soft part of an apple where there's a hidden bruise, a bit of rot.

MADISON

The detective takes up a lot of space compared to his sidekick, a slight woman who seems jumpy and restless. She keeps glancing around Madison's lounge as though searching for something out of place. A hatchet leaning up against the wall or a chalk outline drawn on the tiled hallway. Madison gets the distinct impression she'll grow into her job, becoming officious and overenthusiastic to arrest.

Detective Zavros is wedged in a chair with a mug of coffee balanced on his knee and Archie has taken a shine to him.

'Train goes fast!' he is saying, driving his toy up the front of the detective's ankle.

'No email, text or message of any kind?' the detective asks.

Madison shakes her head again.

'No withdrawal of funds?'

'No.'

'From any account? Credit card, savings?'

Archie makes a high-pitched train-whistle sound and Madison startles. The detective seems unfussed. Madison shakes her head again. 'Archie?'

Her son ignores her, as he often does when engaged in a game. Her own mother would have clipped her around the ear or kicked the back of her legs. Madison is resolved to be nothing like her mother. It terrifies her when the urge to yell bubbles up inside of her. She worries that her genes are irrepressible, that it's just a matter of time before violence erupts. She presses her neatly manicured nails into the palms of her hands and tries again with a softer tone. 'Arch, honey?'

He turns to her with eyes that match his father's.

'Why don't you go get your Lego from your room? You could bring it down and show the policeman.'

His eyes widen and he nods, sprinting away. Detective Zavros lowers his voice. 'What about adversaries, Mrs King?'

Madison mulls it over. 'None that I know of. Baz was—' The other cop straightens with interest. '*Is* . . . well, people either like him or hate him.' Madison looks at the cop again, now making notes. 'I don't mean hate. He's got his ways. Some people like them and others don't.'

'What do you mean by that, Mrs King?'

Madison sighs, 'You know what he does for work?'

'Technically, yes,' Detective Zavros replies. 'I don't know much about lobbying specifically. Does his work make people dislike him?'

Madison studies the detective, 'Where are you from?'

'Me? Northcote.' He nods slowly, as though remembering, 'But it was a different place from what it's like now.'

Madison nods, 'I know. Rougher, right?'

'Something like that,' the detective says, with a small smile.

'Not her though,' Madison says, tipping her head towards the officer. 'She was from somewhere nice.'

Officer Braithwaite lifts her gaze from her notebook.

'Maybe not fancy but decent. Houses with yards, trampolines, that kind of thing. Knew people on your street, juice box in your lunchbox.'

'I'm not sure I get—'

'Look, some people are certain about right and wrong and how you should go about things. Who you should help and who you shouldn't. It's black and white. You're good or you're bad. Simple.' She mutters, 'It's easy if everything has always been easy.'

Detective Zavros leans in, 'Tell me exactly how this relates to your husband, Mrs King.'

'Relates to him being missing? I don't know. You asked about enemies.'

'Adversaries.'

'Right. I'm saying sure, not everyone agrees with him and how he is. If Baz found fifty bucks on the street he isn't going to hand it in anywhere or ask around to see who dropped it. He'd put it in his pocket, same as me.'

'And you're saying that some people wouldn't agree with that. They don't agree with the way he is?'

Madison shrugs, 'I was never looking for a nice husband, Detective. Some people want nice. Some people need nice. It makes them comfortable.'

Detective Zavros looks down at his coffee and takes a sip. 'But were there particular people who didn't like your husband, Mrs King? Perhaps through his work?'

'I don't know,' Madison says, 'I don't ask. His work is his work, it's none of my business.'

'I see. And between the two of you?' He hesitates. 'Everything is all right?'

'Fine. Everything is fine.'

Madison looks over again at the officer scribbling. 'Can you stop that?'

Officer Braithwaite's head snaps up. 'Stop what?'

'Writing everything down.'

'Well, it's my job to—'

'That's okay, Braithwaite.' The detective instructs, 'You can take a minute.'

The officer rests her pen against the page with her lips pressed tightly together.

'Mrs King,' the detective asks, 'did Sebastian have a PC here at home?'

'His laptop is upstairs.'

'It might help us to take a look at it. May we take it with us?'

Madison shrugs. 'Sure, I can get it.'

'Thank you.'

Madison thinks she sees the detective glare at the officer but she can't be sure. She is so tired she feels a bit woozy. Archie rockets down the stairs with a tub of Lego rattling. He runs straight into Madison's legs, the tub lip connecting with her bare shin.

'Fuck!' she growls, clenching her teeth as Lego bricks scatter across the floor. The police officers and Archie all look at her.

Archie's lip started to wobble. 'Mummy!' Tears shine in his eyes.

'Shit, fuck,' she says again, feeling her own tears falling.

'Bad words, Mummy!' There's a sob in her son's throat.

'I'm sorry, I'm so sorry,' Madison says, bending down to pick up the bricks. 'Sorry, sweetie.'

Detective Zavros is quickly beside her. 'Here, let me help.'

They pick up the bricks together as Archie sniffs and Madison's own tears fall on her hands. When the floor is clear, the detective picks up the tub. 'I think Officer Braithwaite knows how to make a castle.'

'A what?' the officer asks from the lounge, fingers still gripping a pen.

'A *castle*,' the detective replies in a low, firm voice. He turns to Madison. 'Is there someone we can call, Mrs King? I don't know if you should be alone.'

Someone to call.

Madison's mother-in-law would weep all over her and then she'd have an extra person to comfort and another mouth to feed. Corey would probably nod off on her couch or say he was coming and not show up. Madison has no friends. Her old boss, Abigail Meyer, would be no help, she's only interested in gossip or proximity to power. Madison has no power and doesn't want to give rise to gossip. She would ordinarily call Baz.

She can feel herself calcifying inside. Before Baz was in her life, Madison had learned to be self-reliant and count on no one.

'No,' she says stiffly, 'I'm fine. I'll get the computer for you.'

RICHARD

'I thought you were taking us for a ride, mate!'

The man sitting across from him is laughing. Richard stares at the photograph on his desk, an image of his wife, Jess, and their boys, Jack, Monty and Harrison. The kids are eating ice creams and Jess is smiling into the camera. She's wearing tortoiseshell sunglasses beneath a big straw hat.

'Jonathon!' the man's wife hisses.

Richard forces a casual smile, 'Sorry?'

'Your talk, you know. All the – prices have gone up, freight is unreliable, materials are out of stock,' he explains, 'taking the mick.' He waves his hand around Richard's office as though that explains it.

'No,' Richard says trying to sound light-hearted but falling short. His voice is clipped, 'I don't take the mick.'

Jonathon raises his palms as though Richard was having a go at him, 'All right, all right!'

Jonathon's wife stares at Richard, conveying a wordless apology, while Richard tugs at his ironed shirt collar. He is uncomfortable in an office and in ironed clothes. Plus, he knows that Jonathon will not forget that his joking jab went unplacated; that Richard didn't kowtow to him. Sure enough, Jonathon sulks in his chair for the next fifteen minutes while they work out a payment plan for the outstanding invoices. When they leave, Richard rests his head in the bowl of his palms.

'Done?' His new office manager, Brooke, is in the doorway.

Richard nods. 'I know I am. With them.'

'Why do we have to make a payment plan when they're the arseholes who missed their payments?'

Brooke is wearing a soft silky pantsuit splashed with bold colour – scarlet, turquoise and dandelion-yellow. Her lipstick matches the blood-red colour on the fabric. She's been with Richard's business for a few weeks and she's organised, efficient and able to take a joke.

Richard shrugs. 'Because the customer is always right and Covid hit people hard and I don't want to spend a minute in court with Jonathon or his lawyer.'

'Fair enough,' Brooke mutters. 'Want to get a drink?'

Richard glances at the clock on the wall of the office. His sons think owning a wall clock is hilarious. They've grown up with clocks on phones. They've never had to turn a clock backward or forward for daylight savings in their lives. It's quarter to six.

'Where are you going?'

'The Shammy.'

Richard remembers that Jess is in Melbourne with Lizzie today but he can't remember what for – photography exhibition? Matinee? Shopping trip? Saoirse, the physio student who lives down the road, is making dinner for the boys. Jack will hate that; Saoirse is only a few years older than him.

Richard glances back at the photograph on his desk. It was from the first family holiday they took just after they moved to Kyneton. Nowhere fancy – just a roadie to Warrnambool; they'd stayed at the campground. Richard was determined to have a good time.

To feel the sun and salt on their skin. To captain them out of the darkness of the previous few months and baptise themselves free of Hawthorn. To cleanse it all away. It was the same year the Meyers went to Paris and the Turners to Disneyland, like nothing had happened, like they weren't all changed. Abigail and Tamsin posted dozens of snaps on social media – Minnie Mouse, peace signs under the Eiffel Tower, macarons, American drugstores and Parisian cosmetic stores.

Warrnambool wasn't Disneyland or Europe, but it was the first time in a long time Richard had seen Jess relax. Laugh. She took most of their family photos but he'd sneaked the camera from her bag and taken that photo.

Richard answers Brooke, 'The Shammy it is.'

•

The Shamrock Hotel roosts on the corner of Lauriston and Mollison streets. Double-storeyed, hen-red with a row of balconies on the upper floor for staying guests and a drive-through bottle-o around the back. There are specials for senior cardholders and a dog-friendly dining area outside. At Christmas Richard books a big table for his workers, somewhere out of view so they can get blind drunk without being spotted by clients. Though new carpet has been put in, the Shammy has plenty of ghosts. Gold prospectors, dusty and deflated; bankers in three-piece suits and hats; wheat farmers.

Richard goes to the bar to buy a local craft beer and get Brooke a gin and tonic. The bartender, Colin, greets him with the same question he always asks, 'How are the fancy folks treating you?'

'I'm still alive. For now.'

The standard laugh from Colin as Richard waits for his beer while leaning on the bar top, enjoying the coolness against the soft part of his arms.

Richard delivers the gin and tonic to Brooke. She grips the glass like it is salvation.

Brooke lives in an apartment above a home interiors store on the main street of town. 'If you can call it town' is her running joke. The locals still swivel to take her in when she walks by. Colin, at the bar, is staring, polishing a glass for too long.

'Does he always do that?' Brooke asks, shifting a sheath of caramel hair over one shoulder.

'Not to me,' Richard replies.

Brooke stirs her gin and tonic with the tiny black straw it came with.

'I'm still getting used to a smaller place, I guess,' Brooke says. She tries to smile. 'I do like Kyneton though.'

'You don't have to,' Richard replies.

'Are you sure?' Brooke snorts. 'People seem to get upset if you don't.'

'They don't want you to leave,' Richard explains. 'That's why they insist it's paradise.'

The first year Richard, Jess and the boys moved, everyone kept saying, 'The air is much better, don't you think?' or 'You'd never go back, am I right?' The Dhillons had appreciated the ardent persuasion. The boys were fine, they slotted in like they'd lived rurally all their lives, but it took a while for Jess and Richard to find their feet.

'You never said why you wanted to leave Melbourne.'

Brooke smiles shyly. 'You never asked.'

'I didn't want to be nosy.'

'Unlike everyone else . . .' Brooke shrugs. 'My marriage fell apart.'

'I'm sorry to hear that,' Richard says. 'I didn't know.'

He takes a deep drink of his cold beer, gratefully noticing the condensation of the glass against his fingertips. 'It's a good place to start over,' he mumbles.

'Well, it was a long time coming. No kids. I needed a change.'

Richard nods, finishing his beer in one more swallow, keen to change the subject away from messy marriages and needing change. 'Shall I get us another round?'

Brooke offers to pay but Richard waves the gesture away. He's old-fashioned. Plus, it means he can walk away from the conversation.

At the bar, Colin nods towards Brooke. 'New office manager, right? What's her name again?'

'Brooke Munroe.'

'Is she single?'

'I'm not her dad, mate.'

Richard's phone vibrates in his pocket. The screen reads 'Unknown number' so he drops it back where it came from. At the table, Brooke is using her phone to check her lipstick. He carries her drink to her and places it on the cardboard coaster.

Her smile is wide and shiny. 'I've been talking about myself too much,' she says apologetically. 'Tell me more about you and the boys.'

Richard lowers himself onto a stool. 'There's not much to tell.'

Brooke pushes at his shoulder. 'There has to be! You haven't brought them in to meet me yet. What are they like?'

'Expensive mostly.'

Brooke laughs loudly. Her teeth are blazing white.

'Also smelly and noisy. Jack is sixteen, Monty fifteen and then the youngest, Harrison, is thirteen.' Richard pauses. 'Someone is always missing the toilet and pissing on the floor.'

'No more kids for you?'

'Hell, no.'

His phone rings again and it's the same notification on the screen.

Brooke peers over. 'Scammer.'

'This is the second call tonight. It could be about the boys.'

'Did they leave a message the first time?'

'No. But I had a weird text message a couple of weeks ago too. I should get it.'

Brooke shrugs as Richard answers the phone. 'Hello?'

'Is this Mr Richard Dhillon?'

'Who's asking?'

'I'm Detective George Zavros with the Victoria Police. We are trying to locate a missing person. I'm sorry it's late.'

Richard grips the top of the table. 'Jack? Monty?'

'Sorry? Oh no. Not a family member.'

'Is everything okay?' Brooke mouths at him.

'Sorry, Mr Dhillon. I didn't mean to alarm you. There is absolutely nothing to worry about. We're trying to locate a missing person, someone we think you might know.'

'Who?'

'Sebastian King.'

The name sends a chill through him. He stands and moves away from the table. Brooke watches him, stirring her gin.

'We understand you were with him the day his son died. We're trying to work out if his disappearance had anything to do with that or if you knew where he might be.'

'That was nine years ago.'

Detective Zavros hesitates. 'Yes. It's a long shot. But we are following all avenues of enquiry—'

Richard cuts him off. 'We're not close.' He paces around the entrance to The Shammy. 'Where'd he go missing from?'

'Well, that's the thing. He was in Bendigo.'

'Bendigo?'

'For work.'

Kyneton sits almost equidistant between Melbourne and Bendigo. Practically smack bang in the middle, depending on which route you take.

'He just . . . vanished?'

'I thought he might have come to see you, or your wife—'

Richard's stomach lurches. 'What are you trying to suggest?'

'Nothing. I'm not suggesting anything. Mr King was in Bendigo, we know that for sure, and you and your wife live in Kyneton. It's just one line of inquiry.'

'We haven't seen him.' Richard moves aside to let a couple come into the pub. 'We haven't seen him since the funeral.'

'Right. Of course. So neither of you has seen Mr King?'

'No,' Richard says flatly. 'Neither of us.' He can hear Detective Zavros making notes. He asks, 'How long has he been missing?'

'A few days,' the detective replies.

'Is Birdie okay?'

'More concerned for their daughter.'

'They've been through a lot.'

'I'm sure we will find him,' Zavros says. 'We tend to.'

Richard hesitates. He has wished, more than once, for Sebastian King to disappear.

'If you think of anything, please get in contact with Victoria Police. Just ask for me – Detective Zavros. George.'

'I will.'

'Oh, and please let your wife know. If she has had any contact or knows anything, I'd appreciate speaking to her directly.'

'Leave it with me.'

'Thank you for your time, Mr Dhillon. I'll let you get back to your night.'

Richard nods and turns towards Brooke, who's staring at her phone. He realises that she's very pretty. He pockets his phone and returns to the table. Colin's laughter rings out from the bar. It reminds Richard of Alex Turner. Alex and Baz King had been thick as thieves back in the day; Richard was the third wheel, the odd one out.

'What was all that about?' Brooke asks. 'The phone call?'

Richard shakes his head. 'Nothing really.'

'It sounded serious.' Brooke leans over conspiratorially. 'Apparently scammers are going *nuts* these days. They'll try anything.'

Richard drinks the rest of his beer too quickly, nodding. 'That's the truth. Anything.'

•

Brooke tells Richard about her family. Her father was a bricklayer and her mother a singer – she toured with Jimmy Barnes. But she died right after Brooke got married and that was the beginning of the end of the relationship.

Only half of Richard is at the table and in the pub. The other half is taking a dense pillow to Sebastian King's smug face.

'I think I married him to make Mum happy. And then when she was gone . . . I dunno,' Brooke says, 'he lit nothing inside me. You know?'

Richard clocks that they haven't eaten any dinner and he won't be able to drive home. Brooke is on a roll. She tells Richard that she'd wanted kids but her ex-husband hadn't been keen. Now, she says, slurring, he's with a woman who has twins.

'*Twins*, can you even believe it?!'

Richard thinks of Paloma Albertini and her girls. Strangely, he's forgotten their names. He wonders if his brain did that on purpose – wiped the slate clean. He fetches a big bottle of chilled water and makes Brooke drink a whole glass on his watch. Then he remembers: *Rose and Queenie*. He slaps the table with his palm and Brooke roars with laughter, asking what the hell that was for. He contemplates telling her about Joe King. He hasn't ever told anyone in Kyneton but he doesn't imagine Brooke will stay in Kyneton long. The child psychologist they saw once in Melbourne told Richard and Jess to talk about Joe and what happened to show the boys they had full permission to share their feelings. They didn't.

Colin brings two tequila shots to their table.

'On the house!' he says, looking at Brooke.

Later, on her way back from the bar with more drinks, someone turns up the music and Brooke realises it's Jimmy Barnes. 'Can you believe it?!' she cries.

She dances at the table, singing along. Then she gets emotional and it's awful to watch her cry. It makes Richard feel uncomfortable when people cry. He reaches an arm around Brooke's shoulders in a half-hug and rubs the top of her arm.

'I'm sorry,' he says, really meaning, 'Please stop'. He passes her a paper napkin from the holder on the table. Brooke sniffs and says they could probably do with more tequila after all that and Richard couldn't agree more. He rushes to buy two more shots to keep Brooke in a not-crying state.

The music switches to Beyoncé's 'Single Ladies' and Brooke is happy. She claps to the beat and three guys near the bar turn around and watch her hips swinging from side to side. Colin cheers.

'We should probably hit the road,' Richard suggests.

Brooke doesn't want to go, but Richard promises to order hot chips from the local takeaway shop on their way to her apartment. Colin seems disappointed as they wave and head off.

•

Outside the pub, Brooke veers from left to right across the pavement, her hipbone occasionally bumping into Richard's. Her laughter clatters down the quiet streets like empty glass bottles. He leads her to the takeaway shop, where she lolls in the green plastic chair out the front waiting for the chips to bubble and brown in the deep fryer.

When they have cooled a little, Brooke snatches the chips from Richard's hands and crams them into her mouth. When he reaches out for them she dodges away with the packet. He reaches, she dodges, cackling. All the way down Mollison Street they play this game and Brooke's laughter grows louder and louder. It makes

Richard feel good. Jess no longer laughs at his jokes. Jess doesn't laugh much at all these days.

'What's in Bendigo?' Brooke asks when they reach her apartment.

'What?'

'Bendigo. You just said Bendigo.'

'No I didn't.'

'All right, crazy,' Brooke surrenders. 'Have a chip then.'

Richard accepts a handful and they lean against the wall next to her door.

'How are you going to get home?' she asks.

'Actually, I don't know.'

They laugh in unison. The chips have left salt on their lips and fingers.

'You don't have to go home if you don't want to.' Brooke reaches for his hand. 'You can stay here.'

Their fingers lace together easily, lubricated with chip grease. She smiles at him.

'I'm married,' he says.

'I know,' she replies.

Her lips on his are strange and foreign and Richard feels as though he's hovering an inch or so beyond his body. He hasn't kissed anyone other than Jess for over twenty years. He notices all the differences. Brooke's lips are fuller and she presses more insistently at him. Her mouth is somehow wetter than he's used to and she smells different – her skin, her hair, her perfume, all woody and barbed like lime and crushed pine needles. Like one of those Aesop stores Jess likes so much. He suddenly can't breathe.

'Are you okay?'

'No. Oh god.' He disentangles his fingers from hers.

Brooke looks as though she's been slapped.

'Shit. I'm sorry . . .'

His senses instantly sharpen. He notices the hint of autumn cool in the air and the acrid stink of chip grease. The bitter tang of hops lingers in his mouth and he sees the way Brooke's lipstick has smeared beyond the line of her lips. The pain of rejection flickers across her face. She reaches into her handbag.

He begs, 'I shouldn't have . . . I don't know what I was . . .'

She finds her keys and shakily pushes them into the lock of the door.

'Will you—' Richard's tongue is so thick and gummy, he can't seem to speak in whole sentences. 'Will you be okay?'

Brooke raises her palm. She tosses her head, her other hand on the door in front of her. Before Richard can say anything else she moves quickly up to her apartment, springing from step to step. There is a half-formed apology on his lips when the door swings back and closes in his face.

•

Goosebumps freckle Richard's arms. The darkness has coagulated. He walks back past The Shammy and sees Colin stacking stools on top of the bar. He reaches his parked car and unlocks it to fetch his jacket, feeling both cold and stupid. He keeps walking down Mollison Street with thoughts punching out in time with his heavy feet.

You fool.
You fool.
You fool.

He feels nauseous.

His heart is beating rapidly and he's so hot he has to take his jacket off again.

He has never been disloyal to Jess for a minute and now he's just kissed one of his staff.

He pins it on hearing Baz's name again.

He feels like his life might be unspooling.

He knows exactly who to blame.
He last felt like this nine years ago.

•

After the ambulance left with the Kings inside it, Alex Turner had poured whiskeys and looked panicked. There weren't any jokes he could make to lighten the mood. Without jokes, Alex was nothing. Richard's sons were stunned into silence. When they finally got home, Richard put Jack into bed in the clothes he was wearing. Harrison had stripped off and clambered into his favourite Princess Elsa dress. Monty, only five then, had tears streaming down his face but didn't make a sound; he would remain the most sensitive of their three. Richard robotically made lunchboxes for the next day, stacking them neatly in the fridge, even though none of them would be going to school. He put the dishwasher on. Eventually he sat at the end of his own bed like a visitor.

Jess sobbed. 'I'm so sorry,' she kept saying. 'I'm so sorry, Richard.'

Richard felt the memory of the weight of Joe's body in his empty arms. He saw his hair darkened by the water and his skin lifeless. Baz and Jess had come out of the bathroom together in that very moment. Realisation shuddering through Richard like electricity. One afternoon, one moment, and his whole life had slid sideways.

Hours seemed to pass with him at the end of their bed before Richard rose on unsteady legs and undressed. He switched off their bedroom light before slipping under the covers. The dark shape beside him now seemed unfamiliar.

Jess's hand found his shoulder in the darkness. 'Richard?'

His eyes squeezed shut at the sound of her voice.

Richard had loved Jess the first moment he saw her. She'd been standing at the bar in a club on Smith Street that no longer existed. She and a friend ordered two bottles of those radioactive green pre-mixed drinks. Jess's wavy hair had been straightened so severely that static strands stood up around her face like a halo. She wore a low-cut top, black skirt and lace-up boots, like a strong yet sexy character from a video game who could run up walls or ninja flip down brick-lined alleyways. The friend was complaining, waving her hands around with a face full of scowl while Jess listened dutifully.

Richard fell for the way Jess looked at her friend with patient concern. He fell for the way she stood tall in those kick-arse boots. He fell for the soft expanse of creamy skin from her neck to her bust. When he worked up the nerve to speak to her, he fell for the way she laughed at his jokes and leaned into his drunken kisses. He loved that she was studying towards a business degree. He loved that when they left the bar together, she drank an enormous raspberry Coke at Hungry Jack's in about two minutes flat (they ended up stuck to the outside wall of that Hungry Jack's, exploring each other's skin with frantic fingers and mouths). Richard fell for the way Jess had things she wanted to do and goals to achieve – lots of kids and a house with a swing in a tree out the back. Later he would wonder if he'd fallen in love so instantly with Jess because he believed falling in love instantly was possible. Because he'd wanted to. But he could quickly imagine a life with Jess and that sealed it for him. Soon after, they had built that life.

But that night, in the dark after Joe died, Richard felt like it was all swirling down a drain.

•

It was Richard who decided they would move away. They would leave the whole shitty lot of them – Baz, the Turners and the Meyers; they would start fresh. They would go somewhere where Birdie King wouldn't be at the playground or the school gate or

McDonald's, looking like she wished death had taken her instead. Richard would find a way for them to start over. He would find a place and a way for them to fall in love again.

Richard lay still in bed and made plans as the dawn turned the light in the room bluish grey. He felt Jess's body weight shift as she surrendered to sleep and he lay a pillow between their heads for Harrison in case he climbed up in the morning to sleep with them. He stared at the ceiling and figured out how to leave Hawthorn and his job and sell the house. Richard built things from scratch or made new what needed repairing. Their life was simply a fixer-upper. He could rip it down and put the pieces back together.

•

His phone vibrates in his jacket pocket.

'Lizzie?'

Her voice is a hiss. 'Where are you?'

Richard glances around him, the streets eerie in the milky moonlight. 'Heading home.'

Lizzie swears under her breath.

'Are you still in Melbourne?' he asks.

Liz is curt. 'No. I'm at your house. Where you're supposed to be. I'm in your bathroom. Jess doesn't know I'm calling you.'

Richard feels queasy. 'What's going on?'

Liz ignores him. 'You're not driving, are you?'

'No. I'm walking.'

He can almost hear her roll her eyes. 'Where are you *exactly*?'

Richard pauses and looks around again. 'At the corner of Wedge and Piper.'

'I'm coming to pick you up,' Lizzie instructs. 'Wait at The Stockroom.'

When Lizzie turns up, he finds out he's too tall for her Honda. Jammed against the glove compartment, his knees ache.

Lizzie fishes around in her door pocket and retrieves a crushed muesli bar. She flings it at him. 'Eat this and sober up.'

Despite being stuffed full of chips, Richard obeys.

'Who were you drinking with?' Lizzie asks suspiciously.

'A colleague.'

'Which one?'

Richard can still taste Brooke on his lips. 'The new office manager.'

Lizzie takes a corner too fast and Richard's knees crash together like cymbals. She wags a finger. 'Do *not* tell Jess that.'

'Is everything okay?'

Lizzie snorts. 'Don't you notice anything?'

'Is Jess . . . hurt?'

Lizzie sighs. 'No. Not hurt.'

They drive without talking for a few minutes, the silence and darkness pressing in on them. Eucalypts flash past, reaching for the sky with bark hanging like peeling skin.

Richard grips the empty muesli-bar wrapper as they turn into his driveway.

'Are you coming in?'

Lizzie stares at Richard as though deciding what to say and what to censor. 'I need to get home.'

Richard unfolds himself from the car seat. 'Thanks for the lift, Lizzie.'

'Don't thank me, just talk to your wife, okay?'

'Okay.'

She shakes her head. 'Tell her I'll call her in the morning, yeah?'

•

Richard finds Jess sitting out the back of their house. She's in one of two big grey moulded-plastic chairs they bought one another for Christmas; it seems to swallow her up. She's smoking a cigarette and wearing one of Richard's jumpers, a huge red thing his mother knitted. It reminds him of a lung. She's staring out at the swing they hung in a tree when they first moved in.

Richard lowers himself into the chair beside her and she doesn't even turn her head, still blowing smoke into the black night.

'Apparently everyone vapes these days,' Jess says weakly.

'You haven't smoked in years.'

Jess shrugs. He follows her gaze up to the night sky. The stars remind him of glitter from one of the boys' Kindy pictures.

'I'm pregnant,' Jess says. 'I went with Lizzie to Melbourne to see Dr Brown.'

The chair is suddenly icy beneath Richard's palms.

'I was going to get an abortion.'

Richard wishes he wasn't drunk. He feels like he's going to throw up. Instead, he finds himself crying.

'I'm sorry,' Jess mutters in a hollow voice. 'I had to say it all in one go.'

Richard swears. He uses the sleeve of his jacket to wipe his face. 'You were just going to get it done? Today?'

Jess looks out across their garden. 'Don't know. Maybe not. I don't think it's that easy for starters.'

'Would you have? If it was that easy?'

Jess pauses before answering, 'I'm not sure.'

Richard remembers all the other times they learned they were pregnant. The surprise and joy, the planning and celebration. Monty, so soon after Jack – just a year! – who had taken their breath away but they'd still been thrilled nonetheless. Then Harrison, only two years after Monty, also longed for. Three was a crew. Team Dhillon. A noisy, wonderful, calamitous gang of boys.

Richard runs a hand through his hair. 'Who else knows?'

'Just Lizzie.'

He has to press his eyes shut tight to make the thought of a baby inside of Jess real. It can't be real; she's just going through changes. She'd been teary and unpredictable over Christmas and

New Year, then so quiet the last couple of weeks. But Richard knows how to use a search engine; he knows that mood changes are typical during perimenopause.

'I forgot to take the pill,' Jess explains.

'I told you I can get the snip.'

She shakes her head. 'It was my mistake.'

They look out at the night and watch the stars shiver in the sky. Richard decides he will not tell Jess about the phone call from the detective or Baz King going missing. They have done too much to change their lives, to make things new, clean and safe.

He remembers the birth of each of their sons. The way they stormed out of Jess like tornadoes, leaving rips and ruin in their wakes, changing everything. He remembers the waves of elation as they proclaimed, 'It's a boy!', each time feeling like a victory. The clammy perfection of their toes, dark hair, wormy little fingers and squashed little lips. The ceaseless wonder at the fact that he and Jess had made each of them – a miraculous production of femurs, fingernails, follicles and everything in between.

Then, reluctantly, Richard remembers the other things too. The bone-crushing exhaustion. The tears – his, Jess's and the boys'. Feeding. Changing nappies. Fevers, mastitis, vaccinations, doctors' visits and never getting a break. Wondering if it would ever bloody end. The startling way such a tiny creature can mess up your sleep and life, break your body and bomb your relationships.

Richard knows they can't have this child without other things splintering. It's a dumb idea not even worth contemplating. And yet his stomach is chilled with something that feels like grief. Grief, greasy chips and booze.

JEMIMA

Jemima knows her hair attracts attention so she has covered it with a cap. She tucks as much as she can underneath it and makes sure her face is plain, makeup free. Wearing long pants and a loose shirt she can almost pass as a tradie apprentice, which she hadn't planned on but is pleased about as she arrives at the wide, tree-lined road in the St James Estate. The street is full of vans – builders, gardeners, electricians, cleaners, furniture deliveries – all busy keeping pretty houses pretty.

She hasn't told anyone where she is. She's used to doing things on her own, though she wishes she didn't have to. Archie isn't old enough to share her life with or to ask his thoughts on things and she's envious of the Albertini girls, always having one another. It wasn't supposed to be like this of course; she should have Joe.

Jemima finds the house she's searching for easily. It rises up behind a solid stone fence and neatly clipped hedge. The gated driveway has two security cameras mounted on a pole, she makes sure to steer clear of those. The house is like a wedding cake, and possesses a square tower topped with a terrace, stone urns on each corner. The façade is fussy – ledges and columns and tall arched windows – all painted in a smooth, soft off-white that reflects the summer light.

She's walked through the house. Not in person but online, through photos, floor plans, maps and videos from the last time it was for sale. In one sales video the real estate agent – palms up, hair slick, suit crisp – describes the architecture as Italianate. The extension, which Jemima cannot see but knows is there, is modern with a black, marble-lined kitchen and walls made of double height steel windows. There's a subterranean gym, wine cellar and four-car garage, nestled within ancient, bluestone walls. There's a room upstairs simply labelled 'Retreat' on the floor plan. Out the back of the house, among palm trees, oaks and an expansive lawn is a tennis court and a pool. The real estate agent in the video keeps using the words generous, gracious and refined; adjectives Jemima can no longer marry with the man who lives inside.

Jemima stands in the sun, watching and waiting and unsure what she is waiting for, the heat fierce on the tops of her hands and burning through her clothing. She's sweaty and slightly dizzy. She shifts to sit beneath a small tree on the opposite side of the street, leaning against the trunk and appreciating the shade from its leaves. She watches a woman carry a flower arrangement into a house, so big she can barely see around it.

Jemima's mum will get a message from her school letting her know that Jemima didn't show up today. She'll find a way to explain it away; since the cops arrived with the news that her dad was missing she's been able to get away with a lot. Madison and her Mum are both distracted, deep in their own thoughts about her father's whereabouts and how they feel about him vanishing. Both are sure he will pop up eventually, in that attention-seeking but also nonchalant way that her father has. Jemima has seen the way her dad effortlessly commands a room, makes women laugh and blokes flock to him to shake his hand or thump his back. She imagines him, out there somewhere, chatting up a barmaid in a pub or brushing country dust off his expensive shoes. He's probably clapping his arm around some salmon fisherman or goat farmer or mine owner or whoever he has to butter up this week. Then he'll wake up in a hotel room and have a neon Berocca for breakfast. He'll listen to a news bulletin while brushing his teeth before saying to a journalist on the phone, 'Now come on, Gordo, we both know that's not entirely true. Let's not be one of those people.'

He will call her, Jemima convinces herself. Eventually. Soon. Won't be long now. With ease and confidence in his voice and swatting away the distress and commotion. She's not sure how she will feel hearing his voice and imagines the conversation they will have in various forms.

Jem, darling, it's me. (Assertive and reassuring.)
Dad?
There's been a huge mistake. It's a funny story.
They thought you were dead. (Soft whisper.)
(Laughter.) *Oh no, sweetheart. Not dead. Not yet. I'm on my way home.*

Jemima? Hello sweetheart. It's Dad. (Calm.)
Dad? Really?
I hear there's been a bit of drama. (Gently teasing.)
Where are you?
Storm in a bloody teacup. I'm fine. You okay, darling? You've been doing what I asked?

Jem-Bear? It's your dad . . .

A car slides into the driveway of the house and Jemima straightens. The driver pulls up close to the intercom system and Jemima watches as the car window lowers, the man inside pulling the sunglasses off his face. It's Alex Turner. Father of Wyatt and Charlie, husband to Tamsin, friend of her dad's. He leans out the window and speaks but Jemima isn't close enough to hear what he says and she's suddenly conscious of the security cameras and how she might explain her presence. She dips her head, cap brim shielding her eyes and pretends to tap on her phone. When the gate opens and the car vanishes beyond the fortified entrance Jemima tries to slow her breathing. She realises this is what she came for – to see something for herself, to see Alex. Now that she has she's not sure if she's relieved, uneasy or both.

She glances back down at her phone and wishes for instructions.

GEORGE

The Jolly Wanderer Motel is exactly as George pictured it and nothing like the sort of place he imagines Baz King staying at. The walls are grubby peach stucco. It's single-storeyed apart from the reception building, which presumably houses the owners above it. Each room has a car space out front and there are three cars parked already – two large utes and one family car. George's phone rings as he pulls into a guest car park.

'Braithwaite?'

'Hi George, you in Bendigo?'

'Just reached the motel. What have you got for me?'

'The companies search into Mr King. It all looks pretty legitimate. He owns his lobbying consultancy, obviously. Then there's another company with joint ownership, I need to look into that further.'

'What about business associates? Has he done work for anyone dubious?'

Braithwaite gives a rare laugh. 'Depends what your definition is. I'd say everyone he does work for is at least a bit dodgy; his job is to make them look pure and flawless. Do you want to know about the companies he represents who use offshore child labour or the ones that get away with chucking poisons in our rivers simply by paying fines for "errors made"?'

George rubs his face. 'God.' He steps out of his car, 'Keep digging, see what comes up. I'm going to interview this kid.'

Myna birds protest as George hangs up, walks into the motel reception and presses the tinny metal bell.

A man appears from a side door, slightly out of breath and red-cheeked.

'Copper?' he asks.

'Detective Zavros. You must be Bruce.'

The man nods and huffs. His thin short-sleeved shirt strains against his belly; his trousers, conversely, are loose and wrinkled. He hitches them up as he indicates towards a room down a short hall.

'He's in there,' Bruce says with a nod.

Since the newspaper article, George had been fielding calls about sightings. He'd been to three pubs between Melbourne and Bendigo, interviewing two men and a woman respectively, who represented a spectrum of tipsy to completely inebriated. Local Bendigo cops got wind of a kid selling prescription meds with Sebastian's name on the bottle. They'd given George a call.

'You're not the same one who came to have a look at his room,' Bruce says, suspicion in his voice.

'No,' George concedes, 'but I reviewed the report several times.'

'Left it neat,' Bruce says.

'Is there anything I should know about Oliver before I interview him?' George asks.

Bruce snorts. 'That he's a thieving little turd? Caught him nicking towels last week too. Does that help you?'

George pretends to laugh.

Bruce leans in. 'He's my sister's stepson. Had trouble at home, you know how it is.'

'I'll go easy,' George promises, opening the door.

•

'Oliver? I'm George.' He holds out his hand but the kid doesn't take it. He's in a grey hooded sweatshirt frayed at the cuffs with the hood pulled up.

'You're not in trouble,' George says, sitting on the only other chair in the room. It's an office chair and the wheels slide as his backside meets the seat. There's a faux oak veneer table between them. 'If you were in trouble we'd be at the station, see?'

The boy sniffs.

George takes a notebook from his bag. He studies the kid in front of him and imagines the life he lives.

'I've got a missing person,' George explains. The boy's eyes meet his. 'I think it's the guy who had those pills you tried to sell.'

'That's nuthin' to do with me,' Oliver says quickly, face retreating back into the sweatshirt.

'No, I don't imagine it is,' George agrees. 'But that's what I'm interested in. Not busting some small-town kid for trying to sell . . . whatever the pills are.'

'I'm not a kid,' Oliver mutters.

'Do you know what the pills were?'

Oliver shrugs.

George lowers his voice and holds out his palms, 'Look Oliver, we don't have anything on you. No pills, just hearsay. We're not going to charge you with anything. You might as well be honest with me.'

'I don't help cops.'

'What about kids? This guy has a son and a daughter. I'm just trying to get him home to them.'

Oliver shifts uncomfortably in his chair.

George presses, 'You found the pills in the room where Mr King was staying?'

'I clean sometimes. My stepmum's brother owns this place.'

'Where were they?'

'Under the bed. Rolled there, I guess.'

'Would you say the bottle was full?'

'Maybe half.'

'Do you remember anything about the label? The name of the medication?'

'It was something zole. Tropuzole? Rizole?'

George makes notes. He thinks of the pills in his own bathroom, including omeprazole for heartburn. 'And did you find anything else? Keys? Wallet? Anything like that?'

Oliver scoffs. 'I wish. Was he rich, this guy?'

'Why do you say "was"?'

Oliver scowls. 'I dunno. 'Cause he was here and now he's missing. I don't give a shit about him.'

George changes tack. 'Did anyone buy the pills or seem interested?'

Oliver shakes his head, 'Nah. Stupid. Made nuthin'. Took one and it did nuthin'.' He sighs. 'Chucked them. Waste of time. And now I got no job.'

'I'm sorry to hear that. Like I said, we won't be pressing any charges.'

'What do you think they were? The pills.'

George thinks it over. Baz King was fit and in good health, he prided himself on it. He seemed like the type to refuse antidepressants or mental health–related medication. Madison had told George he'd had knee surgery; perhaps he still took something for the pain.

George clears his throat. 'Really not sure,' he replies. 'If we had one of the pills, toxicology could run tests and let us know.'

Oliver's hood falls back a little. 'Is that where they find out what drugs are in a body?' His eyes widen as George nods. 'That's cool.'

'It would be,' George mutters, 'but there is no body.'

MADISON

'Coming!'

Madison stares at the closed door. It could do with a paint. Jemima opens it, slightly puffed.

'Hi Jemima.'

'Hey. Are you sure you want me today?' Jemima asks, right off the bat. 'With . . . everything?'

'Of course,' Madison replies crisply. 'It's your day with your father. With us.'

Jemima shrugs. 'Okay.'

'How are you going?'

Madison hopes Jemima won't really tell her. The girl looks like she hasn't slept for days. Madison hasn't either but she doesn't let it show. Jem's t-shirt needs a wash and hangs off one shoulder revealing a pink bra strap.

Jemima delivers the standard line. 'I'm fine.'

'No school?'

Jemima doesn't look her in the eye, 'Curriculum day.'

Madison knows it's a lie. She imagines that another person might reach out to pat the girl's arm or offer a hug. Instead, she hears herself asking, 'Right. Got everything?'

Jemima holds up a finger and returns into the house.

It's no secret that her stepdaughter doesn't like her; Madison gave up trying to get her to long ago. She didn't like any of her mother's boyfriends so it's to be expected. In some ways it makes it easier for her to draw a line through Baz's first family completely. Madison and Archie are all he really needs now.

Jemima returns holding up her sunglasses to Madison like evidence. 'Good to go.'

As they walk to the car, Madison notices the overflowing recycling bin by the side of the house. It's stuffed with wine bottles mostly, some spirits. Jemima catches her stare, murmuring, 'We had some people over.'

Madison has lived with Baz King long enough to spot an unlikely story.

•

The freeway is congested but Madison takes some back roads to get to Archie's preschool. They're fifteen minutes early when Madison parks the car. She wishes she'd stayed in the traffic; at least it would have given them something unimportant to talk about.

'Did you have the same cops as us?' Jemima asks. 'The big guy with the beard and the younger woman—'

'Who looked like a horse,' Madison finishes.

Jemima's eyes pop. 'Shit!'

'Language,' Madison snaps.

'So I can't say the s-word,' Jemima says, chewing it over, 'but you can say someone looks like a horse?'

Madison scowls. 'It makes you sound cheap. And she really did look like a horse.'

'Isn't that body shaming?'

'People love horses.'

Jemima's expression is a mixture of surprise and amusement. 'I guess so.'

'Anyway,' Madison says, 'yes. We had the same cops. George something and the other one. Officer Braithwaite. I didn't like her.'

'Yeah, clearly,' Jemima mutters.

Another car has parked nearby, dark and shiny-new, with a father inside, looking out at Madison and Jemima. Jemima looks away.

'Have they found anything?' she asks.

Madison shakes her head. 'Not yet. But they said that they will. They usually do.'

Jemima looks dubious. 'That's what they said to us too: "they usually do".'

They sit in silence for a few moments.

Jemima asks, 'Does Dad often forget his phone?'

Madison hesitates, recognising the opportunity to give her stepdaughter a small piece of comfort. 'That can happen to all of us.'

Jemima slides her sunglasses up the bridge of her nose. 'Yeah.' Her shoulders drop a few centimetres. 'You know how bad he is at directions without the maps app. He probably just got lost.'

'Probably,' Madison agrees.

Jemima pushes the button to lower her window a bit, letting in a cool soft breeze. 'I didn't get to tell him that I've switched to take Business Studies this year. For my other option.'

Madison studies the girl's face. 'Why Business Studies?'

Jemima returns her gaze. 'Why? Why do you think?'

'For your dad? I'm sure he wouldn't expect you to . . . That's great.'

Jemima shrugs. 'Well, he shouldn't get too excited,' she mutters. 'I sucked at Textile Design, which he told me was a waste of time.' She squints at the side mirror. 'Is that one of Dad's friends?'

'Pardon?'

'The guy behind us. He's just sitting there with sunglasses on, not looking at his phone or anything.'

Madison turns around in her seat. The man looks down at his lap. 'I don't know. I don't recognise him.'

'He seems shifty.'

Madison keeps staring at him so when he looks up again, he appears momentarily startled. He starts the car and indicates to pull out.

'Weird,' Jemima says.

They watch as his dark car glides away. Voices outside the car distract them. Three women are walking towards the day-care entrance holding phones and keys.

'That man,' one of them clucks. 'Some people get more than their fair share.'

'It's such a mystery,' another replies. 'I always wonder where I would go if I didn't want to be found.'

'I'm not sure you *can* get lost these days,' says a tall woman in overalls. 'Phones, credit cards, CCTV . . . we're being tracked all the time.'

There's nodding and agreement. The first woman says, 'You are so right. All the time.'

Madison feels herself trying to shrink.

'Madison!' There's a light tap on the window glass.

'Kate! I didn't see you there.' Madison rolls down the driver's window. 'How is Oakley?'

The woman puts her sunglasses on her head. 'Oh Madison, I'm so sorry. I just heard about Baz. Are you doing okay?'

Jemima glances at Madison and then down at her hands, wedged between her knees.

'Yes, I'm okay,' Madison says then gestures at Jemima. 'This is Baz's daughter, Jemima.'

Kate thrusts her arm through the window and across Madison to shake the teenager's hand. It's awkward for everyone. 'So nice to meet you, Jemima. Madison talks about you all the time. She says you're her bonus daughter.'

Madison has never said that but she smiles anyway. 'He'll be back soon,' she says with conviction. 'It'll be a big joke. Baz loves jokes. Right, Jemima?'

'Right,' Jemima agrees, playing along. Then she adds, 'Not that anyone will be happy to see him.'

Kate's false eyelashes flutter. 'Sorry?'

Madison says quickly, 'After a stunt like this! Exactly!' She laughs nervously.

'I'm sure!' Kate agrees, clearly not sure. 'We'll have to have you all over and Baz can fill us in too. He'll have some explaining to do.' She points at them. 'Call out if you need anything?'

'I will,' Madison replies.

'Anything at all,' Kate stresses.

They watch her return to the two other women, their chatter now whispers.

'They seem nice,' Jemima says with sarcasm.

They remain in the car as the minutes tick by and more people arrive – nannies, mothers, dads, grandparents. They pass by the car like a parade.

'Maybe we can get ice cream after,' Madison thinks out loud. 'Somewhere quiet. Archie would like that.'

'How is Archie?'

Madison's reply is light and swift. 'He's fine.'

'Is he worried about Dad?'

'Look, Jem, I . . .' Madison licks her lips. 'He doesn't know yet. I didn't want to worry him.'

Jemima nods, murmuring, 'Dad will be back soon.'

'Exactly. Your dad travels a lot and Archie is used to that. I don't see any reason to worry him.'

They will have to go in soon, to fetch Archie, but neither of them are moving. It's getting hot inside the car.

Madison asks, 'There was something I found in the house the other day. Only small. A silver earring. Did you lose one?'

'Earring?' Jemima takes a moment, thinking. 'No.'

A woman heading into day care with her baby in a stroller spots Jemima and Madison in the car. She does a double-take and startles like the two of them have extra heads.

Jemima is no stranger to that look. She unfastens her seatbelt. 'I'll get Archie.'

'Thank you,' Madison whispers.

ALBERT

The wine bar is shoehorned between a baby clothes store and a Mexican foodstuffs store – both closed – with a nondescript door. The city exhales a foul breath of petrol fumes and the stench of uncollected rubbish and piss. Albert pushes against the bar door and lifts his hand to a bartender with a moustache and a flat cap. Pouring red wine into a glass, the bartender nods towards the back of the bar, where the doors open up into a garden. Albert spots the back of Birdie's head – hair sauce-red and mussed up. She's wearing one of her favourite mini dresses covered in dark green sequins.

She twirls around when he strokes the side of her arm. 'Hey! How did you know I was here?'

'Edgar called me.' He kisses her soft cheek. 'Where's Jem?'

'She's with Madison and Archie.'

'Is she okay?'

'Sure, why?'

Albert frowns. 'Her dad is missing.'

Birdie rolls her eyes. 'Baz is full of shit and we both know it. He'll turn up.'

Albert glances around the bar. 'Why are you here, Birdie?'

She drums a tall stool with the palm of one hand. 'Sit, sit, sit! Have a wine with me.'

'I think I should get you home.'

She leans towards him, hair falling in her eyes. 'But *I* think you should have a wine with me, and I have better ideas than you.'

Albert scratches his head, glancing back at the bar. 'I'm going to get you a glass of water.'

Birdie playfully pushes him away.

When Albert returns with a jug of water and two glasses, Birdie's arm hangs like a loose scarf around the neck of a woman he's never seen before. He gives a restrained smile.

Birdie screeches, 'This is Tina, Albie! She's my new best friend.'

Tina has large earrings that glint in the festoon lights. Her silk shirt slips and slides as she moves, laughing. She says, 'What a gorgeous woman. Is she your gorgeous woman?'

Albert looks between the two of them. 'I'm not sure.'

'Her hair!' Tina says, lifting up a strand of it. 'Look at her lovely hair!'

Birdie tips her head forward and shakes it.

Tina lurches towards Albert. 'Says her kids have the exact same hair.' Points at him, finger unsteady. 'Is it true? The exact same?'

'They do!' Birdie squeals with delight. 'Tell her, Albie.'

Albert begs, 'Birdie, drink some water. Have you had anything to eat?'

Tina loops her arm over his shoulder. 'Ooooh. This one is a cutie. Where did you find him?'

Birdie grins, lips loose. 'He was my kid's teacher. Weren't you, Albie?'

Tina roars. 'Naughty! I'm into it.'

Birdie's face is briefly sad, 'He's lovely and I'm ruining him. Aren't I, Albie?'

Albert presses the glass into Birdie's left hand, short nails painted black and rings stacked on thin fingers. 'Drink this and I'll get you some food.'

'Ruining him bit by bit by bit . . .' Birdie says, swaying.

'Water. Drink,' Albert instructs.

'No!' Birdie hollers, glass launching from her hand. It shatters on the ground loudly and several drinkers look over. Tina slips out from under Birdie's arm and seems to vanish.

'Birdie,' Albert says firmly, 'you need to stop drinking.'

She picks hair out of her mouth and tosses her head. 'I can do what I like.'

He catches her wrist gently, trying to get her to look at him. 'Listen, Edgar will stop serving you.'

'Why? Is my money no good?' She turns towards the bar and shouts, 'Is my money no good for you, Edgar?'

The man at the bar looks up and over her head to Albert. Albert holds up a finger, asking for patience. A knot of frustration pulls tight in his stomach.

'Birdie, please, just let me take you home. We can have some dinner.'

She looks around, patting the sides of her dress. 'Where did Tina go? She liked my hair.'

Albert sighs. 'I think she left when you smashed the glass all over the floor.'

'Party pooper.' She sits on a stool and almost misses, having to right herself before she tumbles off. She never loses her grip on the large wineglass in her right hand.

'Is this about Baz?' Albert asks.

Birdie sniffs. 'Is what about Baz?'

'This. The drinking, the—'

'I'm having a good time! Me and Tina! Getting on like a house on fire.'

Albert stands closer, touching her knees, and murmurs, 'You told her about the kids?'

Birdie shrugs.

'Did you tell her about Joe?' he asks.

Birdie waves a hand in front of his face. 'I can't remember.'

Albert stares at her for a few seconds. 'You know you can talk to me about him, right? I'll talk to you about him. You don't have to find some random stranger in a—'

Birdie interrupts, 'I talk about Joe plenty. At Griefshare . . .' Her left hand flutters in front of her face.

Albert catches it. 'Yeah, but that's not me. That's them. I'm right here.'

Birdie pulls her hand away. 'Stay for one drink. A teeny tiny one.' She pinches her finger and thumb together, grinning.

'Don't change the subject.'

'Baz drinks with me!'

'Baz? When did he—'

'It's nothing!' she interrupts, slurring. 'Why aren't you any fun anymore? What happened to you?'

'I am fun,' Albert snaps. Then says, 'Birdie, you know this isn't fun, right? This is . . .' He looks around the garden. There's a young couple necking by a potted lemon tree, a small group of women wearing matching t-shirts and an older guy who looks like he's waiting for a date to arrive. He keeps straightening and looking hopeful anytime someone pops their head out the bar doors. None of them are people that Birdie or Albert know. 'This is pressing the eject button.'

Birdie screws up her face. 'Awww, go to hell. Everyone drinks. Look around, Albie. Everyone drinks, see?'

He shakes his head. 'Not like this, they don't.' He sighs, leans in and rests his hand against her face. 'I love you.'

Birdie flinches and he pulls away. He stands back a few inches. He glances up at the clear moon held by the deep blue of night.

He smiles sadly. 'I'm going to go now. You can follow me out the door or you can stay.'

Her voice is petulant, testing. 'I'm having a good time.'

'Are you? I can't keep doing this.'

'Come on!' She tries laughing.

He shakes his head again. 'No. No more.'

'Lighten up!'

Before he leaves, he whispers, 'You're drowning yourself, Birdie.'

PALOMA

Paloma lies on the bed the same way George's cat, Valentine, is lying in the sunshine on the floor: bare, sprawled and satisfied. It's the most indulgent she's been with her time in a long while. George carries two cups of hot coffee, passing her one as he steps carefully over her large leather handbag. The contents spilled out after being hurriedly dropped last night. George places his cup on the top of the dresser drawers beside the bed before reaching down to gather up the mess for her – pens, wallet, glasses, two packets of gum and loose papers.

He hesitates, looking down at a piece of paper in his hand, 'Sorry, I didn't meant to pry.'

Paloma blows on the coffee, 'It's okay.'

'Belwood?' He turns the paper to face her, an article about a housing development going ahead with council approval, 'Nice place to live these days. Thinking of moving?'

'Someone sent me that. I got an envelope with newspaper clippings a few weeks ago and yesterday a second one.'

'Someone?'

'Anonymous.'

'Huh.'

Paloma smiles, 'Curiosity piqued, Detective?'

'Always,' he replies, climbing into bed beside her. Relaxing usually makes Paloma feel anxious, but George is running his fingers over the stretch marks that tattoo her stomach and she is blissfully content. The scars were violet-coloured once but are now silvery and feel like satin.

'People get fixated on things,' she explains. 'I expect you get that too.'

George nods. He kisses the dip above her collarbone and she feels his beard against her skin.

'When do you have to get back home?'

Golden light moves across George's ceiling in swaying puddles. A plane passes by overhead and casts a brief shadow. Last night's dinner had turned into this – being naked in bed with a deep well of happiness inside. Beneath Paloma's skin and fat and bones and even cells – her soul, she might even say, if she was the type to talk about her soul, which she is not.

'Not till this afternoon.'

'Where are the girls?'

'Rose is with Josh and Queenie is staying at a friend's house.'

They don't talk for several minutes. George reaches up for his coffee. Valentine rolls onto his back and lets his legs fall to each side, chin raised and head lolling back.

'I'm coming back in my next life as Valentine,' George says.

'Right now,' Paloma smiles, 'I might already be Valentine.'

She moves her hand to the taut skin of George's rounded stomach before sliding it down to his hip. She likes the way his skin feels. 'Tell me something else.'

'We still haven't found Sebastian King.'

'Did you talk to your sergeant about it? About me and you?'

'Yeah. He said that if you and me and something that happened almost a decade ago qualified as a conflict of interest, he'd have no one left to work on anything.'

'Good point,' she replies. 'Baz was in Bendigo?'

'Yeah, he'd checked out of the hotel. The room was empty and his car gone. We're having trouble accessing the rental car data.' George rubs his face. 'There was a bottle of pills in his room that a local kid nicked and tried to sell on without any luck. But we have none of the pills to test so that's a dead end. I've spoken to the client he was meeting at the Bendigo and Adelaide Bank but he didn't have any idea where Baz might have gone. And I've interviewed Madison and Birdie, of course.'

'Did they recognise you?'

'I don't think so.'

'Was Birdie okay?'

George hesitates.

Paloma sighs. 'She's been through so much. I bet she's worried about Jemima.'

'That girl is really smart. That's the impression I got.'

Paloma nods. 'She is. Still, I need to call Birdie. We used to be closer . . .'

'We generally find people,' George reassures her. 'But it is taking longer than usual, and it's a bit . . . off. Baz King isn't the kind of person who typically pulls a vanishing act.'

'Going unseen isn't Baz's style at all,' Paloma agrees.

Baz King was the kind of St Bernard's dad who assumed she was the nanny. The kind who didn't do classroom help or go to assemblies but turned up for fundraising events and manned the barbecue and made a big show of it. When she joined the premier's office, Baz suddenly became more interested in her, as a means to serving his clients' aims – suddenly remembering the twins' names or noticing when she got a haircut.

'You know,' she says, rolling over, 'I just remembered that I saw Baz a few months ago. Maybe October?'

'Where?'

'A cafe in the city, I can't remember the name of it. Little Collins Street? He was sitting at a table outside – I remember because it wasn't sitting-outside weather. Really cold for spring. It was freezing.'

'Was he with anyone?'

Paloma hesitates. 'Jess.'

'Jess Dhillon? The photographer, right?'

'Yeah. She was giving him something. I don't know what. I was about to say hi but there was something about the moment that seemed too intimate. Like they had a bubble around them and no one else was allowed in. Plus . . .' Paloma sighs. 'I don't really like him. Baz, I mean. I have to deal with his kind at work often enough.' She looks at George who seems deep in thought. 'Have I got Jess into some kind of trouble?'

'No. Should she be in some sort of trouble?'

'Well, she got herself into trouble with Baz all those years ago but I don't imagine that's still going on. She and Richard and the boys moved to Kyneton and started over.'

'They had an affair?'

'I told you that already, didn't I?'

'Nope. But that's interesting. How has Richard coped?'

'Well, he has his construction business. It's been pretty successful, I think.'

George clarifies, 'I didn't mean work, I meant psychologically. His wife is cheating on him and he witnesses a drowning, that's got to mess with a person.'

Paloma smiles at him. 'This seems like the kind of conversation I should have a lawyer present for.'

George tips his head. 'Sorry. Occupational hazard.' He strokes Paloma's hair. 'I do remember you from that day. With the girls. Wet hair in towels, sitting in your lap, both trying to fit in the space. And Birdie begging. She kept saying, "Take me, take me instead."'

'I remember that too.'

George says, 'I'd seen bad things before. Of course. Suicides, car accidents, that kind of thing. But Joe, he was so . . . whole. And still . . .'

Paloma presses her eyes shut tight.

'It did me in,' George says. 'I quit a few months later.'

Paloma looks down at George's hand. She's never really looked at someone's hand this closely, except for maybe the girls when they were younger. Now, she looks at George's hand and finds every freckle and hair and chewed fingernail astonishingly perfect. She weaves her fingers through his and squeezes.

'I wasn't supposed to be there,' Paloma says. 'I didn't want to be. I think Tamsin wanted to set me up with Albert. My mum thought I needed friends who had kids so I promised her I'd go.' She unravels her fingers. 'They weren't my friends. I didn't like any of them apart from Birdie – she's a good person. Baz King on the other hand . . .' Paloma mutters. 'It might be better for a few people if he didn't come back from wherever he is.'

They lie in silence together for a few moments with only the sound of Valentine washing himself, rough tongue over thick fur.

'Sometimes . . .' George says softly, 'I miss believing in God. It was easier thinking that someone else was sorting out justice. Less pressure.'

Paloma sighs. 'I can understand that.'

She breathes in the warm scent of George and the lemony balm he uses in his beard, feeling as though she might be able to lie next to him, like this, for the rest of her life.

'You gave the kids stickers,' she says, recalling.

'I used to carry them in my pockets.'

She murmurs into his skin. 'It did us *all* in.'

GEORGE

The house is neat and modern – painted black with white window frames, plants in big grey concrete pots by the front door. The hedges lining the driveway are kept trim. A man George vaguely recognises answers the door.

'Richard Dhillon?'

Richard's expression is blank. There's no bright shirt or shorts, no pulsing, jangly energy like he had nine years ago.

'Detective Zavros,' he explains. 'George.'

'Did I speak to you a few—'

'On the phone a couple of weeks ago, yes. I was wondering if your wife was home.'

George hears voices inside – boys squabbling. One yelps with pain while another laughs.

Richard hesitates. 'Jess is resting. Hang on.' He turns from the door and shouts inside, 'Boys! Take it outside!' He turns back to George. 'Come on in.'

'I can come back another time if—'

'Won't make a difference, it's always like this.'

George steps inside. In the entrance, there's a wall of family photographs in big square frames: a baby in a garden sitting in a plastic tub. Three boys – all pulling faces – wearing hoodies. A couple, in black and white, looking down at a brand-new infant. A trio of sons in the surf, water foaming around their middles. Richard beckons George towards an open-plan lounge and kitchen. He motions towards an L-shaped lounge, covered in the detritus of family life – dirty trainers, an inside-out t-shirt, an unruly heap of clean laundry to be folded, papers and a laptop on the coffee table, several unwashed glasses and plates. George seeks out an empty spot and sits. In the kitchen, Richard fills an electric kettle. When he returns to the lounge he scoops up mess as he talks.

'You're here about Baz King? Have you found him?'

'I'm afraid not. Not yet.'

George watches Richard's jaw pulse, as though he's biting down hard. 'I have a few questions that I thought you or your wife—'

'That's right. Jess. Hang on.'

Richard goes to the bottom of the stairwell with an armful of laundry, dumping it on the bottom step. 'Honey? Can you come down for a moment?'

'I really appreciate it,' George says. 'I don't expect I'll take up too much of your time.'

Richard nods. 'Coffee? Tea?'

'Tea, thanks. White.'

Richard goes to the kitchen but George's gaze returns to the stairwell. A woman descends slowly. She's wearing a long woollen cardigan, tightly held around her, and leggings with bare feet.

George stands. 'Mrs Dhillon. George Zavros. I'm a detective for the Victoria Police. I'm really sorry to bother you.'

'Oh.' Jess's eyes are wide. 'A cop.'

'Sugar?' Richard calls out. They both turn.

'No, thank you,' George replies.

The woman sits down on the couch opposite. She touches her neck. 'God, I look awful. I'm a bit tired.'

'I won't stay long, Mrs Dhillon,' George says.

'You can call me Jess.' She looks worried. 'Is this about the boys?'

Richard brings over three mugs and places one in front of each of them. He avoids eye contact with George.

'No, Mrs Dhillon. It's nothing like that,' George assures her. 'I'm sure your husband told you I called a couple of weeks ago about a missing person.'

Jess pales and glances at Richard. It's a look that George mentally notes.

'Sorry,' George explains more slowly, thinking of the affair Paloma explained last night. 'Sebastian King?'

Jess's expression is blank.

'Madison or Birdie might have told you? Or the Turners? I usually find that news travels faster than I can. You are friends with—'

'A long time ago,' Jess interrupts.

'We moved,' Richard adds. 'We left all that. Them. I mean, Melbourne.'

'I see. Of course.' George speaks slowly. 'Mr King went missing from a work trip to Bendigo and I have a query you might be able to help me with. It's about something Mr King recently downloaded onto his computer.'

He reaches into his folder and brings out a print of a photograph.

'I don't have my glasses,' Jess mumbles. She reaches over to the coffee table and picks up some black frames, fingers quivering. George passes her the print.

She rubs her forehead while looking at it. George vaguely recollects the golden-blonde woman at the barbecue all those years ago but she didn't look like Jess does now. The woman in front of him is depleted.

Richard moves closer to the photograph. 'Is it Joe?'

Jess nods.

'I don't understand,' Richard says.

'Why did you want to ask us about this photograph?' Jess asks, voice quaking. She passes it back to George as if she suddenly can't get rid of it quickly enough.

'Baz had downloaded it to his PC. Other things – his search history, recent emails – seem to have been meticulously deleted. But this, it seems to be a photo of a hard copy he'd uploaded and saved.' George points. 'And it has this watermark on it.'

He watches Richard out of the corner of his eye.

Jess says slowly, 'That's the name of my business – JD Photography.'

'You took this photo?'

Her voice is hollow. 'I take a lot of photographs. That's Baz and Birdie's son, Joe, but he died around ten years ago. I expect you already know that.'

'I was wondering how Baz came to have it on him,' he asks.

'It's *his* son,' Richard reiterates, inching closer to his wife.

'Yes, I understand that.'

'How would Jess know—'

George tactfully interrupts, 'It's just that it looks like a more recent print . . .' He studies them both. 'I understand that your business, Jess, wasn't set up until a few years after you left Hawthorn.'

Jess is temporarily mute.

'Mrs Dhillon?' George presses. 'Have you had any contact with Mr King recently?'

She shakes her head.

'It's okay if you have.' He glances at Richard. 'I'm just trying to put the pieces together.'

'Jess?' Richard's voice is panicked.

'I saw him,' Jess replies with conviction. 'It was a while ago. Months. I gave him the photo.'

'You arranged to meet him?'

'Yes. In the city. At a cafe.'

'Where in the city?'

'Little Collins Street.'

'With what purpose in mind?'

Jess glances out the window. 'To give him that photo.' She's avoiding Richard's gaze. 'Nothing happened.'

'What made you want to give him that photo? Now?'

'I . . .' Jess hesitates then shrugs. 'I don't know.'

'What else did you talk about?'

'Him, his work, Archie and Jemima. Kyneton, photography. But it was all small talk really.'

'How did he seem?' George leans forward. 'Can you remember anything else from the conversation? Anything unusual or memorable?'

'He seemed tired.'

George looks at Richard, who seems to be trying to arrange his face into a benign expression. 'Tired?'

'Yeah.' Jess seems lost for words. 'I hadn't seen him for a while. We're all a lot older, I guess.'

Richard is glowering and trying very hard not to.

George says, 'Mrs Dhillon, I think we might have to see you at the station to take a proper statement. It could be useful for our investigation. I'll get my colleague to arrange a time.'

Both Jess and Richard nod, resigned.

George studies her face. He tries to place her in that scene nine years ago. So many of his recollections from that afternoon have remained vivid; Jess is not one of those. Richard is there, George can even remember the print on his board shorts. He's right in the midst of it all. Richard had tried to resuscitate Joe and was holding Birdie up as her body lost its ability to remain upright.

George has witnessed people like Richard in every crisis. Helping, bracing others, fetching tea, piling the sandbags, directing efforts. Richard is the kind of person a paramedic looks for – the unelected captain, the one who knows what's going on. Quick to lead and clear-headed. George recognises them easily because he's one of those people too.

The fact that George cannot properly recall Jess from that afternoon means he can guess the kind of person she must be too. Jess Dhillon is one of the ones who vanish. Evaporated by fear or incapability; one of the people who panic and bolt or simply fade into the background, trying to make it all disappear by disappearing themselves. The ones who cannot accept what is happening right in front of them.

'Thank you again for your help.'

As George returns to his car his phone rings. It's Officer Braithwaite. He takes a moment to get himself into his seat before answering.

'Hi George, sorry to bother you.'

He closes the car door to afford himself some privacy before putting the call on loudspeaker. 'You're not bothering me, what's up?'

'The company I was telling you about that Sebastian King has joint ownership of – I've looked into it a bit more and it seems as though it's another consultancy but this one is for construction and real estate development.'

George frowns. 'Construction? That seems odd.'

'I thought so too,' Braithwaite agrees. 'Plus, I didn't clock the name of one of the other owner until I went back again and checked.'

'Who?'

'Mr Alexander Turner.'

George slides his car key into the ignition, 'Interesting. I might need to pay the Turners a visit.'

JESS

Richard returns from a run, slapping *The Age* newspaper down on the kitchen bench. 'Is it his?'

Their son Jack has a huge bowl in his hands filled with six Weet-Bix. Jess had counted them as he piled them in. Breakfast Tetris.

'Who even buys a newspaper these days?' Jack scoffs, spoon in mouth.

'I think you'd better eat that in the lounge,' Jess suggests.

When her son is gone, she says through clenched teeth, 'Are you seriously asking me that?'

'Yes.'

'Bloody hell.' She shakes her head. '*You* didn't even tell me he was missing.'

'I've had enough of Baz King for one lifetime. Haven't you?'

'He's *missing*, Richard.'

'Yeah, but not when you arranged to meet up. Behind my back! Answer me – did you sleep with him?' He points at her stomach and looks like he might be sick. 'Is that his?'

Jess glances towards the lounge. Jack has turned on the television and is hunched over his moon-like bowl, long legs bent up like an oversized toddler.

'No,' she hisses. 'That? No, *that's* not his.'

Richard wipes sweat from his upper lip. 'You wanted to get rid of it.'

'I'm old, Richard. *We're* old. I'm exhausted.' She grips the kitchen counter. 'I can't believe you're asking me this.'

'Why wouldn't I ask you?'

'Because it's yours. Because I'm your wife.'

'That hasn't stopped you before.'

Jess wobbles, wounded. 'We left all of that. You made a plan and we started over, remember?'

'You say that like you didn't want to.'

'I'm *not* saying that. Who do you think I am, Richard? What do you think I'm capable of?'

'I don't know,' Richard says, eyes deadened. 'Why don't you tell me?'

'What's that supposed to mean?' Jess's voice rises.

'Tell me, truthfully, why you arranged to meet him.'

'I . . .' Jess hesitates. 'I don't know.'

'Yes, you do. But you don't want to say.'

'I've thought of him, I guess. I . . . it was exciting.'

'Christ.' Richard wipes his face with his palm. 'Which part? Screwing him in the bathroom when he was supposed to be looking after his kid or the kid dying part?'

Jess looks stricken.

'Have you thought of him when we've been having sex?' Richard's face is bloodless with rage.

Jess hesitates and then nods. 'If you want the truth then that's the truth.'

'I knew it, I just knew it.' Richard jabs at the paper. 'And look at this garbage. There's a piece about him being missing, going on about his career, his consultancy, his "larger than life" personality. Like he was a captain of bloody industry.' Richard looks disgusted. 'Somebody to be *admired*.'

Jess glances at it, despite herself. There's a tiny photo of Baz in a suit. She recognises it as an image taken from his company website which she had previously searched.

'Look at him,' says Richard. 'Look at what it says – supported the property development work of Mr Frank Agosti – that guy's a bloody crook and everyone in construction knows it. Rolf works for him, Alex works for him; it's wrong. He wins contracts he should never win. It's corrupt as hell.'

'The media just want a story, Richard,' Jess consoles. 'A character.'

Richard is pacing now. 'It's not who he was! Baz King was a cheat. A terrible husband and a useless father. Where's all of that?'

'Please,' Jess whispers. She hopes Jack can't hear them.

Richard wheels around to face her. 'You're going to defend him?'

'No, I wasn't saying—'

'That piece of shit almost tore our family apart! He left his wife and daughter and let his son drown. Now it's happening all over again.'

'Stop it!' Jess screams. 'He's *dead*!'

Richard sways a little. 'How do you know that?'

'I don't!' Jess says, her voice cracking. 'But I don't think he would just vanish.'

'Well, you'd know. You two are such great pals.' Richard shoves the newspaper so hard it skates off the end of the kitchen counter. The pages burst apart, take flight and flutter to the floor. 'Baz King being dead would be best for everyone.'

He strides out of the kitchen as Jess grips a drawer handle, steadying herself. She takes four slow breaths and goes to the cupboard, taking out a glass. She's at the sink filling it with water, hands shaking, when Richard returns. His eyes are wild.

He holds his phone up to her. 'You know, I thought this was a prank from one of the contractors.' He reads out the text message. 'Keep your bitch wife away from my husband.'

'What?'

'I got it a few weeks ago and thought it was a dumb joke.'

'I don't know who that is . . .'

'Just tell me now. Is the baby his?'

'No!' Jess insists, heart thudding so hard the sound is filling her ears. 'I've told you no!'

Richard's phone trembles in his white-knuckled hand. 'I called the number when I went out.'

'And?'

'Madison King answered.' He squeezes his eyes shut. 'Don't say a single thing, Jess. I'm packing a bag.'

'Where are you going?'

'I tried to make it all go away but it never does.'

'Richard, please don't—'

'I'll stay in town. At the Shammy.'

'For how long?'

His eyes search hers. 'I don't know.'

MADISON

Madison looks at her call history to make sure she didn't imagine it. There it is again – his name: Richard Dhillon. He'd hung up when she answered but there was a tiny pause right before he did. A lot could be squeezed into a tiny pause. A full blooming of realisation. Clarity, hurt, betrayal. Madison feels the glittering pleasure of revenge in her gut.

Archie is at her legs.

'Play with me, Mummy?'

Madison hates playing. She'd never done it as a child so it is foreign to her. It makes her feel incompetent. 'In a minute, darling.'

Playgrounds she can do, if it just involves being an audience or pushing a swing.

'How about we go to the park soon? Take some bread? For the ducks?'

Archie's face creases. 'Nina says bread is bad for ducks.'

Nina is new at Archie's day care. She has a lot of opinions. Last week she informed Archie that his small packet of chips was part of the reason the world was burning up. Archie was bereft about it. Madison had to buy a small plastic jar to put loose pretzels in for his lunch. She just has to hope Nina won't complain about the plastic.

'Why,' she asks through teeth close to gritting, 'is bread bad for ducks, darling?'

'Nina says it makes their tummies sore.'

'What do they like to eat then?'

'Bugs, I think. Worms?'

'Ah.' Madison shrugs. 'I don't have any spare worms. Maybe we could just go to the park anyway and see them.'

Archie lights up. 'Swings?'

'Yeah, I'll push you on the swing.'

He disappears happily into the lounge to watch *Bluey*. It's an episode he's watched many times before – the one where the daddy is trying to get Bingo and Bluey to school on time but the pups make him late with loads of games. Bluey's dad, Bandit, is a ridiculously generous parent. He always plays games. When Madison became a mother she hadn't expected to be outclassed by a cartoon dog. Or a preschooler named Nina.

Standing by the kitchen sink, Madison taps the kitchen counter. She notices a barely perceptible red wine stain on the benchtop and gets out the cloth and spray cleaner. It's gone in seconds. She will tell Detective Zavros her suspicions about Jess Dhillon and Baz. When her phone rings, she half-expects and half-hopes it will be Richard.

'Hi sis,' Corey says when she answers.

Madison sighs. His voice has that edge to it. Like he's about to ask a favour.

'What's up, Corey?'

'Just calling to see how you and the little man are holding up?'

Bullshit, Madison thinks but doesn't say. The first time she'd noticed her brother lying she was four years old. He'd told her that Santa Claus sometimes got delayed by all those big countries – China, Russia, America – because they had so many kids, see, and didn't make it to Australia until a day or two later. The lie was evident even back then. She knew who'd put the soft drink and lollies under her pillow the following night, and it wasn't their mum or the latest stepdad. Plus, Corey had gone off for a walk Christmas Day, off towards the 7-Eleven, wearing a big jacket even though it had been sweltering hot.

'We're okay,' Madison replies. 'About to head to the park. You wanna come?'

'Nah,' Corey says. 'I've got some things to do. Just wanted to check up on you.'

'Thanks. But we're fine, and Baz will be home soon, I'm sure.'

There's a hesitation in Corey's voice that Madison clocks.

'Is he still into Superman?'

'Archie?' Madison asks.

'He was into superheroes, right?'

'Spider-Man.'

'Spider-Man! That's it. I was talking with The Wiz – Frank – and he was asking how you were. Said he knows a guy who does toys. Fancy ones. Says he has a kid's car with Superman, no, Spider-Man on the side.'

Madison nods slowly, catching snippets of Bandit, Bingo and Bluey in the background, coming from the lounge. 'Ah huh.'

'He'd like that, wouldn't he?' Corey asks. 'A little Spider-Man car?'

Madison frowns. 'What's this about?'

'Nothing, nothing!' Corey laughs. 'Frank just worries about you. You and Archie. With Baz gone, wanted to check you were all right.'

'I told you already, we're fine.'

'Sure,' Corey says, too quickly. 'Yeah sure, right. He just wanted to say about the toy car and I thought Archie would like that, you know, and he wanted to make sure you were holding up.

That you knew you could count on him, could talk to him, if you ever needed anything.'

'We don't need nothing.' Madison's chest tightens. 'Anything. We don't need anything.'

'That's great, sis. I'll tell him.'

Madison licks her lips, thinking. 'Has Baz done something?'

'Sorry, sis? Done something?'

'Has he done something to piss Frank off?'

Corey mutters. Madison can't catch it.

'What has he done?'

'Nothing!' Corey replies. 'Nothing that I know of.' He lowers his voice. 'Why? Do you know of something, Mads? That he's done?'

Madison grips the edge of the kitchen counter. 'No, I don't know of anything, that's why I'm asking you. Why is Frank Agosti wanting to give my kid a car?'

Corey attempts a laugh but it sounds hard won. 'Mads! Chill out. He's just being nice and he knows a guy who does fancy toys.'

Madison recalls the times she has met Frank Agosti. Outwardly charming, with shiny shoes and neatly pressed shirts and a good, firm handshake. But his eyes slid around the room as though checking for weak spots, searching for vulnerabilities. She'd seen that look in several of her stepfathers and when his gaze landed on her, she gave him back a cold stare. She knew his type, and his kind of charm only worked once. Unless you were Madison's mother.

'Frank isn't nice, Frank is smart,' she says. 'What does he know about my husband?' From the lounge, Archie calls out for her.

'Is that Arch? Does he wanna say hi to Uncle Corey?'

'No, he doesn't.'

'Okay, okay, Mads.'

'Don't call me that.'

'Sorry. I'll let you go. Go to the park, get to the playground.'

'Where is he, Corey?'

'I don't know.'

'Does Frank know where he is? If he's at the bottom of a goddamn cliff, I'll—'

'Chill, sis,' Corey interrupts. 'I'm sure he'll turn up, eh? That's what you said, right?'

Madison's heart is racing. She presses her palm to her chest.

'If he does – *when* he does – you just let me know, okay?' Corey asks in a small voice.

PALOMA

Paloma closes the door to the meeting room and stares at her phone for a few moments before dialling.

'Have you got a story for me?'

'Hi Gordon.'

'Please tell me it involves the prem and a fetish.'

'You're already making me regret this call.'

'Sorry, sorry, sorry,' Gordon says with a sigh. 'I'm a dirtbag and even I don't need to know about that.'

'This isn't about the premier.' Paloma chews her lip. On the table in front of her, three empty envelopes, loose newspaper clippings and other documents including photocopies of contracts are spread out across it.

Gordon says, 'Go on, Paloma, I promise to not be a dick.'

Paloma smiles warily. 'Don't make promises you can't keep.'

'Yeah, yeah, shoot.'

'It's about the Belwood Community Centre. I wondered if you knew anything about it.'

There's a pause at the other end. 'The one that burned down?'

'Yeah, it was turned into apartments. The land, I mean, afterwards.'

'A bit before my time but I could find out.' His voice curls, finding its journalistic sensibilities. 'Why?'

Paloma considers how to answer. 'I've been receiving some mail . . . It's probably some weirdo or vigilante, hard to know. Articles and documents relating to the centre and the apartments that came later.'

'Anonymous mail?'

'Yeah.'

Gordon clicks his tongue. 'If this becomes a thing, will you let me have it?'

Paloma sighs. 'Only if you help me. But I want to know everything.'

Gordon agrees quickly. 'Deal. I'll work on it now.'

After she hangs up, Paloma stays in the meeting room for a few more minutes. She spreads out the sheets of paper in front of her like a tarot deck. The first envelope had been easy enough to ignore but now she'd received three and it felt like there was something she wasn't getting. Paloma hates misunderstanding a punchline or leaving a puzzle unfinished. It grates at her that there must be meaning within the bits of information.

Her fingers fall, as always, on the picture of the girl. It's one of those overpriced school portraits that she always buys of her own girls. Kids look strange and uncomfortable in them, not at all like themselves. Hair is brushed painfully smooth, ponytails tightened, smiles look as though they've been stickered on. Paloma picks up the photo. The girl has dark eyes and hair, just like Queenie and Rose. Her teeth are delicate white pearls and she has that look in her eyes of a girl who wants to please, who wants to be liked. She's much younger in the photo than the age she was when she died. Paloma wonders if the family chose this photo for that reason; perhaps at this age she'd been more consistent and reliable, more pliable, less trouble.

The next thing Paloma picks up is a trashy tabloid article. She wishes tabloids had outgrown headlines like this one but that doesn't seem to be the case. It reads: 'Girl Dies in Pool Fire! Boiled Alive!' and the article explains that Quinta Fernando was sixteen when her body was found among the charred remains of the Belwood Community Centre.

TAMSIN

Abigail Meyer stands on Tamsin Turner's doorstep with a takeaway coffee in hand. Her thin body is all rods and ropes. Tamsin feels giddy. Abigail hasn't dropped by to visit Tamsin in years – so long that Tamsin can't remember the last time.

'Tam! It's your party tomorrow. Can you believe it?' As much as it's possible with cosmetic injections, Tamsin raises her eyebrows. 'You heard about Baz King, right?'

Tamsin invites her inside, blood rushing. She asks Abigail if she can get her anything but the woman barely eats so she waves the offer away. Tamsin makes herself a coffee with her Nespresso machine – black so it doesn't take long – as Abigail curls into a sofa. She's wearing black leggings, a Camilla and Marc cropped t-shirt, white trainers and a full face of makeup. She smells like duty-free perfume counters and steaming-hot hair straighteners. Tamsin feels the adrenaline kick in from having Abigail around, like she's in the dip of a rollercoaster.

'There's a detective coming around,' she says slyly, cheeks flushed.

'Get. Out.' Abigail's eyes widen.

•

Tamsin remembers the first time she saw Abigail at St Bernard's Primary. She drove a black Range Rover and had long, sleek, perfect hair, like a doll. She didn't always pick up the children because her nanny, Madison, usually did that for her, but when she did, she hung back under the shade of a tree, not talking to any of the other mums. She looked at her phone and ignored them all. Then one day she suddenly turned to Tamsin and said nonchalantly, 'You see the photos of Kate Middleton?'

Stunned that she was being spoken to, Tamsin replied carefully, 'The holiday photos? In France?'

'Yeah, the topless ones,' Abigail said, 'apparently they're going to sue the magazine.'

'Oh.'

'They're just tits. Who cares? I don't know about her. You?'

Tamsin hedged her bets by saying something noncommittal like, 'Yeah, I don't know.'

Then Abigail screwed up her face so her huge sunglasses rose on her precise cheekbones and declared, 'She's a bit dull.'

It didn't take long for Abigail to fill most of Tamsin's life and thoughts. Abigail's voice was the one in Tamsin's head when she tried on clothes, she was in her thoughts when she purchased a holiday cottage in Daylesford, thinking that the two of them could stay there for long weekends and spa treatments. Tamsin lol'd at the criticisms Abigail made about others (everyone was either too dull or too much) and made sure to answer her texts and calls promptly. Because Abigail wanted to set up Mr Lee and Paloma, Tamsin had invited them both to her barbecue. Because Abigail nursed the thrilling hunch that Jess Dhillon and Baz King were screwing, Tamsin invited them too. Then Abigail didn't come in the end – she'd had a migraine. And of course, everything went horribly wrong.

But Abigail wasn't Tamsin's first friend in Hawthorn. The Turners moved to Melbourne from Dubai when Wyatt was six months off starting school and Tamsin pretended to be happy to be back in her homeland. But in truth, she missed the UAE with its blistering skies, beautiful hotels and maids. She really missed having a maid. In Australia there were endless mounds of laundry and full dishwashers and meals to cook. In Australia she had to pretend not to be resentful.

Birdie's daughter, Jemima, and Tamsin's son, Wyatt, were put in the same class. On their first day, Tamsin and Birdie stood at the classroom door and watched the two children play before class started. Wyatt was a handful, Tamsin was quietly glad to see the back of him, but Birdie hid tears watching Jem in her new environment even as Joe wove around her legs. It took Tamsin a while to figure out Birdie was the wife of the slick and charming Baz King. Baz and Birdie were like chalk and cheese.

One Monday morning, Tamsin asked Birdie if she'd like to go for a coffee. One coffee turned into a regular event – every Monday after school drop off they headed to a cafe with little Joe in tow. Talking to Birdie was easy. Birdie had been on a path to becoming a speech pathologist but had given it up when she had the kids. Tamsin could relate to that. She'd been a flight attendant in another life, pre-Alex and becoming a mum. Birdie was nothing like Tamsin's friends from Dubai or even high school. She was never on the latest diet; she didn't go to the gym; she didn't know about fashion or celebrity gossip – she barely read a magazine. She was sweet and plain and passé – like a supermarket croissant. Dependable. Kind. Plus, Tamsin felt good about getting Birdie out of the house, as though she was doing a spot of volunteer work. Some Mondays, Birdie looked so sleep-deprived and starved of adult company, she gripped onto her coffee cup like it was the only thing getting her through.

Tamsin's life settled. She got a cleaner and did a juice cleanse that had her shitting through five kilos of body weight in a week. That's when she had the conversation about William and Kate under the tree. Abigail asked her to go to Body Pump class with her on Monday mornings. She couldn't go to the cafe with Birdie, it was just logistics. She stopped standing near Birdie at the school gate because she was usually busy chatting with Abigail; it wasn't personal.

Abigail's pointed, blush-pink nails tap against her takeaway cup. 'What does this detective want to know from you?'

'Not sure,' Tamsin says, coyly.

'I heard Baz was in Bendigo. Near *Kyneton*,' she says. 'Are we thinking the Dhillons?'

Tamsin is thrilled to feel the hairs on her arms stand on end. Her currency is in the things Abigail Meyer doesn't know; she needs to mete those out.

'Baz King, eh?' Abigail says, sucking in air. 'Remember when he had that cycling accident and wrecked his knee? I thought the guy had nine lives. Everything that happened to him, he always bounced right back.'

'True. Like hooking up with Madison after him and Birdie . . .'

'Well, that was to be expected,' Abigail says with a snort. 'Birdie couldn't keep it together. Not being mean or anything. Obviously.'

'Obviously,' Tamsin repeats.

Abigail whispers, almost to herself. 'Your party is going to be epic, Tam.' She stretches and yawns, her limbs long and fluid. 'God, I've had a morning. Been round at the Agostis' helping Priss choose curtains.'

Tamsin tries not to look surprised. Frank Agosti's second wife, Priscilla, is Rolf Meyer's sister. Rolf introduced them, and soon afterwards, Frank's first marriage crumbled and Priscilla was living in his seaside mansion. Tamsin finds her a bit insipid but Priscilla is undeniably beautiful. Lean, blonde and perpetually delicate-looking, like one of the princesses in the Japanese cartoons Charlie watches.

'She can't make a decision,' Abigail complains, 'about *anything*.' She puts on a high voice. 'Abi, what backsplash should I get? Which handle? What about the marble counters?'

'She's lucky to have you.'

'Poor Frank,' Abigail says. 'She's just hopeless.'

Frank is Alex's full-time client; he has a legal practice but it's more for show than anything else. Tamsin can't remember the last time he had a client other than Frank, Frank's family or various businesses. Not that she asks much or he tells her much. Alex's work is as opaque as it is dull, in Tamsin's opinion.

'I'm surprised she needs to do anything,' Tamsin says, envy creeping into her voice. 'The house is stunning. Surely she doesn't need to spend any more money on it.'

The Agosti house is on Shakespeare Grove in the St James estate. It has floor-to-ceiling windows and the glass is polished every month. A full tennis court. A gardener. A pool and steam room. A gym and housekeeper's quarters. Their kitchen cabinetry is black and as shiny as satin, like all their expensive cars kept in the huge garages under the house. Beautiful brass tapware. Bathrooms with expensive Parisian candles and plush Missoni handtowels.

'Right?' Abigail agrees. 'She burns through money like it's nothing.'

Abigail is exactly the same, but Tamsin doesn't say anything.

'Poor Frank,' Abigail says again and looks off to the side. 'He tells me about it. It's hard for him, you know. So many people rely on him.'

Tamsin opens her mouth, but there's something about Abigail's concern and kindness towards Frank Agosti that makes her shut it again.

'He needs a friend. Someone who gets it.' Abigail picks non-existent fluff off a couch cushion and Tamsin feels a bit light-headed.

•

After Tamsin welcomes him in, Detective George Zavros comes through to the lounge. He glances at Abigail who doesn't stand to greet him.

'This is Abigail,' Tamsin explains.

He tips his head, 'Abigail Meyer?'

She sips her coffee coquettishly. 'I won't say anything. Pretend I'm not even here.'

'Oh no, you're welcome. Actually, you might be able to help.' Abigail's eyes shine.

'Is Alex here? I was hoping to speak to him too?'

'Oh no,' Tamsin apologises, 'he wanted to be but he had to work.'

'Ah,' the detective replies, 'that's a shame.'

Tamsin perches on the edge of an occasional chair.

'I couldn't help notice that you were having the Kings – Sebastian and Madison, as well as Birdie, over for an upcoming party.' He pauses. 'Your invitation is beautiful by the way, don't think I've ever seen anything like it.'

Tamsin dips her head with false modesty. The party was a late-night brainwave she'd had as she burned up with perimenopause. Tamsin had been so lonely. She'd been watching a Martha Stewart special on throwing memorable parties on Foxtel because she couldn't sleep. Then she'd seen Vaughn, the letterpress guy, at the fancy stationery shop on Chapel Street. Vaughn was so attentive and his curly hair spilled over his eyes like a Renaissance portrait; Tamsin got swept up with it all. The invitations cost her a fortune but she knew it would all be worth it if it turned things around for her. If it gave her the spotlight she was missing so dearly. If it brought her back into Abigail's orbit. The last time they had been close, really close, was when everything fell apart for the Kings.

Tamsin replies, 'It's nothing really. Party, sure. You can say party.'

'I was wondering what the motivation was for it. The timing?' Zavros checks his notepad. 'Who have you invited?'

'The Kings, Abigail and her lot, of course, the Dhillons—'

'You invited the Dhillons?' Abigail interjects, fingernails clacking gleefully against her paper cup.

Tamsin looks between the two of them. 'I thought it would be nice. We've been in the new house for a while. It's summer. Our kids all went to school together, you know, their first year . . .'

'Right.' Detective Zavros nods. 'They were in Mr Lee's class at St Bernard's Primary, I understand.'

Tamsin says, 'Now they're sixteen. They're getting so big! You should see them. It's frightening.'

She gives a nervous laugh and looks to Abigail for confirmation. Charlie, her eldest, recently told Tamsin she's non-binary. She wants her mother to use the pronouns 'they' and 'them'. When Tamsin texted Abigail about it last year, hoping for support or at least attention, Abigail sent back laughing-face emojis and said it served Tamsin right for shortening the girl's name from Charlotte to Charlie. Conversely, Abigail's daughters – Camilla and Indigo – are such girls; they look like Kardashians. They have long sleek hair and wear flesh-coloured crop tops and white sneakers. They get their nails done and know how to apply contour makeup. Tamsin wants to shop for handbags and Pandora charms and go for pedicures with her daughter. Instead she finds Charlie going through old photo albums, ripping out the photographs of herself in ballet leotards or looking deeply unhappy in a white dress at her first communion. Alex dismisses it. 'It's just a phase. Don't give it any attention,' he says. But Tamsin knows it's not. She knows it deep in her bones.

'I imagine they grow up really fast,' the detective says kindly. 'Had you been in any contact with Sebastian King lately?'

'We're friends,' Tamsin answers. 'He works with my husband sometimes. I see Madison, of course. She goes to my gym.'

'Your husband and Mr King own a company together.'

'Sorry? Oh no, I don't think so. Alex is a lawyer.'

'TK Consulting?'

Tamsin shrugs, 'Never heard of it.'

The detective stares at her for a few moments and makes some notes before turning to Abigail. 'Do you have much contact with Sebastian or Madison, Mrs Meyer? Madison was your nanny, wasn't she?'

'Yes, she was,' Abigail replies. 'We're all really close.' She smiles tenderly at Tamsin.

'I'm so sorry. This must be a really difficult time.'

'Very,' Abigail says emphatically. 'Madison is great, such a lovely girl. But she's a lot younger than Baz, I'm sure you already know. And she doesn't come from the same . . . Her family . . .'

The detective clears his throat and offers, 'A different socio-economic background?'

'Yes, exactly.'

'Do you mean to say there was discord between them?'

Abigail blinks. 'Oh! Discord is a strong word. I just meant that they're different, like you said.'

Detective Zavros pauses for a moment and then asks, 'Do either of you know anyone who would want to harm Sebastian?'

Abigail suddenly laughs. 'Sure! Right, Tam?'

'I don't know.' Tamsin is startled.

Zavros looks between them, waiting. 'Can you tell me—'

Abigail adjusts her tone. 'Who doesn't have a few enemies?'

His expression remains neutral and Abigail looks to Tamsin for backup, but she's silent.

'Unless,' Abigail says, with a judgemental exhalation, 'you're boring.'

•

Later, Tamsin sits in front of the television with Alex, a Thai takeaway and a glass of wine so big she has to hold it with both hands. She's exhausted from the day, from Abigail making her blood race, the detective, and preparing for the party.

'I spoke to that detective today. About Baz King. He wanted to speak to you.'

'Hmmm.' Alex is watching a replay of last year's US Masters. He nods, mouth full of slippery pad thai. 'I told you I was busy.'

Tamsin drinks from her glass. 'Abigail dropped by. The cop asked us if we knew anyone who'd want to hurt him.'

Alex keeps his eyes on the Augusta course, 'Hurt Baz? Nah.'

'That's not what Abigail thought.'

Alex doesn't reply.

'There must have been some people who didn't like him. He was pretty sure of himself.'

Tamsin prods at her noodles, watching bright red oil swim on the bottom of the dish. 'Abigail said he and Madison were having problems.'

Alex reaches for the massaman beef. He takes the largest chunk of potato. 'How would she know?'

'She just knows things. Madison used to work for her, after all. And then there's Richard Dhillon. I mean Baz isn't exactly Richard's favourite person.' Tamsin arches an eyebrow.

Alex tries to put the whole spud in his mouth but it's too hot. He has to spit out half. His eyes don't move from the screen. It's as though he'd prefer she was in another room. A golfer takes a putt. Tamsin watches the ball roll into the hole. 'Are you listening to me?'

Alex reluctantly turns from the screen. 'I don't really want to talk about it. You sound like one of those podcasts you're always listening to.'

'What do you mean?'

'The crime ones. You know.'

'You don't want to talk about it?'

'They'll find him, Tam. He's just missing.'

'Abigail said—'

Chewing, Alex interrupts, 'I thought we were past all that.'

'What's that supposed to mean?'

'Abigail. I thought we were over what Abigail Meyer thinks about everything.'

Tamsin's lips clamp shut. Alex used to make jokes about them being 'dykes' and Tamsin would smack his shoulder and tell him to stop being such a dirtbag. But in private, she thought about it. The two of them, her and Abigail, in another life and on another planet. Abigail was so lithe and shiny, it was as though she'd stepped right out of one of the LA reality shows Tamsin couldn't stop watching. Plus, she seemed to have a core of steel. She found everyone so unexciting and pathetic, Tamsin wanted to be Abigail's favourite person. She wanted to be her.

For a time Tamsin dodged Abi's scathing judgement. She was her Best Friend – the only one good enough. Then there was the drama of the barbecue, at Tamsin's own house. It was awful and terrible but there was a rush that came with it. There was something addictive about being at the horrible, throbbing centre of it; an obscene light cast from it. After Joe died, Tamsin lost another three kilos in a week without trying. She could have been a supermodel. Her doctor said later it was because of the body's adrenaline surge response during grief. It was all so dizzying and Tamsin looked amazing, or so Abigail said in admiration. But after the drama of Joe's death died down and Birdie and Baz split and Abigail's Madison married Baz, Tamsin wasn't at the centre anymore. She was a top that ran out of spin.

Tamsin couldn't seem to hold Abigail's interest. She exasperated her. Abigail made snide comments about Tamsin's shoes, she offered 'feedback' about the renovations Tamsin had done in the kitchen. She teased Tamsin about wanting to become a real estate agent – 'You're not going to become one of *those* women, are you?'– until Tamsin gave the idea away. One night, when Abigail and her husband, Rolf, came over for dinner, she sat next to Alex and made jokes all night about the way Tamsin fussed over the food, about how she needed to 'just relax'. Her and Alex had roared like old chums. Tamsin tried to be more agreeable and laissez-faire, to 'just relax', but Abigail was making plans with other people, the newer, younger mums at St Bernard's. Not having Abi's attention left Tamsin desperate and lonely. It made her feel pointless.

Tamsin takes a deep breath and drinks more wine, thoughts racing. Before Tamsin started planning the party and distracting herself with expensive invitations, she'd started wishing for her children as they were when they were toddlers. She'd wanted to read Charlie books about fairies and tuck her sweet girl into bed with the thick Ralph Lauren lilac doona she got on sale at David Jones – sixty per cent off! She'd longed to cuddle a tiny Wyatt, slumped on the couch, with his little thumb going in and out of his lips while he watched the movie *Cars* for the hundredth time.

Thank god she'd got herself out of that pathetic, time-warp spiral, she thinks. Sad nostalgic housewife – so boring.

On the wall beside the television is a photo of the four of them – her and Alex, Wyatt and Charlie – in a silver frame. She'd used the photo for a family Christmas card a few years back. Alex's arm is around her and the snowy mountains of Verbier serve as a stunning backdrop. Charlie is in a purple snowsuit, squinting into the camera, and Wyatt, in red, is smiling with too many teeth. The perfect family snap.

'Abigail was saying that Frank finds Priscilla difficult,' Tamsin says. 'Do you think she would be difficult? She's always seemed nice to me.'

Alex grunts.

'Abigail says she can't make a decision and she spends all of Frank's money.'

'Does she now?'

'You're his lawyer, does she spend all of his money? She always looks immaculate but she doesn't seem too splashy. Surely Frank Agosti has plenty to go around.'

'Frank does very well.'

'And Priss? She's sweet, right? Could Frank help with the investigation somehow? He could probably hire a private eye, don't you think?'

'Alex?' she prompts.

Alex doesn't reply. His face is green, lit by the grass showing on the screen.

She reaches for her phone. There are no messages from Abigail.

BAZ

Marriage. What a shitshow. I'm not sure why we still do it. I suppose it starts out well enough with good and simple intentions. Love, honour, obey, try not to mess it up too badly.

To begin with, Birdie was easy. Uncomplicated. The first time I saw her she was dancing to Natalie Imbruglia. It was that 'Torn' song. She had on a long swishy skirt with a top that tied at the neck. Her hair was a red flag in a slow summer's wind — almost liquid. We were at a party at someone's flat; neither of us could remember whose place it was later. When she brushed past me in the kitchen she smelled like incense and spilled cider. She smiled. A little kid's grin — a bit too much gum and eyes vanishing into wrinkles — like she'd known me her whole life, and something inside me popped like a firecracker. Birdie had optimism. She wasn't prissy or polished, she wasn't aloof. She made me laugh. She had a kind of innocence that made me believe I could be endlessly impressive to her, constantly surprising.

I felt sick when she was walking down the aisle, her hair now stiff and crispy from too much hairspray. She was on her father's arm, beaming madly at everyone like she had in the kitchen that first night, while her dad looked at me like I'd just shat on his lawn.

He knew. Birdie and I had just reached a marrying age in the same place, at the same time. It felt like the thing to do. Birdie wore her grandmother's dress. It was a bit daggy and didn't fit her snugly, but that's Birdie for you – sentimental. She gets teary at YouTube videos with dogs in them. Birdie's mum made the bouquet herself and bless her, but she's no florist. I bought a suit from Hugo Boss. Now that suit was perfection – slim-fit, fully lined, button cuffs, structured linen-blend in chambray sky blue. Plus, Magnanni shoes from McCloud's in burnished cognac leather. Mum gave me a white rose from her garden for my buttonhole and a pressed linen handkerchief with the initials of my father's father for my trouser pocket. When Father Michael gave us the go-ahead, Birdie kissed me in a feverish way you're not supposed to in church. I broke it off and laughed. Everyone there laughed too. And we went back down that aisle husband and wife, getting showered in confetti that got mixed up in Birdie's hair.

I was wrong about being endlessly impressive. After we had Jemima my glitter lost its sparkle. Birdie was wrecked-tired and I had no new material. Charm is a finite resource. We fought and then we got tired of fighting. Joe came along but he wasn't really a decision, just what happened next. There were suddenly three of them with their luminescent hair and strong wills. Birdie and I became flatmates more than lovers, circling around each other in the house, two separate species sharing the same habitat. I had affairs. I'm sure Birdie knew about them but she didn't say. Birdie got too drunk every now and then and we never talked about that either. Her drinking gave me permission to mess up in my own ways – it was a relief to be honest. As long as Birdie had her vice I could keep all of mine.

Joe's death didn't split us up. It looked like it did, which, I'll admit, was convenient. No one challenged us about it, unless you count my mother who was torn to pieces when I told her. Our marriage was falling apart long before Joe died. Times were difficult when Jemima was born but in retrospect she was an easy baby, if there is such a thing. With Jem there was one Birdie for one baby and the ratio worked. When Joe came along it all went to shit. The kid hated sleeping. He screamed his lungs out whenever Birdie tried to put him down. He needed very specific circumstances to nod off, which changed regularly. First, being joggled about in a baby carrier for hours on end with a white noise machine nearby. Then being pushed in a stroller over a bumpy footpath at pace. Then driven in the car with the radio on. Infant Joe was a dictator. Birdie insisted it was colic but the doctors wouldn't confirm it.

When I got home from work, Birdie was usually in tears. No dinner cooked, mess all over, milk leaking through her shirt, the house looking as though there'd been a break-in. As soon as I was in the door, Jem wanted to use me as a climbing frame and Birdie needed me to get takeaway. It was like that all the time — crisis and chaos. The nights were long even with Birdie doing all the wake-ups and feeds. The girls in the office felt so sorry for me. Birdie took our angry baby to various specialists but they weren't all that useful. One night I arrived home to the kid red and hysterical, laid out naked and covered in oil. Someone told Birdie that a few drops of lavender in almond oil, massaged in, would do the trick. He was almost impossible to pick up, like noodles in soup, and the two of them, mother and son, sobbed over each other while Jem fell asleep in front of Peppa Pig.

You hear people say, 'We grew apart', but by the end I barely remembered the together part. Joe's death split everything into Before and After. It was such a deep and wide chasm we couldn't go backward or forward. We limped along for a couple of years but by the end there was nothing left of the marriage. All that remained of Birdie was the mum part. Once Joe was gone she doubled down and poured everything into Jemima. She could barely stand me touching her. You're not supposed to say it's a 'wife's duty', not anymore, but I felt like I was begging for any scrap of affection. I told her she could buy nice clothes but she never did. Then she started drinking a lot more, especially after dark when Jem was in bed. She wasn't a loud drunk, if anything Birdie usually got quieter, sliding into the darkness herself. I'd find her in the mornings curled up in Joe's toddler bed, the doona barely reaching her toes. It was as though she was trying to vanish too.

Birdie was the one who insisted we see that batshit therapist – Dr Patel – to try and talk it through. The doc wanted us to talk to Joe as though he could hear us. Birdie seemed to love that but I couldn't see the point. Talking to Joe when he'd been alive was purposeful, like I was loading up his little brain for his future development, dropping coins into a piggy bank. He could go to Harvard; he could be a lawyer! Not now. Talking to a non-existent Joe hurt and felt hollow at the same time. Dr Patel quietly warned us that 'over eighty per cent of marriages end in divorce following the loss of a child' but the writing was already on the wall.

Then there was Madison. Aside from her age, Birdie and Madison couldn't be more different. Madison is pragmatic and rational – nothing fazes her, nothing sticks. She's great with numbers and details, dates and plans. She doesn't make a fuss. She's brilliant with Archie, if not a bit over-protective; soaking up parenting books as though someone might spring an exam. She's a tough nut to crack – she keeps things tamped well down. All that slick and rigid coolness in a soft, warm, compliant body is sexy. If Birdie is an open book then Madison is a puzzle. There are things she keeps hidden even from herself.

Madison moved in pretty quickly. It felt good to have someone in the house again. She played music I'd never heard of, put cut flowers in vases and cleaned in her underwear. I felt young again. Hopeful. Without a family or a ton of friends around, she spent most of her time making sure I was okay, or cooking, working and going to the gym. She'd finished up with the Meyers and was managing a clothing store in Brunswick. If it was one of my days to have Jem, Madison could look after her without a worry; she'd been the Meyers' nanny for so long after all. Life was nice with Madison in it. Easier and sweeter. Home smelled like fresh lemons. When we walked into a room *together, people noticed. They didn't look at me like they had been, that I was a reminder of terrible misfortune; Madison erased that. People looked at her instead – beautiful, young and steely as hell. Less than a year later we were married in Bali. Madison bought a white sundress at a market in Ubud and wore it with a frangipani flower behind her ear. I was in shorts and a cream shirt. It was stinking hot and the sweat trickled down the backs of our knees; Madison's hair stuck to her bare back. It was spontaneous – Mum had a sook about not being invited. We sorted out the official paperwork when we got back to Melbourne. Or at least, Madison did.*

When Birdie found out we were married, she lost it. Jem was staying over with my mum when she came to the house late one night and smashed a beer bottle on the front door. She'd tried AA meetings but they clearly hadn't stuck. I told her to stop making a scene and she kicked in the letterbox. She was jabbering like a fool: 'Don't you dare mess up that girl in there. Don't do to her what you did to us.' I told Birdie I'd get custody of Jemima if she didn't get it together. That hit her like a sack of cement. She wasn't the woman I'd seen at the party all those years ago, lithe and vibrant and swaying to Natalie Imbruglia. When I got back inside, I wrapped my arms around my sweet new wife and said, 'She's nuts.'

A few months later, Madison was pregnant. She stopped working around Christmastime – the store wasn't paying her nearly enough for all the hours she did and she was big and tired. Plus, it was embarrassing having a wife working in a clothing shop. Girlfriend, maybe, but not wife. Being pregnant suited Madison; she learned to knit and made dozens of tiny cardigans.

At the first ultrasound scan we were asked if we wanted to know the gender and Madison, ever-practical, replied with a firm yes.

'It's a boy,' the radiographer replied happily.

I was numb.

There was Joe at the poolside, grey and already gone, Richard Dhillon trying to bring him back. There was Jess Dhillon, behind me, putting herself back into her clothes. There was Birdie, mouth open and heart outside of herself.

Then I looked down at my new wife on the radiographer's bed and stared into her cool, grey-blue eyes, into her soft, young, hopeful face. Our son wouldn't look like Joe. He wouldn't have Birdie's hair. He wouldn't die. Everything would be different. It was a do-over.

'Isn't that wonderful?' I said to Madison, kissing her smooth forehead, part-relieved, part-terrified.

A son.

Another son to hold tight but never tight enough.

A gift and a threat, forever mine to adore and dread.

That's the trouble with love – it raises all the stakes.

ROMA

Roma Sherman hasn't been to the property since winter. It had been a hard and arctic day then, the sky like frozen milk, the roos in the distance looking twitchy. She'd pulled a rock from the ground and taken it home with her; a craggy ivory-coloured stone almost as big as her two fists pressed together. It was the kind of thing her grandchildren might do and perhaps that's why she did it – to remind her of them. To think of what they might do here one day. It remains above the fireplace in her lounge, white and solid and the size of a human heart. Staring at it last night got her thinking she should come back.

Roma opens the car door to release Lenny and he bounds out like a dog half his age. The land takes years off him; she swears it each time they drive back to the city, age piling back on like a wet blanket. Now he is off – springing through the early morning, heading towards the gums, kangaroos, and probably snakes too. You can't keep a dog from being a dog, Roma reasons, refusing to fuss over the thing. Fred hadn't taken the same approach. Lenny was his dog – Pomeranian mixed with griffon mixed with something with longer legs but god only knows what. Fred – smitten – had spotted Lenny in a pet store and asked very few helpful questions.

'Off you go then,' Roma murmurs, though he's already halfway to the horizon and cannot hear her. She is used to issuing permissions. With Fred gone, Lenny is now hers but she can't shake the sense it's temporary; that she's just minding him for now. She's perpetually annoyed that the pet-sitting isn't over yet. It's the same at home without Fred there – it doesn't feel like her own place. The house and everything in it, Lenny included, was Fred's domain. He'd been a graphic designer once but never ambitious, not like Roma. In his last few years he had become singularly devoted to painting, mostly watercolours. Their terrace in Hawthorn is littered with them. Roma both hates them and can't throw any away. She's much more comfortable in her judge's chambers where people rarely use her first name and she gets to wear a costume.

She steps lightly over the uneven ground, careful not to roll an ankle. It's been six years since they bought the land, an old gold-mining parcel near Whroo. Fred had a vision for it: a series of small buildings – one for them, one each for the girls and their families, plus an amenities building with kitchen and bathroom. It would be communal and functional, living among nature and looking up at the stars at night. Fred was a dreamer. He'd found the place when he came up to take photographs of birds and gum trees. 'Good As Gold!' the listing bragged. Fred suggested they could set up an off-the-grid Airbnb, which Roma promptly rejected. It was bad enough hosting their own children and grandchildren let alone families of total strangers. She simply stalled. She figured they'd buy the land, spend forever sorting out what they'd do with it, and Fred's enthusiasm would eventually fade. Then they could sell it for a tidy profit and chalk it up as a successful land-bank.

But instead, Fred himself faded. He was half the man he'd once been by the time they worked out there was cancer in the depths of his bowel.

Remarkably, now that Fred's gone Roma doesn't want to sell the land. It feels important not to. Fred's fanciful ideas about family holidays and living beneath the big bowl of the sky now seem a bit sweet. Utterly impractical but endearing.

Roma whistles but Lenny doesn't return. She listens for the sound of him rattling among the undergrowth. In the meantime a galah streaks across the sky and startles her.

Roma moves easily, sinewy and fit for her age. She expertly braces her knees as she steps into a dip and whistles again. There's a faint bark in the distance, then Lenny's barks become more frequent but no closer. The dog couldn't give a rat's about Roma, his loyalty died with Fred.

'Lenny! You shitbag!' Roma yells into the wild.

Following the sound of barking leads Roma near to what Fred used to call 'The Ridge'. Fred liked to position himself up here with a thick quilt around his shoulders, painting or just looking, watching the birds ride the thermals above the ironbarks. He'd let the ants bite his ankles and came home happy as Larry and covered in marks. He said they'd have to build a rail up here, something else for Roma to stall on. She peers over the edge now and spies Lenny snapping at a myna. She sighs as the bird lifts off and Lenny circles back, yapping.

'Get up here! Stop carrying on!'

She's sick of it all. The dog she didn't want, the house that feels cold and empty, the widowhood she wasn't planning on.

'Lenny!' she bellows.

Then she spots something in the bushes below. It's white. She squints again. She takes the prescription sunglasses off the top of her head and slides them over her ears.

She says something she can't recall later, something unlike her. Because in among the scrub there is something that shouldn't be there. As far as Roma can tell, it's a shoe.

A shoe attached to a leg.

A leg attached to a person.

A hand, twisted unnaturally, the thin golden glint of a wedding ring.

FOUND

JESS

Jess knocks on a door with a brass number three nailed on it.
'Richard?'

She rubs her arms to try to warm them up and wishes she'd brought a coffee with her. She'd been too nervous to have breakfast and now her stomach is growling. Her morning sickness is passing. At the other end of the verandah a woman with a vacuum unlocks a room and waves. She's the publican's sister who cleans the rooms, everyone knows her by her nickname – Minnie.

'Hi,' Jess says. She waits for the woman to go in before knocking again.

'Richard? Are you there?'

The Shamrock Hotel is unfussy and robust; pub downstairs, accommodation upstairs. Locals stay more than out-of-towners because tourists prefer petite, cosy cottages and converted churches.

Jess breathes deeply and rests her forehead against the silent door. She'd left Jack in charge of the boys. All three had barely glanced up from their screens when she informed them she was going out.

'I'm going to fetch your father,' she'd said.

'Hmmmm.' Only Harrison replied, as though she'd said milk or bread.

Halfway to the front door she heard him murmur, 'Lucien's parents are getting a divorce. His mum is a lesbian now.'

'We're not getting divorced, Harry!' she yelled, wrenching the front door open and hoping it's the truth.

Jess traces the brass number three with her index finger and knocks again. More urgently now.

'Richard?'

Nothing.

Even before deciding about this baby, Richard had booked a vasectomy with a local doctor the day after she told him. The one thing she'd wanted to 'sort out' on her own and she couldn't pull it off. Richard was so good at taking charge, it came naturally to him. He'd noted the vasectomy surgery in her phone's calendar, writing 'Reproductive Responsibility day'. He'd even added an eggplant emoji.

She misses him. The stale jokes and the way he whistles around the house. The certainty of him. The shape of him under the doona with one foot stuck out for temperature control. She feels off balance without him; as though someone has lopped off an essential part of her. She'd thought about leaving him so many times but the fantasy never looked like this: her cold, pregnant and begging with a cheap hotel room door.

'Richard!' she calls again. 'Let me in.'

Minnie pops her head out of the other room. 'It's Jess, isn't it?'

Jess swallows and tries to smile. 'Yeah. Sorry, I think my husband is asleep in there.'

'Richard, right? The builder.' The woman shrugs. 'I think he went out.'

Jess looks at the time on her phone. It's only nine in the morning.

Minnie must be around her mother's age, with cropped silver hair and a compact figure as though she herself is made of hospital corners. She has two pink stud earrings in each earlobe.

'Do you happen to know where?' Jess asks. 'Did he say?'

'Said he was off to the city.'

'Melbourne?'

'Yeah.' Minnie sounds unimpressed, as though you'd never catch her in the city.

'Melbourne?' Jess repeats, puzzled.

Minnie closes the door of the room she's cleaned and unlocks the next one along. She tips her head and the earrings, all four, seem to glint in thought. She puts a hand on her hip, giving herself a wing. 'For some party, I think he said.'

GEORGE

Sweat creeps down the back of George's neck, his spine and into his boxer shorts. He wants to tear off his beard like it's a bad disguise. The junior not wearing full protective gear signs him in at the outer cordon.

The cordon tape and police vehicles are garish against the bush and baked ground, making it look as though the circus has come to town. Whroo is in the middle of nowhere. When George did a Google search, it came up as 'Ghost Town'.

A familiar voice calls out to him, 'George?'

He recognises the crime-scene officer beneath all her gear. Mostly because she has pink-framed glasses.

'Hey Joyce, how's it going?'

'Could be worse.'

They'd last seen each other at an arson investigation – an insurance scam gone wrong. The smell had been stomach lurching: charred plastic and flesh, burned hair and electrical wires; at least two of the officers had vomited on arrival. But Joyce conducted herself as though she was at the Melbourne Flower Show. Even humming as she worked.

'Where is he?' George asks.

Joyce points to a spot among a clot of trees. Other officers, anonymous in their protective white coveralls, complete various jobs while making sure to remain on the forensic stepping plates.

'And the car?'

'Above the ridge. Hard to see. Odd place to take a stroll,' Joyce says pointedly. 'I've got a couple of officers checking it over.'

'It's the rental car of a missing person I'm looking for. Taken us a while. We had a glitch with the car data.'

Joyce shrugs. 'I'd say that's your guy then. Been gone a week or a bit more?'

'Yup.'

'There you go.'

She's frank too, George remembers that now. Not all cops are the same, in George's view. There are the helpers, who want to make the world better, the folks who want to boss people around, and the clear-headed puzzle-solvers who see only data in bits of skull or exploded internal organs. George is a helper and Joyce is a puzzle-solver.

They both watch a blue wren bouncing along the branch of a shrub. His turquoise head feathers are so audacious they appear neon. They're not always so colourful – the males change colour from dull brown to startling blue every breeding season. This little show-off is early, a jarring contrast to the matter at hand.

Joyce looks down at her notepad, and George thinks of the person Baz seemed to be from all the interviews he's conducted and the way Paloma described him – *going unseen isn't Baz's style*. More breeding-season wren than regular wren, George thinks.

'Can I ask you a question, Joyce?'

She glances at him, glasses catching the light.

'Do you think he fell? Or was he pushed?'

Joyce's gaze travels from the cluster of crime-scene officers, taking photos and marking evidence, up through the whispering trees and to the ridge above. She lightly taps her pen against the pad. 'I couldn't say with clarity, Detective. There's been rain.'

George nods. 'No footprints.'

BIRDIE

Birdie watches her daughter sleeping. She's jittery, like her skin wants to escape her. Jemima is still wearing yesterday's makeup – turmeric-coloured eyeshadow and wonky eyeliner – and her limbs and sheets are everywhere. Birdie watches her chest rise and fall, just checking. When Joe and Jem were little she did this a lot; when they were really tiny, she'd watch the pulse in their fontanelles. She looks down at her daughter's feet. She's only got one sock on – a white one with red hearts all over it.

Toni, Jem's girlfriend, had come over last night. Slight, pretty and a bit ghost-like with pale hair and pale skin, a protective charge in her eyes that stirred territorial feelings in Birdie. As though Toni was daring Birdie to make a wrong step and she'd snatch up Jem's heart in a tight fist, where it belonged. Still, Birdie had liked her. She liked how strongly Toni felt about her daughter and she liked that Jem had something good to cling to in the midst of her father's vanishing.

Birdie holds Jem's bare foot, her daughter's warm skin full of life. Her bedroom smells awful. Musty and humid, viscous with hormonal sweat, desire and angst. She has a collection of mugs on her bedside table, some with tea still in them and one with a gummy, bacterial skin. Her floor has a trail of boots, crop top, bra, skirt and the other sock.

Above Jemima's bed is a small shelf holding a series of photo frames.

One is of Jem and Joe, their faces covered in ice cream.

One is of Archie wearing Spider-Man pyjamas.

One is of Jem and Baz, faces squashed together in a selfie.

The fourth is of Birdie and Jem and Albie. Like the jam in a sandwich, Jem is in the middle.

The photo was taken after a dance concert, back when Jem used to dance. Birdie had spent an hour plaiting and re-plaiting Jem's French braid before spraying it so stiff with hairspray it felt like plaster. In the image Jem's lips are painted fuchsia and her cheeks are two red apples. Albie, towering over them both, looks straight at Birdie.

She wishes she didn't miss him so much. It burns inside her all day long, exactly as she feared it might.

'Mum?' Jem is sitting up on her forearms.

'Hi sweetheart.'

She rubs her face, making the makeup worse. 'How long have you been there?'

'I'd rather not say.'

Jem falls back on her pillow. 'You're a real creep, you know that?'

Birdie squeezes her foot. 'I know it, sweetheart.' She looks back at the photo.

'What's up?'

'I'm thinking of going today.'

'Going where?'

She crawls up the bed to lie beside her daughter and Jem shifts to share her pillow. 'Tamsin's.'

'Is that a good idea?'

'It's a new house,' Birdie says softly, 'I don't know. I thought it might be the brave thing to do.'

Jem nudges her mother's shoulder. 'I'll come with you.'

MADISON

'Mummy, it hurts.'
Archie is tugging at the waistband of his green shorts. Madison has tied the drawstring twice; the first time they hadn't been tight enough and now they are too tight and Archie is sitting on the floor with his face scrunched up and little legs pumping.

She wants to scream or smash something. Instead, she reaches out to him, 'Shall we try something else? Your red ones?'

Archie nods, yanks off the green shorts and leaves them on the floor for Madison to pick up.

He skips into the lounge in his underwear, flicking her a mischievous look over his shoulder as he goes. Again, she notices that his eyes – devilish, delightful – are just like his father's. Sometimes she has felt jealous of this, this shared face which she does not have. Though she's never admitted it, when she was pregnant she had wished for a daughter. Someone who looked like her, whom she could give the kind of childhood she'd never had. She'd imagined daisy chains and plaiting hair, ballet classes and getting their nails done together.

Madison pinches the bridge of her nose and fetches a glass of water. She feels a headache starting to creep up her forehead.

Last night she'd received an email from Zaina Thomas, the divorce lawyer, following up on their meeting last month. She'd deleted it.

She can hear Archie playing with pieces of a wooden train set, tipping them all out in a noisy clatter. She scans the kitchen, looking for something to clean and put in order but it's pristine. She hadn't been able to sleep last night, thoughts hot and churning and keeping her awake so she'd padded downstairs to wipe benches and reorganise toys. Including the train set Archie will have now spread over the floor.

So many times she had wished Baz was the kind of father who would come home before the night set in and lay on the floor with their son, clicking the train tracks together, making little cities and stations, building bridges and tunnels. She could make dinner without Archie wrapped around her leg, listening to the two of them *choo-choo*-ing and laughing, delighting each other. It was the kind of scene she'd watched in movies and on TV shows and longed for herself. A warm, safe and happy home with a father who was a permanent fixture, a reliable presence. Her phone, on the dining table, rings and she leaps towards it. It is an unknown number.

'Baz?' she asks, breathless.

'Mrs King?'

'Who is this?'

'Hawke Fire Alarm Services. We noticed on our client records that the alarms in your home haven't been checked in over a year. We were wondering if we could find a time to—'

Madison hangs up and sinks into a chair at the table. She pushes the phone away and drops her head into her hands.

Archie's tiny hand grips the fabric of her shorts, his voice soft and worried, 'Mummy?'

Madison inhales quickly, 'Oh hey!'

'Mummy okay?'

Madison runs her fingers through her son's hair, 'Yes, yes, I'm okay.' She looks down at his bare legs and the Spider-Man underpants, 'I meant to get you those shorts.'

Nine years ago, she had been trying to get sunscreen on Camilla's bare legs and shoulders at Tamsin's barbecue when Birdie had brought her a bottle of Coke. It had felt like there were three kinds of people that day – the parents, the kids and a separate category just for Madison: the staff. Being the nanny meant not being allowed to sit with the mothers or whinge about the kids' poor behaviour. It meant looking enchanted by children who often treated her like a punching bag or personal servant. On that summer's day it felt like everyone else belonged to someone, belonged in a family, apart from her.

Archie curls his toes on the tiled floor, he's got a toy train in one hand, 'Can we go swimming?'

'What's that, darling?'

'At the party. Can we go swimming?'

'Oh,' Madison suddenly feels a bit woozy, 'There's a pool but . . .'

'Please?' Archie begs.

Madison takes his shoulders in her hands, 'Only if you are wearing your floaties, okay?'

'Okay.'

She gets closer, making sure to get his direct eye contact, 'No floaties, no pool, I mean it Archie.'

He wriggles out of her grip, 'I wanna watch *Bluey*.'

She straightens and nods, 'You can watch *Bluey*. I'll get the shorts.'

She glances at her silent phone across the table and thinks of what she will do when Baz is finally home. Wondering what she will want to do first – hold him in her arms or throw him out the door.

ROMA

Roma is at the Rushworth police station, Lenny peacefully curled up in her lap. When she arrived at Rushworth, officers suggested she leave Lenny in the car, but Roma suddenly felt odd without him.

'Judge Sherman?'

She looks up at the bearded detective and nods. 'That's me.'

'George Zavros. I'm the detective on a missing persons case we think might be linked to the body you discovered.'

'Who is he?' Roma asks. 'The missing person.'

'The body hasn't been formally identified, clearly, but we think he might be a man named Sebastian King. Have you heard of him?'

Roma glances skyward, thinking it over, 'I recall seeing something in my newsfeed. King, did you say?'

'Yes, he was from Melbourne.'

Roma replies, 'I don't know him personally. Though his name is familiar.'

George takes a seat beside her and opens a notepad. 'I know you've been over this but can I ask you some more questions?'

'The dog found him first,' Roma replies. She knows how this goes – she will be asked the same questions twenty or thirty or more times and she will have to find a way to make it efficient and bearable to repeat.

'On your land in Whroo,' George prompts.

'My husband and I bought it a while back. He passed away eleven months ago.' She doesn't wait for the detective's sympathies. 'I bring Lenny up when I need to get out of the city. It reminds me of him. Fred, I mean.' She pauses for a short moment. 'Lenny was barking and when I put my glasses on I could see the man's shoe. It took me a while to get down there. I'd say he's been there a few days, Detective . . .'

'Zavros.' He nods. 'Yes, I'd agree with you.'

He reaches out to pat Lenny. The dog lifts his chin obligingly.

'He's not mine,' Roma explains. 'He's my husband's. His name is Lenny.'

'Hi Lenny.'

'The man, Sebastian, was a mess.'

'I'm sorry you had to see that.'

'The birds had got into him I'm afraid.'

'Yes. I gathered that from the forensic team.'

'Is there anyone we can call? Someone to be with you, or to take you home?'

It's the fifth time Roma has been asked that question and each time it feels like a knock to her composure. She is a proudly capable and contained person but even she didn't expect to start her day with a dead body.

'And the head . . .' she murmurs, 'it was cracked right open. Like a nut.'

THE PARTY

Alex is by the front door when Tamsin comes down in the morning. He's holding his keys, ready to take Wyatt to his morning swim squad. He's on his phone so Tamsin is careful to walk quietly, making sure not to startle him. She takes in his broad shoulders and the neat press of his expensive shirt, feels a pleased twang in the deep of her gut.

'They don't know anything,' he's saying into the phone. 'Stag's been on their tail. Nothing to report. Kindy, supermarket . . .'

She pauses on the step. Usually Alex speaks with authority, swagger. This morning he's curled over his phone, sounding urgent, desperate.

'You know her brother. They come from nothing. They're not smart.'

Now Tamsin's stuck on the step between upstairs and downstairs and unsure which direction to go. She remembers telling her children that if they don't have anything nice to say about a person, they shouldn't say anything at all. Truth is that neither she nor Alex stick to that rule. She presses her hand against the wall, getting balance.

Alex sniffs. 'The mother of the girl? I doubt it.'

Then, 'Sure, I'll find a cop. I'll talk to people.'

Tamsin almost turns back up towards their bedroom but Alex says, 'Leave it with me,' and hangs up. He turns and catches her eye and seems to recalibrate, puffing back up to his usual Alex stature.

'Morning.'

'Hi love,' she replies, voice tender but with a wobble.

'What do you need me for?'

'Ice?' Tamsin requests.

'How many bags?'

'Five.'

'Right.' He sounds vexed already.

•

Later, Tamsin stands in front of the fridge frowning at the shelves. The checklists in her head keep jumping around, merging and splitting. She should've hired servers like Abigail suggested. A local cafe is delivering food, but keeping track of the logistics in her head feels like herding cats. She tugs on her earlobe.

Charlie walks into the kitchen wearing men's flannelette pyjamas, glancing at the glasses covering the benchtop. Tamsin has laid them out in rows: champagne, wine (red and white), beer and water. Her eldest picks up a champagne flute and twirls it by the stem. 'How many are coming?'

'Around forty?'

Not everyone had RSVP'd. Because of Baz, Tamsin didn't feel able to press guests for a response. Besides, there were plenty of people not from St Bernard's days coming. Neighbourhood friends, new friends from St Brigid's and St Florian's. It wasn't a reunion, she reminded herself, with a dismissible pang of self-reproach.

She passes boxes of napkins and straws to Charlie. 'Can you make these look nice?'

Charlie nods. 'Who are they? The people coming?'

Tamsin counts beer bottles. 'The Meyers, the Mitchells, Sue, John and their two—'

'The Dhillons?'

Tamsin licks her lips. 'Maybe.'

'Birdie and Jemima?'

Tamsin shuts the fridge. She ignores the question. 'How are you feeling about Baz King, love?'

Charlie visibly retracts. 'I hope he's okay. For Jem and her brother.'

Tamsin nods as sagely as she can muster. It feels like the plot of a miniseries. Terrible. Exciting. She presses her eyes shut and opens them again.

She needs to get the new plates out.

•

The bluetooth speaker plays Ed Sheeran. Ed is competing with an orchestra of cicadas. There are already teenagers in the pool – boys doing bombs and girls hanging on the edges in bikinis that show most of their butt cheeks.

Alex is carrying a beer bottle.

'Do you want a glass, hon?' Tamsin offers.

Alex rolls his eyes. 'No, I don't want a bloody glass.'

It's steaming hot already; Tamsin worries she'll have wet patches under the arms of her white linen shirt. The Meyers arrived early so she's fizzing. By the pool, Abigail wears a pair of white denim shorts that she confessed, not-so-quietly pleased, belong to her sixteen-year-old daughter, Camilla. Her tanned arms are loaded with gold bracelets. It seems as though she's had a blow-wave for the occasion. Rolf Meyer is wearing a Lacoste polo shirt and a perfect white smile that probably wasn't the one nature gave him.

Alex fishes around in a kitchen drawer for a bottle opener, even though Tamsin tied one to each drink bucket with a length of black grosgrain ribbon.

'How are we going for ice?'

He slams the drawer shut. 'Fine.'

When the doorbell rings, Tamsin gratefully heads to the front of the house.

In the doorway Archie is on Madison's hip. Her eyeliner is a little crooked, her shirt crumpled where Archie grips on. He sucks his thumb and Madison lifts her chin like a challenge.

Tamsin's voice is high-pitched. 'Madison! I didn't know if you were coming!'

'I shouldn't?'

'No, no, this is great!' Tamsin gestures for them to come inside.

'I didn't bring anything,' Madison's voice is flat.

'We have everything. Come on in.'

Tamsin leans over to say hello to Archie but he burrows his head into his mother's chest. Her heart seems to rise into her throat. He's the same age Joe was and he'd been on Birdie's hip when they'd arrived back then. Too big for it really, but Birdie never seemed bothered by that, she mollycoddled him. Tamsin swallows down guilt. Almost ten whole years had passed. They had to be able to move on. They *had* moved on! Up the road from the old house, at least. They had to be able to throw a pool party occasionally without anyone accusing or judging her.

Madison asks, 'Are Richard and Jess here?'

'Not yet,' she replies. 'They didn't RSVP.'

'Did you text them?' Madison asks.

'Text them?' Tamsin replies, quizzical. 'No.'

Madison seems to chew this over. Her expression is unreadable. Archie slaps her breastbone with his meaty palm.

Abigail rushes in from the poolside. Teenage shorts, arms clanging with jewellery, Tamsin's heart flutters.

'Oh Madison!' Her arms open wide. 'It's so good to see you. We're so sorry about Baz. I can't even imagine—'

'Maybe you should text them to check,' Madison interrupts, looking directly at Tamsin, ignoring her old boss.

•

Birdie hears her name being called as she closes her car door. She turns to see Richard Dhillon coming up the path towards her and is startled by how much he has aged since she last saw him. Jemima gets out of the passenger side of the car with a platter, fruit squashing against the cling film.

'Jem?' Richard asks, getting closer. He awkwardly high-fives her and then says, 'I'm really sorry about . . . your dad. I've been thinking about you all.'

Jemima shakes the fruit back into place. 'Thanks.'

Richard gives Birdie a quick hug and kiss on the cheek.

'Good to see you, Richard. It's been a while.'

'Yeah, it really has. Is Albert coming?'

Birdie feels Jemima staring at her. 'Ah, no. I don't think so.'

All three turn to the house ahead of them. They don't speak for a few moments. They're barely a hundred metres or so away from Tamsin's old house, where Birdie last held her son alive.

'Where's Jess?' she asks, suddenly noticing her absence.

'Don't know,' Richard replies. He's the first to reach Tamsin's new door. It's been painted apricot pink, the colour of cosmetics packaging. Birdie wishes she was holding the fruit platter – it would give her something to cling on to. Richard knocks firmly and they huddle together, waiting.

'Oh hi!' Tamsin announces, looking over the odd grouping. 'I really should prop this door open.'

Jem lifts up the platter. 'We brought this.'

'Fruit! Wonderful! That's so kind, you didn't have to do that. Come in. How are you, Birdie?'

Tamsin and Birdie air-kiss one another's cheeks and Birdie blinks at the sweet scent of Tamsin's perfume, the same one she wore all those years ago.

'Richard, so nice to see you. You didn't RSVP!' Tamsin's laughter is glassy, 'I didn't think you were coming.'

Birdie follows Jem, leaving Richard at the door with Tamsin. She can hear Tamsin asking him about Jess. She tries to keep her breathing smooth and regular as she moves down the hallway. She focuses on all the ways Tamsin's new house is different. She would take Jem's hand if her daughter wasn't holding the fruit platter like her life depended on it; the girl's knuckles are white.

'Are you okay, Mum?' she whispers.

'I'm fine, darling,' Birdie lies.

When they get to the kitchen, Abigail is standing with Madison and Archie. Jemima finds space on the counter for the fruit plate and Archie cries out and lunges for her. Jemima lifts him up, swings him round and sinks her face into his neck. Elated, wheezy giggles erupt from him.

'Hey Madison,' Birdie says.

She can feel Abigail's hungry gaze trained on the two of them, hoping to see conflict, animosity or drama.

'Hi Birdie,' Madison says steadily.

•

After parking, Jess checks her reflection in the rear-view mirror. Her stomach lurches and she wonders if she was wrong about the morning sickness abating. She re-ties her ponytail and tries to smooth the loose curly strands around her hairline. She presses her hands against her eyelids and breathes slowly. Then she gets out of the car and walks straight through Tamsin Turner's front door, which is propped open, and into the house. Her heart is beating so hard it feels like her skin is tingling. When she was last in a home of Tamsin's, she'd done her hair and makeup and not eaten breakfast. She couldn't – there were butterflies in her stomach from thinking of Baz's mouth on hers, the heat of his breath, his skin against hers. Baz King smelled like power. He smelled like confidence and sex.

'Jess?' In the kitchen, Tamsin is holding a platter of fruit. She seems surprised.

Jess murmurs, 'Hi Tamsin.'

A young child squeals from somewhere in the house, perhaps the lounge, and Jess can hear the sounds of kids' cartoons on television. She looks beyond Tamsin towards a pool out the back. The house is even fancier than their old one, plus, there are a lot more people than there had been at the last barbecue and all the children have become teens. One of the Meyer girls lolls on a sun-lounger wearing a pink string bikini. The girl's black winged eyeliner is so expertly sharp it could slice tomatoes into quarters.

'Nice to see you,' Tamsin says, smiling and looking her up and down.

Jess tugs at the hem of her t-shirt. 'I'm trying to find Richard.'

'He's out the back, I think. Maybe by the barbecue?'

Tamsin says something else but Jess doesn't hear her. She's remembering Baz and Alex and her – cooking sausages. The three of them roped together with sexual tension, the mood as high as a kite. Everything hilarious. The sun a bright white blister. Everything about to collapse.

'I'll go out and find him.'

Heading outside, the teenagers in and around the pool don't even look up at her; it's as though she is now invisible. Even Alex Turner almost crashes into her holding a large stainless-steel bowl.

'Shit! Jess?' He peers at her.

'Hi Alex.'

'God. How are *you* going?'

Back in the day, Alex knew all about her and Baz. He was always trying to get them to confess. He was amused by it, seemed turned on by it.

She gives him a tight smile. 'Fine.'

Alex's upper lip hosts a string of tiny pearls of sweat. He angles his body so they have more privacy and whispers, 'Do you know anything about it? About Baz?'

'No. Why would I?' She leans back a couple of inches.

'Come on.' He's close enough that she can smell his breath, 'We all know you two—'

'I've tried to put that behind me, Alex.'

He snorts. 'Have you though?'

Jess spots Richard sitting on a lounger next to Madison King. Madison looks over at her.

'Yes,' she hisses. 'I need to see my husband.'

Alex's voice drops. 'If you know anything—'

But he doesn't finish his sentence because Madison is suddenly between them, smooth blonde hair swinging. She strikes Jess hard across her face with the palm of her hand, making Jess's eyesight go for a short moment. Then the pain flashes bright against her eyelids, burns up her cheek, and she loses her breath and footing.

In front of her, Madison is panting. 'That's for screwing my husband.'

•

In the lounge, watching cartoons with Archie, Birdie and Jem hear the loud voices.

'I told you to stay away from him!'

Archie is using Jemima like a climbing frame, scrambling up her legs and hanging from her hands to watch the screen upside down. The sound of shouting has them on their feet in seconds. Jemima gathers Archie up in her arms as the raised voices lead them outside.

Richard is pleading, 'Hang on, Madison, don't hit her! She's—'

'Don't touch me!'

'One husband isn't enough for you?'

When Birdie and Jem get there, Jess is on the ground and Madison is standing above her, pointing. Richard has his hand clenched on Madison's shoulder while Alex crouches by Jess. Rolf and Abigail stand to one side and Tamsin looks like she might be smiling.

'Mama!' Archie calls out. Still holding him, Jemima takes a step backward.

Madison reaches into her pocket. 'I know what you did! See? I found this!'

It's so small, everyone leans in. Pinched between her thumb and forefinger is an earring – a tiny 'J'.

Birdie hears the pain in Jemima's voice as she whispers, 'Oh Mum.'

'Stop!' Birdie calls out. She closes her eyes for a short moment.

Madison barely notices her. 'What have you done to him? Where is he? Where is my husband?'

'Stop!' Birdie cries again, voice breaking now, 'It's mine, Madison.'

Everyone seems to swivel at the same time, apart from Madison. Madison is the last to look at her.

'It's my earring,' she says, her voice diminished. She holds up her palms like white flags. 'It's J for Jem. And Joe.' Her hands are quivering, 'I'm sorry.'

Jemima's eyes have filled with tears. The crowd turns to Madison, poised for fury, but instead the woman who was the nanny and then the wife but never in anyone's mind a protagonist in her own right, exhales and buckles. The rage seems to evaporate from her, her knees giving way. Richard reaches for her as she crumples. He braces her, just like he did with Birdie when Joe was dead, all those years ago. He stares across at his wife who's holding one hand to her cheek.

'Wow,' sighs Abigail gleefully.

Into the crowd steps Detective Zavros. His partner stands waiting a few feet away, holding her police hat, her face expressionless. George and Madison stare at one another and say nothing for a moment. His cheeks are pink, his hair flattened by sweat. He glances sadly at Birdie, then Jemima and back to Madison.

'You found him,' Madison murmurs.

George nods, looking at the ground.

'Good god,' Tamsin whispers. 'He's dead.'

BAZ

What I wouldn't give to be there for my funeral.
What a show. They should sell tickets.

When my dad died three and a half years ago, his funeral was held on the kind of winter's day in Melbourne that slices through you, the cold searing like a burn. Archie was tiny and wouldn't stop crying; Jem sat up the front of the church with Mum, Madison and me, and Birdie a few rows back in a dark green dress while everyone else wore black. It looked nice with the colour of her hair.

Dad would've been pleased with the way he exited. Influenza led steadily to pneumonia and he was gone within a few weeks — not too much buggering about. For the coffin, we dry-cleaned his best suit and I gave Mum one of my Hermès ties with a subtle pattern in navy and teal. He looked smart. The funeral home did a good job with the makeup. Mum stressed 'not too much please', as though Dad might pounce back to life with a face washer in his angry, manly, homophobic grip. They also gave him a close shave, better than he'd done himself in years, and plucked the hairs from the end of his nose and tops of his ears.

I never saw my dad lay a hand on Mum and I don't think he ever cheated on her as I'm not sure he'd have known how. He flirted sometimes but he was terrible at it. There was a long-running joke about the pretty French waitress at the local 'caff' where he went for the occasional steak and cheese pie. Odette, her name was. 'Ohhhhhh-dette', Dad would joke, 'if only I wasn't already accounted for, right, Patti?' and Mum supplied the obligatory eye roll as though the guy still had it.

The trouble with Dad wasn't cheating or hitting, it was that he bullied Mum in the subtlest of ways. She didn't have a credit card until she was in her sixties, and even then he read the statements and checked over every item. He went to her doctor's appointments with her. He took care of all the finances. He had opinions for the both of them and voiced them on her behalf. He took her wineglass when she'd had too much — usually just the one — and was astonished when she disagreed with him on anything, as though they were practically the same person. Mum got shingles once and I caught Dad in the kitchen squinting at the instructions on a two-minute noodle packet like they'd just been invented. If Dad was in the room, the remote was in his hand and never hers. He reduced her. He so effectively made her a supporting role to him that she barely knew how she felt about things or what her favourite ice cream flavour was. It was as though he moulded her out of clay the day they were married.

So, alive, Dad had been like Vegemite. Love him or hate him. Birdie had never liked him; she hated the way he treated Mum and looked down his nose at her. Mates thought he was a bit of a laugh but also scary — 'Wouldn't want to get on the wrong side of him!' Older men — white and bloated with views on things — thought Dad was great. They saw themselves mirrored in him and found the reflection a comfort. As long as Dad was okay, so were they. I don't think Dad ever had a female friend; he wouldn't have known what to say or do with a woman other than Mum.

But here's the thing with death — whatever grievances were outstanding with Dad, they all evaporated after he died. His slate was wiped clean. He was posthumously softened and simplified;

his character artfully photoshopped. Friends remembered him as a solid bloke, the kind of man that was difficult to find these days: 'a family man' and 'hard worker' and 'good for a laugh'. Problematic qualities like racism and believing fat people were lazy and disgusting transformed into endearing trivialities or were just erased. 'He called a spade a spade!' they reasoned, with affection. His stubbornness became conviction and determination, his narrow-mindedness became reliability, the kind of consistency subsequent generations lack. By the way people talked about him, you'd think Dad deserved some kind of monument: Last Great Australian Man.

In death, Dad's character got a spit and polish. Mum still has a photograph of her and Dad on their wedding day on the hallway table – him in a suit with big lapels and her in a long dress with hair that looks like it was baked with too much bicarb. They are cutting into their wedding cake – nothing fancy, two tiers, the top one probably fruit – holding the knife together. Both of Dad's hands are on top of Mum's.

In death, Dad became the kindest interpretation of that black and white photo – handsome, protective, loving and loyal. It was ungracious to remember him as also bossy, judgemental and mean. We all agreed: Joseph King was a dependable old coot, decent husband and top bloke. Nothing else mattered.

Like Banjo Paterson would say, 'He was hard and tough and wiry – just the sort that won't say die.'

A fair dinkum cobber.

True and blue.

That's what death does to a person. Best brand management ever.

GEORGE

George accompanies Madison King to the automatic doors of the hospital mortuary. They keep opening and shutting like some kind of bad joke. Inside, where he ushers her, the air conditioning is jacked up so high, goosebumps rise instantly on her arms.

He has already asked if she'd prefer to identify the body via photographs but she flatly refused. He looks behind her towards the car park. 'You didn't ask anyone to join you?'

'No.'

'Is anyone on their way?'

Her gaze is almost combative. 'Can it not be done with just one person?'

He hesitates, 'Can it not . . . no. I mean yes. One person is fine. There is a social worker on her way so we can wait here for her to arrive.'

Madison turns her attention to the hallway beyond the small reception area. It's wide and silent, giving away nothing.

'I'd like to do it now. My son is with his grandmother, I don't want to wait.'

'Okay.' George nods.

Madison walks beside him, matching him step for step, and he has the sensation she should be the one leading him. His heart sinks, as it always does during the short walk. Shrill smells of bleach and steel fill his nostrils, silence presses against his ears. There is no chatter or laughter or radio playing like in most workplaces.

Dr Decima Bosson meets the pair at the door dressed in a neat pencil skirt, blouse and sturdy heels. Other times, George has seen her in scrubs and marked with 'decomp' – the mess the body makes as it tries to dissolve. Mid-autopsy Decima always has her blue construction toolbox at her side complete with an electric saw for opening skulls, ladles for bodily fluids, forceps, scalpels and scissors – it's hard physical work breaking apart a body to study it from the inside out. Today, the way she is dressed, Decima could be a lawyer or the principal of a private school.

'Madison King?' she asks. 'I'm Dr Bosson, the pathologist. You can call me Decima.'

Madison says nothing in reply, her face is dark and closed off, as if daring Decima to pity her because she won't allow it. People do that, George has noticed. They hold themselves in. They brick up all the emotional holes and exits and vacuum-pack themselves into a tiny parcel.

Decima continues, 'Detective Zavros probably told you that the deceased sustained head and body injuries so he is mostly covered.' She glances at George meaningfully. 'I'm afraid there has been a significant amount of decomposition, Mrs King. We are also able to identify the body with photographs or dental records if you'd prefer—'

'I'm fine.'

George says, 'Okay, well, I can take Mrs King in now, Dr Bosson.'

'I'll be here if you need anything.'

Inside the room, there's a stainless-steel table and a figure beneath a sheet. Madison stands at a distance from the slab.

George gently lifts up the bottom corner of the sheet. Madison steps forward. The exposed feet are brown and bloated. She doesn't recoil.

'Shall we see the knee first?' George asks gently.

Madison nods. He removes more of the sheet slowly and carefully, as though the body is a sleeping child. The faint, silver line of a scar snakes through dark hair and greenish skin. Whoever the orthopaedic surgeon was, they'd done an excellent job.

'It's him,' Madison says, exhaling.

George replaces the sheet over the leg and goes to the other end of the slab. He waits as Madison's hand goes to her mouth. The colour has left her face.

Her voice is a whisper, 'I thought I could do it.'

'Would you like to wait a moment?'

'I can't do it.'

George nods, 'Of course. Let me take you out.'

When he gently touches her shoulder to guide her from the room it is quivering. What is left of Baz King's face remains hidden by the hospital sheet as they leave.

BIRDIE

Baz is dead but Stevie Nicks makes everything better. Her voice is the one Birdie's father listened to when he was alive, the voice Birdie heard sitting on his knee or dancing on top of his feet in the kitchen. The one that braided them together. Smoky, full of rasp and longing. It wraps around Birdie like Stevie's signature black cloaks. Like Stevie's medievally long golden hair.

The living room light is a sudden blade in her eyes and through her head. 'Darling!' she pleads. 'The light!'

Jemima asks her a question and Birdie has to line up each of the words till they make sense. *Something, something, did you know?*

'Your father?' Birdie asks.

The room swells, the walls go soft. Jemima has a question for her mother that she wants answered but Birdie is having trouble making it out. It's something about his work, about who he worked for.

'Your dad,' Birdie explains, 'did what your dad did.'

And then adds, 'Whatever he wanted to do.'

Now she is thinking of Jess Dhillon. Thinking of the way she was back then. Skin like honey, hair like corn silk, a vision of adoration.

Gin. Neat. Down the hatch.

Baz is dead; Birdie tries to accept it as fact. The thought rolls like a marble. Dead? Dead! He'd been inside her not that long ago, alive as anything. The man she'd agreed to marry, the man who fathered her only children, the person she'd wanted to erase from the face of the Earth on more than one occasion. Even her own father had murmured with a sigh, when he was still alive, *Perhaps it would be better for everyone if he just took himself away.* And now he was. Away.

Is she pleased? Birdie considers the question and cannot decide.

Suddenly, she wants Albert. The wanting rises up inside her like vomit. A keening, a yearning, a 'can't stop it even if you try'. It's grotesque and dangerous, that kind of longing. The kind that leads to loss. She wants the feeling gone so she skips the track that's playing and ends up back at Fleetwood Mac, the notes a balm.

Someone shouts, 'Turn it down!' Perhaps Jemima, perhaps a neighbour. Either way, Birdie giggles.

Albert Lee.

He's too good for her, of course. That is the problem. Pretty, lithe, kind. Sweet and young. *Younger.* But Birdie is more than just older. She is life-worn and ancient. It's embarrassing. Plus, the more broken she gets – smashing herself into tiny, sharp and bitter little pieces – the kinder Albert is. It's too much.

Too much. Baz had called her that – too much. Pasta water frothing over the edge of the pot. An abundance of oranges fallen and rotting in the soil. Summer sun trying to burrow into your skin, trying to fry your eyes out. Too damn much.

That light is on again.

'Turn it off!' she calls out, but arms are lifting her. *Trying* to lift her. It's like moving dripping wet sand in your hands, all the watery bits running through your fingers. What a comedy! Birdie giggles.

Bed. A bed beneath her body and it's a blessing. Birdie lets herself melt into it. For a moment.

'Oh Jem,' she says, thinking of how dear and strong her daughter is. Brotherless and now fatherless. How selfish and terrible she is to think only of herself. Baz is Jemima's father and now he is gone. You only get one! Birdie finds herself crying, tears wetting her pillowslip. Howling from the ache deep in her gut. Her poor daughter. Both of them now – her and Jem – without fathers.

The tears retreat and sleep strokes her cheek.

But she is up again. Eyes forced open, fear gripping her gut. Because if Birdie's not careful, dreams of Joe come in the cooling, creeping night when her mind finally rests and she surrenders to the grief that wants to eat her alive. The guilt. She drank too much, then and now, and left her son in the pool to drown. There is no redemption for that; there is no one worse. She is rotten. A fruit made of bruise – thumb-pressed, stinking ooze, right to the core.

Birdie rolls out of her bed. She slides a bank card into her pocket. She finds shoes – thongs – and shakes her long hair.

Three, four, open the door.

GEORGE

Personal Property of Body #1678, Coronial Services Centre, Victoria.

1. Black Country Road wallet:
   Visa Gold card, Mr S King
   Driver's licence, Mr S King
   NRMA Membership card, Mr S King
   Medicare card, Mr S King
   Medibank card, Mr S King
   Crown Casino VIP card, Mr S King

2. Keys to rental car: Avis, Toyota VPN 1674

3. Tiffany's gold band

4. St Christopher medallion, 18ct, 1.5cm long

5. Photograph (black & white) of young boy, stamp on back: JD Photography

6. Watch: vintage Rolex

•

It's the afternoon when George's phone rings.

He draws her name out with a smile. 'Paloma.'

'George.'

'I just saw you on the news.'

'Oh?'

'Raising the age of criminal responsibility.'

'That clip again. I thought I was off-screen.'

'I spotted you.' George looks around the office to make sure no one else can hear the affection in his voice.

Paloma mimics the premier's voice and quotes, 'We're giving that one more go to try and get a national consensus and if we don't – we won't hesitate to do our own thing.'

'Did you write it?'

'Yeah. A strong man going it alone to fight the big guys – they love that.'

'They really do,' George says. In his mind he paints himself inside a circle with Paloma, and everyone else – 'they' – exist outside of it.

'Long day?' she asks. 'Want to have dinner together?'

George nods, even though she can't see him. 'Reviewing Baz's personal effects and waiting on a call from the coroner.'

'How was Madison? Identifying the body.'

George sighs. 'Okay. As okay as a person can be.'

Paloma murmurs agreement.

'How about I give you a call when I'm done? Bring ice cream?'

'Deal,' Paloma agrees. 'Bring ice cream.'

George returns to his desk and calls Decima's number, apologising for the delay in getting back to her.

'All good, George. I'm not going anywhere. Up to my proverbials with paperwork.'

Decima rarely complains. When she conducted the autopsy on Baz King, George watched through the observation window.

She was adept and thorough, bagging up minuscule bits of grit and embedded clothing fibres. Baz's injuries, she observed, were consistent with trauma and a fall. His head had, just as Judge Roma Sherman described, split open like a nut. Decima estimated that Baz had died very quickly. As for ascertaining whether there had been a struggle or an altercation before his death, it was hard to tell.

Doing an autopsy on a suspicious death was gruelling, gruesome work but, like Joyce the crime-scene officer, Decima never flinched. She took her time dissecting and analysing. She led the other members of her team with gentle grace, wholly dedicated to getting to the bottom of deaths. 'Identity, cause and circumstances,' she reminded newbies, checking the trio off on her gloved fingers. 'These are your only three jobs. Don't forget it.' But that wasn't quite true for Decima, who was also focused on preventing as many deaths as possible. Five years ago she'd assisted the coroner in appealing for a safe injection site for heroin users in Richmond. She didn't want to assess any more dead bodies than she had to.

She says, 'I got the toxicology report back.'

'Alcohol?'

'Strangely, no.'

'Drugs?'

'Nothing recreational. I thought he might be a coke kind of guy, but no. Nothing apart from some medication.'

'What are we talking?'

George hears shuffling papers. 'It looks like Riluzole.'

'Is it a poison?'

'No, it's a benzothiazole. It affects nerves and muscles.'

'Huh. Interesting. I wonder what he was taking that for. Could it be significant in causing a fall?'

There's a hesitancy in her voice. 'Possibly.'

George pauses and straightens. 'What is it used to treat?'

'I need to do some more research but as far as I can tell it's used to prolong life in ALS patients.'

'You've lost me,' George admits.

'Sorry.' He can hear the weariness in her voice. 'I've requested Mr King's medical records so I can figure it out. I wanted you to know it might take a little longer to send the report.'

George nods. 'Of course. Take your time.'

Across the office beyond the glass wall, a police officer waves to get his attention.

'Thanks, George,' Decima says. 'Hey, I saw Mr King's photo in *The Age*.'

George rubs his temples. 'Yeah, I was hoping they'd wait a minute before running that.'

'It doesn't quite add up, does it?' Decima murmurs. 'No note? And in the middle of nowhere?'

'That's what everyone says,' George agrees. 'Not the type to go quietly.'

To take a bow without a curtain call, without an encore, he thinks to himself. The police officer waves again and George holds up a 'please wait' index finger.

'I'd better go.'

Before they end the call, Decima agrees, 'Not from what I read. Not the type at all.'

•

'What's up?' George asks the young police officer. He seems nervous. He has a thin moustache and looks as though he's wearing the cop's uniform for a dress-up party.

'We've got someone in lock-up who keeps shouting for you.'

'Me?'

'Sergeant said I should try and find you if you hadn't gone home.'

George thinks of Paloma. 'I was just about to.'

'They're pretty loud. Maybe a friend?'
'They're drunk?'
'That and interfering with public order . . .' He inhales meaningfully.
'Name?'
'Martina King.'
George sighs. 'Give me a minute.'

PALOMA

Paloma's colleague June stands up from her desk. 'Your phone was going off while you were in the bathroom.'

Paloma dries her hands on the front of her trousers. She finds herself hoping to see calls from Gordon Tuttle at *The Age*. It's been a few days since she sent Gordon photos of the contents of the three envelopes she received and this morning she found a fourth envelope in her letterbox at home. She is spooked; the others had arrived at work so this one feels personal. Paloma finds herself thinking about the contents of the envelopes more often than she would like. Her mind wanders away from her work and her dreams feature pools and girls and lost things. She looks at her phone screen and sees that she has missed four calls from George.

'George?'

'Paloma, sorry.' He sounds a bit frazzled. 'I've got someone here . . .'

'Are you okay?'

'I might need your help.'

'George? Who is it?'

She waits while his voice is muffled, giving instructions to a fellow officer, she presumes. Then he's back in her ear, saying clearly, 'Birdie. Birdie King.'

•

Paloma looks over her old friend. Birdie is barefoot, her soles almost black. She curls them towards her body, like a wild animal, trapped and fearful. Paloma holds out one of two paper cups. 'I have coffee.'

Birdie regards her with mistrust. The floor and walls of the room are painted soft green and the fluorescent lighting makes the sparse space look even worse. Paloma feels like she's walked into a horror movie and marvels that George can deal with this kind of thing daily. The toilet in the cell stinks so Paloma flushes that first before sitting on the edge of the mattress. Birdie's pallid skin has taken on a greenish tinge from the walls. She sits up slowly and Paloma presses the coffee into her hands.

Her voice is hoarse. 'What time is it?'

'Morning. We thought you should sleep it off a bit.'

'What are you doing here?'

Paloma drinks from her own cup, then says, 'George called me.'

Birdie looks young and old all at once, waiting to understand.

'The detective. George,' Paloma explains. 'Do you remember shouting for him last night?'

Birdie closes her eyes. Both hands, thinner than they'd once been, Paloma notices, cling to the coffee Paloma brought her.

'We've been dating a few weeks,' Paloma says, voice lowered. 'Before any of . . . this. He told me you were locked up for disorderly behaviour and obstructing a police officer.'

Despite her fragile state, Paloma wants to reach out and shake Birdie. When they first met at St Bernard's Primary School, Paloma was the underdog and the one to be pitied. Now the roles are switched: Paloma is dressed for work – tube skirt, pressed shirt and heels – while Birdie is knotted up on a plastic-coated mattress.

'Do you remember much?' Paloma asks.

Birdie shakes her head carefully, like it hurts.

'You were at the IGA, trying to buy wine, I think. When they wouldn't serve you, you got pretty mad about it. I'm not sure what happened to your shoes . . . Where are your shoes?'

'I don't know.'

'The officer tried to calm you down and you pushed him.' Paloma sighs. 'That's obstruction.'

Birdie's hands are trembling. 'Does Jem know?'

'I don't think so. Queenie messaged her. She stayed with someone from her writers club last night – Toni? Antonia someone? Queenie told Jem I was taking you for breakfast.' She looks at her coffee. 'Not completely untrue.'

'Am I going to be charged?'

'Not sure.'

Birdie swears under her breath. She brings the coffee to her lips.

'Baz is dead,' she says softly.

The skin under Birdie's eyes is thin and violet from the abuse she has done to herself. The rest of her face is ashen, including her lips. She runs her thumb around the lid of her cup. 'I wished him dead, Paloma.'

She glances up at Paloma, who doesn't respond. 'Sometimes. Often enough. It's terrible, isn't it? To wish your kids' father dead?'

Paloma swallows. There's a surveillance camera in the upper corner of the cell. 'I'm sure you're not the first,' she says carefully.

Her girls' father, Moses, had been a few-nights stand. Paloma wouldn't have continued any contact with him if it weren't for Rose and Queenie. Gorgeous when she met him – tall and languid with huge square palms and a lazy smile – she'd been flattered he was interested in her. But he didn't want anything to do with their daughters. In a way, it was as though he was dead or had never existed.

'Everything seemed to get even better for him after Joe died,' Birdie mutters. 'He was Teflon. He got more clients. He married Madison. They had Archie . . .' She pushes down on the plastic blister on the coffee cup lid. 'Don't get me wrong. We were done. But . . .'

Paloma rests her forearms on her knees. 'No one thinks badly of you, Birdie.'

'I've made a mess of things.'

'I'd prefer to be catching up with you in a cafe.'

Birdie tries to smile. Her eyes fill and her voice almost vanishes. 'They had a *son*, Paloma. A little boy.'

Paloma reaches out to her. 'Honey, let me call Albert. He can come get you.'

'Like this?' she whimpers. 'In here?'

Paloma whispers, 'He'll understand.'

'I'm too old and messed up. Albie deserves . . .' Tears slide down her face. 'I've made mistakes, Paloma. I can't say . . .'

Paloma glances at the camera again and whispers, 'Stop. I know you've been through a lot. More than anyone should have to. Sometimes, when I'm feeling sorry for myself, frankly, I think of you.'

She pauses and licks her lips. One time, when Paloma had been late for school pick-up, rushing from uni in stained jeans and sweat at the back of her knees, she'd found the twins with Birdie, Jem and Joe. Birdie had taken them all to the sports field to play. For the girls' birthdays, Birdie bought them the latest and greatest backpacks and lunchboxes, things Paloma couldn't afford and Birdie knew were playground currency. She'd had Paloma's back in all the quiet and important ways.

'But you need to get yourself together, Birdie.'

Birdie stares at her through pink and swimming eyes.

'You still have Jem and she needs you. She's just lost her father, and whether she's feeling it right now or it's going to hit her later, it will hit her. Do you hear me?'

Birdie nods, head hanging as though by a thread.

'You've got every right to be a mess. But you can't be.' Paloma takes a deep breath. She rests her fingertips on Birdie's leg. 'Go back to Dr Patel. Go back to AA. You have to sort it out now.'

A thick pall of boozy, unwashed scent comes off Birdie, her back pressed against the cell wall.

'We can talk more another time, somewhere other than in here,' Paloma says, standing. 'I have to go to work. I'm going to call you tonight.'

Tears make blemishes on Birdie's grubby shirt.

'I'm going to call you tomorrow too. Every day for a while, okay? All you need to do is answer the phone.'

Paloma waits, watching the wet stains on Birdie's shirt spreading.

'Okay,' Birdie says finally. Her voice is rubble.

Paloma smooths her skirt. 'Now, let me call Albert.'

'No,' Birdie refuses quickly. 'Don't. I'll order an Uber.'

Paloma looks at her friend. In her head she hears a prayer her mother used to say when she was a girl. Paloma used to think it was magic, a kind of abracadabra; now she knows it's Latin. She hasn't prayed for years, not after Pell and all the others before and after him. Still, the words rise up within her. She imagines them draping gently upon Birdie like a protective cloak.

Pater Noster,
qui es in caelis,
sanctificetur nomen tuum . . .

GEORGE

Dr Decima Bosson sits at her desk with a bag of chocolate freckles at her elbow. She offers one to George. 'Dr Martin?' she asks in the direction of her phone. 'Thanks for agreeing to talk. I've got Detective Zavros with me. You're on speaker.'

Dr Kevin Martin's voice is formal and wary. 'Detective, Doctor, hello.'

'We've been able to access Mr King's medical records,' she says, 'but I want to make sure I'm drawing the right conclusions.'

'Yes?' replies Dr Martin.

'You've been his GP for some time?'

'Around eighteen years. I've treated the whole family. Even little Joe.'

'That's great, Kevin,' Decima says. 'It makes my life easier if people have had continuity of care.'

George nods in silent agreement.

'I imagine.' Dr Martin clears his throat. 'Look, it seems pertinent to say . . . Baz and I were friends. It might be difficult for me to be completely objective.'

'Thank you for letting us know. Were you friends before you started treating him, or . . .'

'No, we became friends later. Maybe after a couple of years? Baz is a gregarious guy, fun to be around. Confident.' He hesitates. 'Did I say is or was? I'm still getting used to that.'

George says, 'I get the impression he was a very vibrant man.'

'Yes,' Dr Martin says. 'Very vibrant.'

Decima glances at George. 'I'm going to talk about our understanding so far of his death, Kevin, and you can jump in whenever you like. Is that okay with you?'

'Go ahead.'

'You probably already know that Mr King fell from a height in Whroo, a rural area about two hours north of Melbourne.'

'Right.'

'The injuries he sustained from the fall clearly caused his death and, at this stage, we're unsure if anyone else was with him. We've completed a toxicology report and there are no illegal substances or alcohol evident. No recreational narcotics. Nothing to assume he was under the influence.'

'Hmmm.'

'But we did notice medication – Riluzole – which indicates that Mr King perhaps had motor neurone disease?'

There is a long pause.

'Did you prescribe him that medication, Kevin?' Decima asks. They both know he did. It's clear from Baz's records.

Dr Martin says, 'I did. He was diagnosed with the early stages of amyotrophic lateral sclerosis. Or primary lateral sclerosis, which we hadn't ruled out.'

'Would you mind explaining those terms to us?'

'Amyotrophic lateral sclerosis, or ALS, is a motor neurone disease, the one everyone knows about. Primary lateral sclerosis tends to be slower to progress and impacts the lower limbs first. ALS affects the upper *and* lower parts of the body and can cause a limited life expectancy. Not always but often. Two to five years on average. PLS can end up in ALS too, so it requires a more patient diagnosis.'

'Right. So you diagnosed Mr King with motor neurone disease a few months ago.'

'I did.'

'Which symptoms did he exhibit?'

Dr Martin sighs. 'Baz was fit. He ran, he cycled. So when he got clumsy . . . well, it wasn't like him.'

'The diagnosis must have been a huge shock.'

'It was.'

'Was his wife aware?'

'Baz and I are mates but his health is his business.' Dr Martin pauses. 'Was.'

Decima checks her notes. 'I just have one more question.'

'Go ahead.'

'Are you able to speak to Mr King's state of mind?'

'I'm not a psychiatrist, Dr Bosson.'

'No, but I can't find any records relating to Mr King's mental health. No antidepressants—'

'No, I shouldn't have thought so.'

'I wondered if, as a trusted doctor and friend, you had any views?'

Dr Martin says confidently, 'Baz King was sharp as a tack. Not the kind to let life get the better of him – far from it. He could talk his way into or out of anything, even bad luck. Look how he handled what happened to Joe. He had a good business and a happy family. I've never had any concerns about Baz's mental health. Not when Joe died and not recently.'

Decima nods. She looks to George. 'Anything to add, Detective?'

George holds Decima's gaze, the same conclusion zapping between them.

'No,' he replies. 'Thank you, Kevin.'

MADISON

Madison wakes up to the sounds of Archie downstairs, playing and laughing. Birdie is at the foot of her bed.

'What the hell do you want?'

'It's Baz's day to have Jem. I wasn't going to bring her but she wanted to see Archie.'

Madison regards Birdie through narrowed eyes.

'I brought you tea,' Birdie adds.

'I hate tea. It tastes like dishwater.'

Birdie places the mug on the side table. 'It's peppermint.'

She goes to a chair in the corner of the bedroom covered in clothes and papers. She shifts them onto the floor and sits in their place.

'Why are you really here?' Madison asks.

Birdie shrugs. 'I wanted to say sorry. And check that you're okay.'

'You wanted to say sorry?'

'I *am* sorry. It was so stupid.'

'Did you screw him in here?'

Birdie flinches.

'Did you sleep with my husband in this bed? Our bed?'

She slowly shakes her head.

'Where then?'

Birdie meets Madison's glare. 'The lounge.'

Madison feels like she might throw up. She pushes the mug of tea off the side table with one finger. Hot liquid quickly spreads over the carpet.

Birdie stares at the stain but doesn't move. 'I know this doesn't mean much . . .' Her voice is distant. 'But it was nothing.'

Madison draws the covers up to her chin. 'It's never nothing.'

She had been so sure it was Jess. Baz had been near Kyneton when he vanished – it all made sense to her. She could tell from the look on Richard's face that he'd thought so too. The Dhillons had left Tamsin's house in tears and George had driven Madison and Archie home. Madison had put Archie into his pyjamas early and crawled straight into bed.

'Why couldn't you just let him go?'

'I did,' Birdie insists. 'I have.'

'No. You haven't. Did you see how disgusted Jem was?'

Birdie stutters, 'She was confused, I know. I didn't mean for her to—'

'Find out? Ha. She wasn't confused. She was *disgusted*. You slept with him in *my* house. You're still holding on to the past. To everything.' Madison points at her. 'I've seen all the bottles in the trash and I know you won't let Albert move in.'

Birdie runs her fingers through her limp hair.

'You'll be a sad, sick drunk for the rest of your life.'

Birdie doesn't object. She's all elbows and knees in the bedroom chair.

Archie bursts through the door and hops onto the bed like a frog. He tumbles across the doona and crashes into Madison. 'Mummy! Jem is here!'

Madison kisses his head. He smells like playdough and soap. Her voice is sweet, 'I'll get up in a minute, darling.'

'Jem says she can make pancakes. She wants to stay over,' Archie chirps. 'Can she make pancakes? Can she stay?'

He sucks his bottom lip in under his top teeth, his curls bouncing and pyjamas flapping.

'If she wants to.'

'Yay!' Archie leaps off the bed and races out the door.

She says icily, 'That wasn't about you, to be clear. I want you gone. But Jemima makes Archie happy.'

'Of course,' Birdie says. 'She loves him.'

She stands to leave. The two women stare at one another. Each one a mother. Each one a wife, once. Each one haunted by the same man.

'Get out,' Madison orders.

•

Later, in the early evening, Madison tucks Archie into bed while Jemima is taking off her makeup. He's dog-tired but fighting it.

'Then Jem said – "Archie, if you paint it green and purple and blue . . ."' He can't stop talking. '"We can make a peacock" and I said, "Yes! A peacock!" So we did that, we made a peacock and then after that a boy chicken—'

'Rooster.'

'Yeah, with the red thing on its head. Jem made the eyes so funny – you should see them . . . they look *crazy*!'

'Head on the pillow, little guy.'

'She's really funny.'

'I know, baby.'

She smooths his hair. His forehead is warm from all the excitement. She pushes his favourite Pokémon soft toy into his sticky hands.

'Do you think we could get a dog?'

Madison hesitates.

Archie yawns. 'We could get a dog like Bluey.'

'I'll have to think about that.' She pulls the covers up to his chin, the way she prefers them. He pushes them away and kicks his legs. 'We don't have to call it Bluey. We could call it something different.'

'Time for sleep.'

Archie catches her fingertips as she stands. 'Mummy?'

'Hmmm?'

'If we had a dog, Jem might come over all the time. She likes them. Dogs.'

'Does she?'

His face brightens. 'Yeah. She told me.'

Madison presses his clammy palm to her lips. She walks to the door and pauses by the light switch. 'You going to blow the light out?'

Archie takes a deep breath and blows as Madison flicks the switch. Archie's nightlight glows spectral green in the corner of the darkened room. Madison lets her eyes adjust and watches her son yawn and roll to one side. She waits a few moments, imagining a forcefield around him; it repels heartache, fear, broken limbs, illness and bullies on the slippery dip. Tiny terrible things and huge unbearable things. It keeps out disaster and demons; it keeps him safe.

Archie looks over at her, his eyes obsidian in the darkness.

'Mum? You still there?'

'I'm still here.'

'I miss Daddy.'

Madison nods, her chest aching. 'Me too, darling.'

•

It's two in the morning when Madison jolts awake from a bad dream. She scrambles to Archie's room – he's there in the almost-black when she pushes the door wide open, just where she left him.

Her breathing is shallow as she takes him in, still curled around his Pokémon toy. His mouth hangs open and his cheeks are red apples. He breathes loudly, like his dad used to, and drool is wetting the soft toy in his hot little fists. Jemima is on a mattress on the floor beside him. Asleep, she looks smaller, younger, and peaceful. Madison tiptoes over and sinks down beside Archie, brushing the hair from his face. She shushes, soothing herself rather than him.

In her dream, she couldn't find her son in a busy community pool. What felt like thousands of little-boy heads bobbed in the water and none of them was Archie. Madison had been frantic, screaming his name as water poured down her face and into her mouth. Diving under the surface to try and see his legs, his *Bluey* swim shorts, under the water. No one paid her any attention, no one noticed her fear. When she woke, gasping like she was drowning, her stomach was leaden with cold terror.

Archie flinches under his mother's worried touch, and Madison slowly stands and reluctantly returns to her room. Her head is pounding. There's a sound like a pulsing buzz coming from the top of her dresser. She's disoriented for a moment and then goes towards it, picking up her phone. She doesn't know the number calling.

'Hello?' Her voice is too loud in the quiet darkness. 'Yes, I'm Madison. Corey's sister, yes.'

Within seconds she's back in Archie's room, shaking her stepdaughter's shoulder.

Her voice is high and trembling. 'Jem? I have to go out. Can you look after Archie?'

•

The bright lights in the hospital make Madison dizzy as she rushes through the corridors trying to find someone to tell her where Corey is. A woman stands from her seat at a small reception desk and Madison fires the name at her, 'Corey Leck?'

The woman finds his name in the system as Madison finds her breath and tries to slow her heart rate. 'Upstairs, third floor, ward nine.'

Madison repeats the directions to herself as she gets in the elevator with a doctor in scrubs, an orderly and a woman dozing in a wheelchair. The orderly smiles at her and she realises she doesn't have any shoes on.

She finds the ward quickly but a nurse moves in front of her before she can rush in.

'Hang on. Hang on, love.'

'I need to see my brother.'

'It's past visiting hours.'

'I just got a call. I didn't know he was here.'

The nurse has managed to manoeuvre her towards the nurses' station. Madison looks back over towards the ward.

'Corey Leck,' she says again, impatient.

Another nurse looks up at her from her desk and nods without checking the computer. 'Overdose, right?'

Madison tries not to cry. She grabs hold of the closest wall. The nurse comes around and touches her arm and Madison recoils. When she was small she used to long for touch. She would sit by her mother's knee as she watched television and lean carefully against her leg, feeling the warmth and solidity, until her mother pushed her away. Now, she hates being comforted.

'It's okay, darl, he's okay. But he's sleeping.'

'What happened?'

'Fentanyl, we think,' the nurse says. 'Though I'll let the doctor tell you when she's next in. He probably usually takes heroin but got some of this stuff instead. We've given him naloxone and it seems to have righted things. Mostly.'

Madison's mouth tastes sour. 'How long will he need to stay?'

'Couple of days, I'd say,' the nurse replies. 'Monitor his respiratory response, make sure he gets back on his feet. Is he going to stay with you?'

Madison answers immediately, 'Yes, he'll come stay with me.'

Madison is allowed to go to Corey's bedside if she promises to be very quiet and not wake him or the other patients. Madison agrees, but the nurse whose touch she rejected hovers at the entrance to the ward. Madison sinks into the chair beside Corey's bed. He's so withered that the sheet over his body barely registers something beneath it and his eyelids are thin and lined with blue veins. Madison reaches for his hand. It's bony and dirty, the fingernails yellowed. She places it in hers and strokes the tops of his fingers as her tears fall onto his papery skin.

'Who did this to you?' she whispers. 'If this was Frank, I'll kill him. We'll get you right and then I'll bloody kill him.'

PALOMA

The woman inside the laundromat is lit aquatic green by the last of the lights, before she switches them off too. Paloma watches from her car as she slings a handbag over her shoulder. She's locking the front doors when Paloma gets out of the car and steps towards her. 'Mrs Fernando? Zita?'

The woman baulks, pressing her handbag against her side.

'I'm Paloma, I left a few messages—'

'Are you a journo? There's a guy who's been calling me.'

'Gordon?'

She starts to walk, Paloma barely keeping up with her pace. 'Leave me alone.'

'I'm really sorry to bother you, Mrs Fernando.'

The woman mutters, not turning back or pausing, 'Jones. I'm back to Jones. Not Fernando.'

'I'm sorry. I wanted to talk to you about Quinta and Belwood.'

'I've got to catch a bus.'

'Where are you going? I could drive you?'

'I don't trust any of you.'

'Yes,' Paloma agrees, now puffing. 'I mean no, I imagine it's difficult to trust—'

'You lot print anything!' Zita Jones says, shaking her head towards the pavement. 'Don't matter what I say. Don't matter about Quinta. Just the story. Just getting a good story.'

'I'm not with any papers,' Paloma says. 'I'm with the premier's office.'

Zita wheels around. 'What did you say?'

'I'm with the premier's office. Well, not in an official capacity, I don't think.'

'I already told you lot I'm not taking any money.'

Paloma stops dead. 'What?'

Zita points. 'I ain't taking money and it ain't making it right. She's gone.'

'Did you . . .' Paloma catches her breath and her thoughts. 'You were offered money?'

Zita's head tips. 'Who are you?'

'Paloma Albertini.' She takes a step towards her but Zita matches it with a half-step backward.

'I don't know you,' she replies slowly.

'No. Well, you've been sending me envelopes, right? With clippings, printouts . . . about your daughter? Quinta?'

Zita stares at her for a few long seconds. 'I ain't sent nothing.'

Paloma's brow wrinkles.

'What's in them? The envelopes?'

'Information, I suppose. I assumed you must have sent them to me. My friend – not really a friend, more of a colleague – Gordon told me that you work here.' Paloma gestures back towards the laundromat.

Zita's voice is a whisper. 'Is there stuff about him?'

'Who?'

'The Wizard. Everyone he knows.'

'The Wizard?' Paloma asks. 'Who is that?'

Zita's face is hard again, zipped up. 'I got to go.'

'But I could drive you and we could talk—'

Zita holds up her hand. 'If you don't know about him then you don't know nothing I need to know.'

GEORGE

'Judge Sherman?'

George steps over the rough land towards her car. It's more peaceful out here than he remembered it, without the tents and personal protective equipment, cordons and site officers.

'Roma,' she insists. She's holding her dog but offers the hand not tucked under Lenny's belly.

George nods at Lenny. 'Looks like he wants to be off and running.'

'Don't I know it. That's what got us into trouble the last time.' Roma scratches behind his ear and the dog looks up at her with wiry eyebrows. She places him down with care. Lenny is running as soon as his paws hit the ground. He zigzags towards a few mynas and sends them whirling into the air, crying warnings.

'Let's hope he doesn't find anyone else.'

George gives a tight smile. 'I thought only cops had that kind of humour.'

Roma says wryly, 'You don't corner that market. You ready?'

They tour Roma's land without much talking. The ground is lumpy and walking requires head-down concentration. Hunks of white rock appear under George's feet every now and then, alongside tufts of grass and leaf litter. He watches out for snakes too. Addicts, thieves, drunks he can handle but there's no humanity in a snake.

Roma slows and points towards a cliff edge. George recognises it, of course, but straightens and takes it in without the distractions of a crime-scene investigation. He studies the tops of the trees, silvery eucalyptus leaves moving in the breeze, and a pair of galahs stationed at the top of a paperbark. There are gatherings of red gums and even a dripping, pendulous peppermint willow, which George fancies he can smell in the air. He circles around and surveys the land the way they walked in. He imagines two people side by side. Maybe an argument between them.

Roma says, 'It's different being out here alone, isn't it?'

'Very,' George agrees. 'Thank you for meeting with me.'

Roma shrugs. 'I come most weekends – it gets me out of my head. Lenny loves it. I've grown to enjoy it more and more. Makes you realise how dirty Melbourne is. Or can be.'

George turns to her; her tone is contemplative, like she means something more.

She gives him a weary smile. 'Been a tough week. I'm starting to think things aren't quite as they seem in my world.' She waves her hand. 'Judge Porter.'

George nods slowly. Judge Nigel Porter had been found dead in his Toorak home yesterday afternoon; George had seen the coverage on the news. Judge Porter had been an imposing figure – tall and angular, with a severe face and a reputation for not suffering fools.

'I'm sorry to hear of his death.'

Roma sniffs. 'Are you?'

'Did you work together much?'

'Not if I could help it. You didn't hear this from me, but Porter wasn't serving the state, he was serving himself,' she mutters, then straightens. 'But that's enough of that. You want to see the land so let's see the land. Fred would be happy.'

'What are you planning on doing with it?'

She smiles wistfully. 'I have no idea. I was humouring my husband when we bought it. Thought it was ridiculous. Indulgent. Now I'm not sure I'll put anything on it.'

'It's beautiful.'

Lenny bursts out of long grass with his tongue dark pink and curling. He runs at Roma and scrambles up her shin.

'Oh, you're happy now, are you?' she coddles. Lenny settles into a springy walk beside her ankles.

Roma glances at George. 'Do you think there was someone here with him? Do you think someone wanted to kill him?'

George scratches his beard. 'That's two questions, Your Honour.'

Roma smiles. 'And?'

'I'm not sure, and yes.'

'Having enemies isn't a crime,' Roma dismisses.

'Correct.'

'If there was someone with him, they'd have to have come and then gone. The rental car was still here.'

'True. But the rain might have washed away footprints or—'

Roma scoffs. 'I hardly think anyone is walking out here, Detective.'

'Car tyre tracks,' George finishes. 'But you're right, walking does seem unlikely.'

Roma throws a stick for Lenny but the dog gets distracted and races after something more enticing. A rat perhaps. Hopefully not a snake.

'He lived in my neighbourhood, you know,' she says, peering into the distance. 'Hawthorn. I read about him in the paper. Sebastian King? Spin doctor?'

'It's funny, isn't it? That we come from the same place?'

'It is but I've seen plenty of funny in my time,' George replies. 'Last week one of my officers found out her dad was an exhibitionist. She had to arrest him herself for indecent exposure.'

'Huh,' Roma says, lips twitching.

'It's weird out there.'

'You're not wrong.' Roma looks thoughtful. 'One more query, not about the case. Why do you do this work, George? Do you like solving things or helping people?'

George contemplates the question. 'Both. If I have to choose, then helping people. But I don't have to choose.'

Roma nods. 'Making things right again?'

'Something like that.'

'All the king's horses and all the king's men?'

'I'd like to think we have more success than they did.'

Roma laughs. 'That's always been my motivation too. People complain about things not being right – systems, politics, welfare, whatever – and then do nothing to make them different.

'I always thought I was doing something. Making some difference. These days, I'm not so sure. Maybe I haven't got my hands dirty enough.' She stares down at her feet and then tips her head up at George again. 'I have a confession. I know your sergeant. Old friend of Fred's.'

'Oh?'

'He told me something I shouldn't know.'

George waits, not wanting to be baited into divulging something he shouldn't.

'You were there when Baz King's son died.'

'Ah,' George sighs. 'Yes.'

'What a tragedy.'

'Yes, it was.'

'Some things can never be made right.'

When Lenny returns, grinning and panting, Roma pats George's shoulder and gestures to the open space. She whispers, 'I'll leave you to take it in, George.'

'Thanks, Judge Sherman.'

She doesn't turn around but lifts a hand. 'Roma!'

'Roma. Right.'

George takes a few long slow breaths. He closes his eyes and feels the sun on his eyelids. He waits until he can no longer hear Lenny crashing through the brittle grasses or Roma's sure and steady footfalls. He waits until it feels as though he's completely alone.

In his mind, he dresses himself in Baz's clothing. He slides on Baz's wedding ring, the one now returned to Madison, and fastens his expensive watch. He feels the St Christopher medal against his chest. He even imagines a slightly dicky left knee, which someone like Baz King would take pains to cover to keep up the appearance of youth. He reaches into his pocket and touches the photo of his son Joe. The photographic paper feels wet and slick, like the blood that will later congeal in an unholy halo. George feels his heart swell and lurch, the way a father's would, at the memory of the boy. Then he looks beyond the fall ahead of him and the trees below, the weeping peppermint willow and the galah lovers. He looks out into the big beautiful blue sky. The vast and boundless Australian sky. It can fill a person with possibilities or leave them feeling minuscule, meaningless.

George wonders which one it was for Baz King.

PALOMA

Paloma stares, again, at the text message on her phone – *Meet after work, bus stop. 9 pm.*

Three buses have slowed while she has been sitting at the stop. The first two drivers gave polite waves, the third rolled his eyes when she didn't get on. At ten minutes past nine, Zita Jones takes a seat at the other end of the bench. Paloma opens her mouth to greet her but a man sits between them and Zita widens her eyes. The next bus rumbles up to the stop five minutes later and the man boards while two girls get off looking at a phone between them and giggling.

When the bus has gone and the girls are in the distance, Zita asks, 'Were you followed?'

Paloma looks around. 'No.'

'Are you sure?'

Paloma shakes her head. 'I didn't think about it. I guess I can't say I'm absolutely sure.'

Zita nods, face relaxing. 'Least you're honest.' She scans the street around them, taking in the parked cars, the man across the road jogging and the two girls growing smaller with the glowing phone between them.

'Let's walk then.'

Paloma follows Zita as she heads to a nearby park where the bats are noisy in the trees. The deeper into the park they go, the more relaxed she seems, but she doesn't say anything more until they're sitting on another bench, partially hidden by thick shrub.

'Why did you want to see me again?'

'Why is the premier asking about my daughter?'

Paloma shrugs. 'He's not. Not yet anyway. I'm asking. I work for him and I've been receiving these envelopes.'

'You said.'

'I thought they were coming from you.'

Zita shakes her head and withdraws a vape from her pocket. The fug that fills the air is sweet.

'They're not from me. How many have you got?'

'A fourth earlier this week. This last one . . .'

Paloma had gone to the letterbox in her slippers. She didn't care what her neighbours thought and she had been expecting a package — gifts she'd ordered for Queenie's and Rose's birthdays. The envelope had been sticking out of the mail slot and she knew straightaway what it was because of the same light brown envelope. She hadn't wanted to touch it.

'It was in my letterbox. The others came to me at work.'

Zita puffs. 'So whoever it is knows where you live now.'

Paloma nods reluctantly. 'I'm not too worried for me but my daughters . . .'

Zita looks over to her. 'You have daughters?'

'Twins. Sixteen.'

Zita's mouth softens, 'Oh. Same as Quinta.' The woman's face, weathered and drawn, suddenly seems softer.

Paloma leans towards her. 'Can you tell me about her? I only know what the papers said.'

She inhales. 'Right, like you know how she died, that's all

anyone knows 'bout her. But she'd been sixteen years on Earth and no one talks about that.'

'Tell me,' Paloma encourages.

'Quinta was smart. Walked early – nine months old – talked early, did everything fast. Liked to run. Ran everywhere. Teachers at school would get her to do errands, take notes to other teachers, 'cause she was quick, see?'

'Good little netballer. Played centre.

'Loved her brother. Only eighteen months apart.

'Her dad, well . . .' Zita sniffs. 'He was a loser. But he was good at basketball so maybe that's where she got them athlete genes from.' She gestures to her own body. 'Not from me.'

There is the sound of footfall and Paloma and Zita remain silent as a jogger moves past the bench and continues on the path, disrupting the bats in the trees above who screech and protest.

'Why was she there? At the pool that night?' Paloma asks.

Zita smiles. 'Seeing a boy.'

'The papers didn't say—'

'The cops said not to say anything about him to the press, so I didn't. Said it might make Quinta seem . . . Well, she was fast to everything, you know? Boys included.'

Paloma asks, 'Who was he? The boy?'

Zita looks into the middle distance and sucks on her vape. 'Don't want to say. If you really want to, you can find out. Just not from me.'

'But he was there? That night?'

Zita nods. 'Came late. Too late. Quinta was already inside. He got there and flames were going up. He smelled the petrol and ran. I didn't know about him until later. I read her diary.' She looks down at her shoes. 'She really liked him.'

'I'm so sorry.'

'Yeah, everyone's real sorry,' Zita says bitterly. 'Are you going to do anything about it?'

'I don't know that I can,' Paloma says. 'I don't know who's sending me this stuff or what I can do.'

Zita stands. 'I better catch my bus. Quinta's brother's at home.'

'I'll walk you.'

She shakes her head. 'Better not. Just in case.'

'Who do you think might be following you?' Paloma asks.

Zita smiles, but it's pitying. 'You'll work it out.' She drops her vape into her handbag. 'Or you won't.'

•

The next day Paloma excuses herself from a team meeting. She walks quickly to a spare meeting room and closes the door behind her. She presses Gordon Tuttle's number on her phone.

'Paloma?'

Her heart is racing so quickly she feels breathless. 'What were the findings about the cause of the fire at Belwood?'

'Hi Gordon, nice to talk—'

'Just answer me.'

'Electrical fault, filtration room.'

'Would it smell like petrol?'

'Petrol? Doubt it.'

'I need you to find out about the boy who was there that night.'

'There was no boy—'

'And who presided over the inquiry? Into the cause?'

'Judge Porter.'

'Judge Nigel Porter?'

'The one and only.'

Paloma swears and rubs her face. When she lifts her head, the premier is glaring at her from the meeting room where the team is still gathered. She mouths, 'Sorry.'

Into the phone she says clearly, 'There was a boy, Gordon. We need to find him.'

MADISON

Madison no longer feels fit for the world outside their front door. It is too unchanged, carrying on as it has always done, while she is flooded with emotion. Despair for Corey. Anger at Baz. Confusion. Loss. Uncertainty about the future. Her feet feel like concrete and all her clothes are suddenly tight and rough, too close to her thin skin. She's the wrong shape for regular life, suddenly the wrong kind of human. Maybe not human at all.

Madison's mother called to offer condolences but did a terrible job of it. Made it about herself, cut the call off early and forgot to ask about Archie or mention Corey. She made a joke about the weight people put on when they're grieving and how Madison should 'watch out!' before pretending she didn't really mean it. 'Anyway,' she'd huffed, managing to sound accusatory, 'I suppose you have it all under control.'

Madison almost said no. She needs money. She needs to get Baz's life insurance and income protection payments. But Baz had looked after their insurances because he'd been a consultant for the Insurance Council of Australia and played squash with the chief financial officer for AIA. Madison can only recall that his first name is Paul. He may have been trying to get hold of her;

she has lots of missed calls on her phone. Birdie had called. So had Detective Zavros and even Abigail Meyer, who no doubt wanted to pry, but Madison didn't have the energy to answer calls or check messages. She'd spoken with Patti, of course, who was in tatters and wanted to come over. Madison was too exhausted to look after anyone else. Baz's sister, Rachel, would have to hold their mother up.

Madison jumps when her phone rings in the afternoon, with an unfamiliar ringtone that sounds like a church bell. She figures that Archie must have worked out how to change it. As it tolls, her son looks up at her innocently from beside her feet. He's watching *Bluey* on her iPad.

Madison answers before she has time to remember that she doesn't want to talk.

'Is this Mrs Madison King?'

The voice on the other end is frank but warm. It reminds Madison of an old school teacher.

'Yes.'

Madison's attention wanders to the screen in Archie's lap. He's watched this episode many times over; it's the one where Bluey's dad joins a game of Keepy Uppy – trying to keep a balloon up in the air for as long as possible.

'I'm from the Victorian Coronial Services. We are able to release Sebastian King today.'

Madison pictures Baz waiting somewhere. A bus stop. A taxi stand.

'I don't understand.'

'Your husband, Mrs King. You can arrange for his body to be collected. I presume you've engaged a funeral director?'

Madison's breath catches. 'No.'

'Would you like me to recommend one? They are all very familiar with the collection process and will be able to help you.'

'Yes. Please.'

Archie giggles at the iPad, at Bluey's dog-dad, Bandit. Madison wants to cry.

'Mrs King?' the woman asks. 'Are you still there?'

Madison nods and then remembers to say yes out loud.

'I'm really sorry,' she says. 'I know this must be a terrible shock.'

'He's only been there a few days,' Madison says. 'Does this mean you know what happened to him?'

There's a short pause. The woman says, 'I'm very sorry, but I don't have the pathology report. What usually happens is that when the autopsy is done, samples are taken for testing. Then the pathologist's report is completed. It can take a while, I'm afraid. In the meantime we try and return the deceased to their families so they don't have to delay a funeral.'

Her voice is so rhythmic and calming that Madison finds her breath. 'I see.'

'Hopefully you don't have to wait too long for the report.'

The woman, who is called Penny as it turns out, takes Madison's email address and promises to send her a document with a list of funeral directors who are familiar with the Coronial Services' processes. She says it also lists grief counsellors and reminds Madison of the Lifeline service. By the end of their call, Madison's thoughts have become soupy again. She hangs up and only the *Bluey* jingle remains, filling the soundscape.

Out the window there is a perfect blue sky. Madison imagines her conversation with Baz when she picks him up.

Helluva trip.

We've all been so worried.

Don't worry, darling, I'm here now.

Baz? I went to see a lawyer about a divorce.

And now?

I'm scared without you.

That's the way. You know I love you.

To bits.

To bits.

After tamping down thoughts, desires and feelings for so long, Madison is suddenly awash with them all. She cannot feel her edges. The feelings are liquid and everywhere. There is an ocean within and around her.

LAID TO REST

BAZ

*S*ecrets I keep, deep in my pockets:

1. I blame Birdie for Joe dying.
She should have been watching; she shouldn't have been drinking. Never mind where I was, I was furious with her. When we had counselling, Dr Patel asked if I blamed Birdie and I said, 'No, of course not.' It was a lie.

2. I hated the way people treated me when Joe died.
People acted as though I had a second head growing out of my shoulder. I was a leper. I was cursed. People saw me coming and they did that horrified mental calculation – it's him, do I say something or not say something? Parents clutched their kids when I walked by and I wanted to shout, 'It's not contagious!'
Worse still, people complained about their kids to me, as though I was better off without one of mine. How noisy their kids were, how sleepless, constantly sick, relentless, messy and bothersome. As though I'd wisely returned Joe like a faulty product. I know they were embarrassed about their kids' aliveness but it stung. They wanted to assure me I wasn't missing out on much, ha ha ha.

Before Joe died I was lucky and flying high. Afterwards I was a loser.

3. *After we had Archie, people stopped being horrified by me.*
He's a new dad! A new person! Look at him, his luck has changed! He's come good!

With Archie, I was the hero in the hero's journey.

Madison does all the hard slog – she grew Archie, she gave birth to him, she raises him. And I take the credit, I take the shine.

Take it like a criminal and don't regret it for one second.

4. *I like the grey. The grey pays.*
Madison has a nice life and Archie doesn't want for anything. Jem either. But that all comes at a price and people will lie about what they're willing to do or not do. Fact is, most people haven't been faced with the opportunity. If you could make great money, really *great money, from doing something not quite legal, not quite high moral ground, would you do it? I bet you would.*

How many people have watched pirated movies or TV shows? Tried to pay less tax or parked in a no parking zone? Taken soap and shampoo from a hotel? Nicked a glass from your favourite pub? Kissed someone you shouldn't while in a relationship? Come on. Who are you bullshitting? Me or yourself?

What I have done in my career might lie outside of your moral boundaries, but I ask you – has anyone ever tested where those moral boundaries are, exactly? What would you do for hundreds of dollars? Thousands?

How about hundreds of thousands?

BIRDIE

They meet outside Readings bookstore in Carlton. Albert, early, pretends to study the notices in the shop window.

'Hey Albie.'

They kiss each other's cheeks. Birdie wants Albert to kiss her properly like he did the very first time, here outside the bookstore, but Albert always lets Birdie lead. The one time he reached for her was when she was about to tell him she was no good for him, that she was a terrible person and he should run, rather than walk, away from her. That was the very first time they kissed. They'd been walking late at night, the streets dark blue like rivers and still. Her warning had dissolved in her mouth as Albert pressed her up against the window glass and he had smelled so good. The buckle of his belt, smooth and silver, chilled Birdie's stomach through her thin top. She had felt as though she was lifting off the ground, as though her heart burst out of her and soared somewhere above her head.

'Where did you want to go?' he asks now, stiffly.

'A cafe nearby?' Birdie is anxious. She keeps touching her hair.

'Okay.'

They fall into step with one another. The bottom of Birdie's dress swishes around her ankles and the soles of her sandals gently slap the pavement.

'Thanks for coming.'

'That's all right.'

Several years after Joe died and Birdie and Baz had split up, Albert sent Birdie a text message. It was late at night or early in the morning, depending on how you looked at it, but Birdie replied straightaway. They'd both been awake when they shouldn't have been. Albert asked how she was doing and Birdie admitted that her marriage had fallen apart. Albert tried to be funny by sending a gif of a building being blown up and then erased the message, apologising and hoping she hadn't seen it. Birdie found his embarrassment endearing; it was easy to be friends after that.

'How are you holding up after the news about Baz?' he asks carefully.

'Not great,' she admits, without telling him about being locked up. 'I thought he'd just pop up. Seemed like the kind of thing Baz would do. Vanish, make a fuss, and then reappear. I can't quite get my head around it.'

'And Jem?'

'Jem's okay,' Birdie says. 'But you know how she is.'

'She's tough,' Albert says.

'Yeah,' Birdie murmurs. 'That's what we all keep telling ourselves.'

She gestures towards a nearby cafe where there's a free table by the front window. Albert sits and waits at the table while Birdie buys coffees. She returns with a red face.

'Are you okay?'

'I'm off the booze,' she explains. 'Doctor says it's normal.'

Albert blinks hard but says nothing.

Birdie leans in. 'I've started going to meetings, Albie, and I'm not going to be half-arsed about it. Dr Patel is going to help me.'

He smiles, but it's small and sad. 'That's great, Birdie.'

'I should have done it a long time ago. You've been trying to tell me it's a problem for so long.'

He nods and his weariness eats her up.

'Look . . .' She inhales to give herself courage. 'I'm embarrassed. Ashamed.'

'I've told you how I feel about you, Birdie,' he says softly. 'You don't have to be ashamed with me.'

'I know,' she says. 'But I am.'

Albert presses his lips together, saying nothing. The coffees arrive and Birdie reaches into her bag. She slides a book across the table. 'I wanted to give this to you.'

The book cover has an image of a winter's tree, leaves of orange and blue falling from it. Albert opens it and on the first page there's a black and white photo of a couple. The woman is wearing cat-eye glasses and her hair is thick and wavy. The man looks at her as though she is the moon and the stars.

'It's Jeff's book,' Birdie says, 'The CS Lewis one that he reads from. His wife – the one in the photo – she was a poet.'

Albie looks up at her. 'Thank you.'

'It's not about Narnia.' She says, smiling and crying at the same time.

'Oh Birdie.'

She grabs both of his hands and clings tight. 'It's dangerous to love me, Albert, I'm not joking.'

'Birdie—'

She shakes her head, stopping him from speaking, 'I need to get this out before I lose my nerve.' Her lip quivers. 'I messed up, Albie. I slept with Baz a few weeks ago. Before . . .'

Albert slumps against the back of his chair.

'I'm so sorry.'

'Why would you . . .?'

'Because . . . I don't even know. Because our lives were stuck together?'

Albert looks wounded.

'I didn't mean for it to happen. I felt dreadful about it. Then at Tamsin's party . . . well, Madison found out and everything went to pieces.'

'Does Jem know?'

Birdie nods, 'She's confused. Angry too. After the party and hearing about Baz I drank too much and got locked up.'

'Oh Birdie, no.'

Birdie closes her eyes. 'This is how it is with me, Albie. I'm broken.'

'You're not.'

'I *am*,' she insists. 'I drink too much. I do stupid things. You're so kind and I've hurt you. I push people away so if they . . . go . . .'

She brings his hands to her face and kisses his knuckles. 'I want you in our lives, Albert. I've *always* wanted you in our lives.'

The tears shine on her cheeks. She leans against his hand, his long slender fingers resting on the side of her face. She feels them twitch.

'I've been so scared, Albie.'

Albert's voice is soft and bruised, 'You and Baz?'

He peels his hand away from her face, the warmth of him leaving her skin.

GEORGE

George eats cereal in the lounge wearing only his underwear. The bowl rests on the hillock of his stomach. His phone rings.

'Decima. How are you?'

'Good. I'm calling about Sebastian King. I've sent you my full report.'

George walks into the kitchen and places his bowl in the sink.

'Short story?'

'Short story is – I have no reason to believe anyone else was involved in Mr King's death.'

George leans against the sink.

'I can't find evidence of anyone else being there,' she continues. 'No property, no DNA, no footprints, obviously, though that was problematic. Within the scope of my investigation, I don't think anyone else was there.'

'Do you have a conclusion?'

George can hear her breathing.

'There are really only two options from that assumption. Either Mr King had an accident or Mr King caused his own accident.'

'What's your bet on?'

'His body doesn't offer too many clues either way. Other than the ALS maybe.'

'In what way?'

'It might have made him more clumsy. But that's a supposition.'

'And there was no note.'

'No.'

George drums the benchtop with a thick thumb.

'That's all I can give you, I'm afraid.'

'That's plenty, thanks, Decima.'

'You're welcome.'

Valentine slinks into the kitchen and makes figure eights in and out of George's legs. George squeezes food from a foil pouch into Valentine's bowl for him. Valentine is so keen he gets gravy and jelly on his ears.

'You silly bastard,' George scolds.

While Valentine eats, George looks out and around his apartment. Paloma's place is nothing like his. She's too busy to maintain order. There's always something in the fridge that should have been binned days ago and towers of books in the corners of every room. Nothing matches – couches and cushions, doonas and pillowslips. It's hardly ever peaceful unless it's too early in the morning for Rose or Queenie to be awake, but Paloma's love for her girls is so big and vivid it seems to take up space.

George picks up his phone. 'Mrs King? It's Detective Zavros. I have the pathologist's report. I can drop by later this afternoon.'

•

George and Jemima sit at Madison's kitchen table. Madison is boiling the kettle. A plate of sliced ginger loaf is between George and Jemima, though neither of them reach for it. It's one of many cakes, Madison explains, urging them to eat it. Also lasagnes, shepherd's pies, regular pies, homemade curries and boxes of chocolates, all dropped to her directly or left on the doorstep.

Jem looks the detective up and down. 'Queenie said you were the paramedic when Joe died.'

George nods.

'The guy who gave me stickers?'

'That was me.'

'You gave me a whole bunch, do you remember? It pissed off Jack Dhillon because you only let the rest of the kids have one each.'

'I remember.'

They hold eye contact.

Madison asks from the kitchen, 'Milk? Sugar?'

'Just milk, thank you.'

'And now you're here,' Jemima says wistfully. 'When Dad is gone.'

'I'm really sorry about your father, Jemima. I know you've been through a lot.'

She studies him, speaking lightly, almost as though he isn't in the room. 'Dad would like that – you being there when Joe died and here now. A kind of plot twist. Or maybe an Easter egg. Toni will know what it's called.' She tips her head. 'You know we're burying him in a few days.'

Madison returns to the table with two coffees.

'Thank you for seeing me at short notice,' George says. 'I wanted to speak to you both once I had Dr Bosson's findings.'

George slides papers out of a file.

'These documents belong to the coroner but I'll give you as much information as I can. You can ask me anything. If I can't answer for any reason I'll let you know.' He takes a quick drink of his coffee before getting started. 'The main thing of note is that Dr Bosson and I don't see any evidence of foul play. We don't believe anyone else was involved.'

Jem stares out the window. George follows her gaze but there's only a protea bush out there, the pink blooms moving in the breeze. It's as though she's not listening.

'Okay,' says Madison, unimpressed. 'So what happened?'

'Your husband died from injuries he sustained from the fall. Given the extent of the injuries, we believe he died very quickly.'

'But why was he out there?' Madison presses. 'In the middle of nowhere?'

'We don't know.' George is slow and careful. 'We do know that he either fell or . . .' He pauses and watches Jem, still staring at the protea. 'I'm sorry.'

'It's not *your* fault,' Madison snaps, as though the apology offends her.

They are silent for a few moments. Archie is at day care and the house is much quieter without him. In the past, George used to quickly fill pauses and hesitations. He has learned over time that it's better not to. 'People need to process,' one of his mentors told him. 'Don't let your unnecessary chatter get in the way of that.'

'What else?' Madison eventually asks. 'In the pathologist's report?'

George has practised this sentence. 'Once you are clear on the executor of the will, that person can apply to access the full pathologist's report and Mr King's medical records. But the two most important and conclusive findings are that there was no foul play and we believe he died swiftly.'

'But you don't know how he slipped.'

George checks Jem's face. She's now looking down at her fingers spread out on the tabletop. He turns to Madison. 'No. There had been rain so we don't know how he . . . slipped. We're inclined to assess the death as accidental though. There was no note on Mr King or that you have found since?'

'No,' Madison says firmly. 'He would never do that.'

'Well,' George says softly, trying not to look at Jem again, 'if you would like the coroner to investigate further, we are able to request an inquest. That's a choice for you to think over.'

Madison closes her eyes and presses her fingertips to her hairline.

'I know it's extraordinarily difficult,' George says. 'You don't have to make a decision today.'

Madison shakes her head and mutters, 'How am I supposed to know what to do? I'm planning a funeral. I didn't expect my husband to . . . Look, I know you must see it every day, but I don't. I didn't plan for this.'

George nods. 'Of course.'

'Will requesting an inquest mean we need to pause the funeral?'

'No. You wouldn't need to do that.' He licks his lips, hesitating. 'Did you have any indication that Baz was intending to harm himself?'

'No,' Madison says again, bristling. 'I already said he would never do that.'

Jem locks eyes with George.

'Okay,' George replies. 'An inquest can be a prolonged process so it's worth considering whether it will be worth it.'

Jem's firm voice surprises them both. 'Dad wouldn't want that.' She looks from George to Madison. 'The fuss, you know? The delay, using up everyone's time.'

'Are you kidding? He loved fuss,' Madison mutters.

'It would really hurt Grandma,' Jemima counters. 'You know how she is with the church.'

Madison studies her stepdaughter. 'You could be right.'

Jemima's voice is steady and sure. 'There's no note, right? Dad was fine. He was happy. It wasn't supposed to happen. It was an accident.'

Madison is silent. She nods slowly. 'Look, my brother is sick. He's in hospital and I need to go see him.'

'Of course.' George stands. 'Please don't rush, if you decide you'd like us to continue investigations, we certainly can, just through the coroner.'

Madison nods at him, though her eyes are staring somewhere else.

Jem walks George to the front door where she leans against the doorframe. 'Queenie says you're dating her mum.'

Just thinking about Paloma makes the corners of George's mouth lift.

'She's really protective of her mum,' Jem says. 'But she reckons you're all right.'

'Huh. She said I'm all right? That's big praise from Queenie.'

'It really is.'

George reaches into his pocket and passes Jem his business card. 'If you ever want to call me, here are my details.'

Jem accepts the card but doesn't look at it. As he heads towards his car, she says, 'We don't want an inquest.'

George turns back.

'Things are . . .' Jem pauses. 'It is what it is. That's what Dad would say.'

'Okay.'

'Besides, he would have wanted us to move on. It's what he always did.'

George studies Jem in the doorway. She's like a match with her dark clothes and flame-coloured hair; small and flinty.

She shrugs. 'He got himself a new wife, a new kid after Joe died,' she says without bitterness. 'See? Start a new page, that was his way.'

'You've all been through a lot. Take your time. See how you go.'

Jem's gaze is steady, like an angry cat. 'We won't want one,' she says crisply.

George nods. He wonders what she is not telling him.

PALOMA

Paloma doesn't love sunrises – they come on too fast and are over too quickly. One minute Paloma is waiting in her car in the dark and the next it's light, fragile and tender, and she has to slide down her seat in case she's noticed. Gordon called her last night with the name she'd been waiting for – Benji Tran, the boy who had been meeting Quinta Fernando at the Belwood Community Centre.

'Ask me,' Gordon had teased her.

'Ask you what?'

'Why the name sounds familiar.'

'Tran?'

'He was the police chief's nephew. So you won't see his testimony anywhere.'

'How did you find it then?'

Gordon clicked his tongue. 'I have ways.'

'Have you spoken to him? What does he have to say about it?'

'Not much. Kid is six feet under.'

Paloma winced. 'Are you kidding?'

'Fell on some train tracks. Accident – well, that's the official line. I think the poor boy was probably depressed.'

Paloma closed her eyes tight.

'So,' Gordon asked, 'what's next? There's not enough for me to run a story and I don't know what you're going to do with all this.'

'Neither do I,' Paloma replied.

She's no closer to understanding what she might do with the information now as she sits in her car parked twenty metres from her house, waiting. She scans the other cars around her to make sure none of them is occupied. Zita Jones's fear of being followed has crept under Paloma's skin. She looks briefly at her phone, wondering if she should call George but unsure of what to say, unsure exactly what she is or should be scared of.

Then she sees a figure – bulky dark hoodie, loose jeans – walking down the road towards her house. They have a familiar gait. Paloma feels her breath catch as she slinks down further into her seat. She barely dares to peek over the steering wheel and watch the person move closer towards her letterbox. An envelope appears from under the hoodie and slides quickly through the mail slot. The figure turns, briefly, and surveys the street. Paloma shuffles down again and waits a moment before rising. Her anonymous poster doesn't wait for longer than a couple of seconds, striding back in the direction they came from. But wind catches the top of their hood and lifts it from their face for a moment and Paloma sees the hair it's covering. Fox orange, just like her mother's. She sees Jemima King's delicate, almost feline face framed by the darkness of her huge sweatshirt.

After she has gone, Paloma waits several minutes, catching her breath. Then she presses the name on her phone and holds it to her ear, staring at her mailbox with the edge of an envelope showing.

'George? I need to show you something.'

JESS AND RICHARD

They meet in Trentham. The cafe is housed in a former bank, the walls dark green on the lower half, cloud-white up top, like a flood line. An ancient springer spaniel sleeps beside the espresso machine. Jess arrives first. She takes a table by the door so she can see Richard arriving. Her stomach swoops and crashes with every person who comes in. Her legs jiggle as though readying for escape.

'I ordered you a coffee,' she says when he finally gets there.

'Sorry I'm late.'

'You're not. I was early.' She smiles carefully at him. He's had a haircut.

A waiter delivers their drinks – one soy latte and one long black. He asks if they'd like anything to eat and they look at one another, seeking permission. He hands over two menus and leaves them to decide.

'How are you?' Jess asks.

'I'm all right,' Richard says, guarded. 'How're things at home?'

'Okay. The boys miss you.'

His expression is challenging. 'And you?'

Jess hesitates. She had longed for lust and passion. She'd thought of Baz King so often – the heat of him, the shape and muscle, his wealth its own seduction, the rule-breaking of it all. But without Richard around, she misses the things that previously drove her crazy: his same old jokes and daggy clothes, the way he hyped up the boys till they were wild and laughing right before bedtime. She misses the way he smells – sawdust and something else that is uniquely him and can't be explained. She finds herself at the kitchen sink staring out of the back window. She forgets why she walked into rooms. She keeps losing her keys and has to hide several spares under pots by the front door. The house is quiet and sad. The kids are quiet and sad. Jack is furious with his mum; he blames her for Richard leaving, showing his anger with roiling, mutinous silence. Harrison is simply confused, and Monty – despite living most of his life in Kyneton – asks if they're going to move again.

Jess says, 'I miss you a lot.'

'Tell me the truth about the photo they found.'

She reaches for his hands but Richard doesn't offer them. 'I found the image in an old archive file on my computer. It was from the school athletics day. It was boiling hot. We were all close to passing out, so Tamsin went to her boot and got out two huge golf umbrellas for shade and Birdie found a little umbrella for Joe, one of Jem's old ones – ballerinas and ballet shoes all over it. Joe loved it. He went off singing and spinning it around his head.'

'Was Baz there?' Richards asks.

'No. None of the dads were. None that I remember. Joe played while I took pictures and it was nothing really, but special too, that moment. I called to him, he turned and I got that photo.'

Jess feels as though there's a glass cloche over that day, steaming with insufferable heat and thrumming with significance because of what was to come soon after. The mums under Tamsin's umbrella joking about hot flushes, the kids grizzling and needing water bottles re-filled, and Joe, sweet and content, completely unaffected. Twirling and grinning in a world of his own. It was almost as though he had one foot in the hereafter.

'And you went to give it to Baz.'

'Yeah,' Jess confesses. 'I found an email address on his company website. I got in touch and said I had something for him.'

'Recently?'

'A few months ago. Spring.'

Jess remembers the afternoon. It was frigid. The kind of Melbourne day that is ruthless and inescapable. Cold that grips your bones and finds its way into your ears.

Baz was sitting outside as though it was January warm. He didn't look like she remembered. He was smaller somehow.

'I found this,' she'd said to him, breathless with the cold, breathless with the circumstances. Jess passed him the photo. Their fingers touched and his were like ice.

'Oh,' he'd said, like his heart was in his throat.

They'd talked for a while about things that weren't exciting – the kids, their houses, politics, life. Every time he mentioned Archie or Madison, Jess had willed her jealousy to settle down. Then Baz had said, 'I suppose you've got other things to do? In town?'

Jess had licked her dry lips. 'No. I came to see you.'

Richard hesitates, thinking, and then asks, 'What were you hoping for?'

'I don't know,' she replies carefully. 'Something, maybe.'

'Something . . .' he repeats. 'I know I'm not everything you wanted.' He holds up his hand when she opens her mouth to interrupt. 'I'm a realist, Jess. You're not. You'll always want more and I love that about you too.'

'I do love you, Richard.'

'I know,' he says. 'But I'm not dumb. I know that I love you more than you love me. We don't talk about it, but it's true.'

'I'm sorry,' Jess says.

Richard shrugs. 'I get what it is and I've made peace with that. You're always seeking, that's how you're wired. But . . .' He pauses, looking out the window. 'I want to know. I don't want to be the last to find out.'

Jess leans in. 'There's no one else. There's nothing else. He's *dead*.' She adds, 'I know I couldn't move on before but he's dead and it's all done now. Finished.'

The version of Baz Jess saw at the cafe on Little Collins Street has been erased from her mind. But she keeps the old version of him filed carefully away. The one that makes her feel desired and bad, who helps her find an orgasm when one is just out of reach.

Richard reaches for her hands. 'I kissed Brooke.'

Jess startles. 'You what?'

'The new office manager. We were drunk. Really drunk. It was the night you'd come back from Melbourne and—' He points towards her belly.

'Okay,' Jess says slowly, 'you kissed Brooke. Hang on, you kissed her or she kissed you?'

'I guess she kissed me.'

Jess nods and then laughs.

'Why is it funny?'

'I don't know.'

She finds it sexy, Richard being desired by another woman. She says emphatically, 'Come back home.'

The waiter returns to the table, nodding at the menus, 'Have you decided yet?'

Jess and Richard stare at one another across the table.

PALOMA

Paloma waits by the school gate as girls stream out in lots of twos, some threes and a few bigger groups, but it's hard to fit them all side by side on the pavement. Some of them are chatting, thumbs hooked around straps, a lot of them are looking at their phones. One pair are taking endless selfies – lips puckered, tongues out, fingers in victory signs.

'Hi Jemima.'

She's holding the hand of a slip of a girl who has long blonde hair down to her waist, so blonde it's almost white. The girl stares at Paloma, assessing her.

'Hey Aunty P,' says Jemima.

Back when she and Birdie spent more time together, before Birdie took to drinking during the day and Paloma could no longer stand the smell of vodka or gin on her breath, Jemima used to call her Aunty P.

Paloma smiles. 'It's been a while since I've heard that one.'

'This is Toni.'

'Hi Toni, nice to meet you.'

Toni nods and glances at Jemima.

'Who are you here for? The twins—'

'Nothing to do with the twins. I was wondering if I could talk to you. It shouldn't take long.'

Jemima hesitates before saying, 'Sure.'

Toni drops her hand and the girls lean towards one another, murmuring. Paloma looks away to give them privacy, their whispers suddenly seeming like one of the most intimate things she has seen for a while.

•

Paloma takes Jemima to a nearby cafe and they sit at a table far away from the counter and girls buying big plastic cups full of bubble tea. They order coffee. Jemima shrugs her bag off her shoulders and tucks it neatly under the table.

'How've you been holding up?' Paloma asks.

'I'm okay.'

'It's a pretty crazy time.'

'Yeah.'

Paloma takes a bracing breath. 'What do you think happened to your dad? Do you think Frank Agosti had anything to do with it?'

Jemima looks up sharply.

Paloma lowers her voice, 'I know it's you who's been leaving the envelopes for me.'

The expression on Jemima's face falters a little. Their coffees are delivered to the table and they both thank the server. Jemima stirs several spoons of sugar into hers.

'Was it always you?'

Jemima nods. 'He asked me to drop them to you and gave me the dates. He bought me a new phone and earbuds to do it, so I said I would. I stick to my promises.'

'Five packages?'

Jemima nods again, 'Some to your work, some to home. I guess he wanted to make sure the last ones didn't go to anyone else by mistake?'

'There aren't anymore?'

'No, that's it.'

'Did you look at what was put inside?' Paloma asks. 'Did you listen to the phone call he recorded?'

'Yes.'

'So you know as much as me.'

Jemima nods. 'Frank got someone to burn down the community centre so he could get the contract to rebuild. Judges, cops, council – all in on it. And Dad. Dad knew about it and he helped make people look the other way.' She fixes Paloma with a steady stare. 'He was good at that.'

Paloma nods. 'He was.'

'What are you going to do about it?'

'That's a good question. I wanted to talk to you about that.' She studies the girl in front of her. 'I've given it all over to the police.'

She watches Jemima's face but she doesn't flinch. Paloma had spoken to George, the two of them stayed up most of the night connecting dots. Working out how Alex and Baz's company received kickbacks from Frank's construction and real estate development companies, and how police and officials had been manipulated and bribed to ensure Frank's businesses won tenders. Paloma wanted to protect Jemima and George agreed so they had to figure out who in the force she could pass the information to and who could be trusted. They decided together that the source would remain anonymous. The same went for Gordon Tuttle, Paloma would never tell him who had given her the information.

'Good.'

'They won't know where it's come from but it's pretty damning,' Paloma warns. 'I don't know how it will reflect on your dad or the other people involved. Quite a few people, like you say. I can't promise anything.'

'I know.'

'It's going to have an impact and you've been through a lot already. Are you ready for that?'

Jemima surprises Paloma by laughing.

'What's funny?'

'This is funny.' She takes a sip of her strong, sweet coffee. 'Are you kidding? I'm not ready for any of this.' She returns her cup to its saucer with a clink. 'I wasn't ready for Dad to get me to mule his secrets, I'm not ready for him to be dead.'

'I'm sorry.'

'It's not your fault. I'm glad it's gone to the cops.'

Paloma asks, 'What about your Mum or Madison? Do you think you'll ever tell them that the documents and recording came from your Dad?'

Jemima shakes her head and mutters, 'He did the right thing this time. But he doesn't get to be a hero.'

She runs her finger around the lip of her cup. Her short nails are painted purple. They sit without talking for a few moments, listening to the hiss of the espresso machine and percussion of cups, plates and cutlery.

When she speaks again, her voice is tender. 'Paloma?'

'Yes, sweetheart?'

'What did you think of my dad?'

Paloma's eyes widen. 'I think he was complicated,' she says delicately.

Jemima tips her head. 'I know you didn't like him.'

'Well,' Paloma says slowly, 'your dad doing all of this – that surprises me. So maybe I didn't know him very well.'

Jemima mutters into her coffee, 'Maybe nobody knows each other well.'

'Maybe,' Paloma concedes.

'That girl?' Jemima adds softly. 'The one who died in the pool? Who Frank helped to kill?'
'Quinta?'
'She was my age.'

HAWTHORN WRITERS CLUB, 'SUMMER STORIES' SUBMISSION
POST TRAUMATIC (IN FOUR PARTS)
BY JEMIMA KING

Part 1

The therapist told me I probably have PTSD. It's what soldiers get when they've been to war. It means I've experienced something so dreadful it's stuck in the place in my brain between past and present, and now I carry it with me everywhere I go. To the supermarket, to school, to the beach. It's a shadow lurking in every corner. A demon. It corrodes everything.

Maybe it stands for:
Past
Terror
Soul
Destruction

The girls at school want to talk about what happened. They think it's dead interesting to have a dead brother. They want to know how it happened and what it feels like and why and what now. But not in a kind, trying to understand way. More in a jabbing a finger into the wound kind of way.

Talking about what happened to my brother doesn't help. Talking about it erases nothing. Plus, I'm no good at it. That's because trauma, they say, gets stuck in a part of your memory that's not reliable. It's not like other memories – going to Fiji or a first kiss. Those memories turn like pages, one after another. Those memories are orderly and neat, with a beginning, a middle and an end. We shelve those memories nicely, like books.

Trauma is an exploded mirror ball. It's not orderly at all. Bits go everywhere. Bits go missing. Bits get stuck in everyone around like shrapnel. We all carry a fragment or more. They're sharp and silver. I have pockets full of them. If I push my fingers in, the tips come out bloody.

If you wanted the whole story, the how-it-happened, you'd have to get us all together. The kids: Charlie, Wyatt, Rose, Queenie, the Dhillon boys and Meyer girls, me. Plus the mums: Mrs Turner, Mrs Dhillon, Aunty P, Madison and the dads. We'd all have a piece to share, and even with all of us, all of those pieces, it still might not make sense. Maybe one of us would look like a liar.

Perpetual
Triage and
Sensory
Disruption

My memories of that day include wearing a new swimsuit. It was printed with scales. Mum said, 'I was going to wait till Christmas,' but gave it to me anyway. It smelled of new lycra, all sweet and rubbery, with a big plastic sticker still in the crotch. I couldn't find my goggles and that made me hot and mad. Tamsin Turner's pool had little tiles all over the bottom in different kinds of blue. There were fancy snacks for the adults and fancy chips but the kids got packets of plain chips and Indigo Meyer said, 'Our mum doesn't let us eat this stuff,' but ate three packets anyway.

I remember my mum's scream went on and on like a siren and it hurt my ears and inside my chest as though my heart was ripping apart. And I raced across the pool with Charlie Turner but that must have been before. Surely I didn't get in the pool after Joe had sunk to the bottom like a heavy stone.

When we got taken to watch TV, Queenie and Rose sat on their mum's lap and I wanted my mum but she wasn't there. After that day she wasn't there for a long time. Sometimes her body was there but she wasn't. We were too old for *The Wiggles* but we watched it anyway.

The ambulance guy gave us stickers. I got more than everyone else.

Mr Lee – he was still just our teacher then – came late. He gave me a hug and it felt like he really meant it. His sadness was like a scent. Mrs Dhillon had her top on inside out and Dad yelled, 'Jesus Christ! Oh god! Jesus Christ! My son, oh dear god, my son! How?' Afterwards he was sobbing. Afterwards he was saying, 'He was with the mums. I left him with the mums.' The mums are supposed to be safe as houses but they weren't and everything that was black is white and everything that was white is black. If the grown-ups can't make sense of it – I've got no hope.

Then there's Joe in the coffin. Later. He looked like he was sleeping and I wished to touch him and wake him up but I was scared.

And before all of it – Joe and I had a fight in the car. He'd broken the toy I'd got inside a chocolate egg and I went off at him, *really* off at him, yelling and screaming and kicking my legs at the back of Dad's seat. 'It can be put back together,' Mum said and 'Quit it, Jem!' Dad roared. All I cared about was that tiny toy that fit in the palm of my hand and I hated him for busting it. I hated my brother with a blistering rage. With his sticky rabbit and sticky-up hair and big eyes. I hated him and wished him gone and then he was. This is the piece that cuts the deepest and hurts the longest – I wanted Joe gone and then he was.

Part 2

Archie feels like a do-over. I spoil this little brother like crazy and love him more than almost anything else.

He hates that there was a brother before him. He wants to know who I like best but I won't say. Instead, I tell him made-up stories with him as the hero and take him to the park and sometimes to the movies and sneak him sweets and one time a chocolate egg with a toy inside even though it snagged my heartstrings.

Archie likes bugs and Joe never liked bugs. Archie likes noise and splashing in the bathtub and making the floor wet; Joe was a quiet kid. Archie eats spicy food and throws himself down the slide at the playground so fast it makes my stomach hurt watching him; Joe was gentle and took his time with everything. Archie likes balls and trampolines and moon hoppers; Joe liked kaleidoscopes and rocks and those things that you look down and everything is in multiples, the way a fly sees the world.

It's weird to think that Archie is the age Joe was when he stopped being. Joe will always and forever be four years old. I'm the only one of the two of us that kept getting older.

Part 3

Like an insensitive prick, life goes on.

I met someone last month in writing club. Toni knows about Joe. She knows about PTSD.

Toni says things like:

'I read somewhere that it is no measure of sanity to be well adjusted to a demented society,' and 'The system is a goddamn fiasco,' and lately, 'I really really like you, Jemima King.'

I know I scare people off. People like me do that; tragedy marks us like we got hit with a rotten egg. People don't want to get too close in case the stink is catching. Maybe I seem crazy or weird or contagious to a lot of people but not to the ones who count. Though it's taken me some time, though it'll take me more time, maybe all the time I get, I'm no longer so crazy to myself. One day soon Archie won't beg me to play hide 'n' seek every time I go around to Dad and Madison's. He won't want to smash sticks into the earth or go as high as he can on the swings. Soon enough my little brother will be learning letters and reading stories for himself. He won't adore me like he does now. And I won't be able to protect him by dressing him in a red cape, the both of us pretending he's invincible and a costume can save him from bad things happening. That's the price for carrying on, for living.

Part 4

The other funny thing about getting branded with tragedy is that people treat you like you're fragile and might shatter if placed too directly in the sun, and people also treat you like you can handle anything. What is that about? Teachers pair me up with the refugee kids in class, the ones who whisper their secrets to me over *Jane Eyre* or a Bunsen burner. Adults tell me things they shouldn't as though Joe's death made me one of them. Broken people share broken things with other broken people. Other times I get a wide berth, a side eye, a sad turn-down of the mouth. *Poor Jemima.*

I am the storage unit for a lot of secrets that shouldn't be mine to store:
My mum drinks too much.
My dad did bad things with bad people.

Perhaps, from all our shattered and silver pieces we can make a kaleidoscope. Is that too cheesy to say? Maybe. Turn out our pockets, shake it up, and make a new picture. Perhaps I use too many metaphors. Perhaps Toni and I will kiss on a tram as it swings into Bourke Street and not give a shit about anyone or anything. Perhaps anything and everything.

Perhaps
The
Score
Is un**D**ecided.

PALOMA

Paloma clicks the meeting room door shut.
'I shouldn't be here,' Zita says, her face chalky.
Paloma had found a room she could hire by the hour in the centre of the city, part of a shared office space for freelancers.
She reaches towards Zita. 'It's okay, it's safe.' After a few moments, she says, 'Ready?'
Zita nods, her hands trembling. Paloma tips up the envelope and the thumb drive falls into her palm. She presses it into her laptop and selects play.

Voice 1: G'day Alex.
Voice 2: He's furious.
Voice 1: Sorry?
Voice 2: He's furious, you twit. Don't give me your spin, I watched you invent it.
Voice 1: Mate, I'm not telling anyone else what to do. It's just me. I'm tired of it all.
Voice 2: Well, he won't have it.

Voice 1: Why not?

Voice 2: Because you know too much and because he needs you, that's why.

Voice 1: What does he need me for? He's got everyone he needs in his pocket already. Porter, Tran, you know he does. Anyone not on the take he's got dirt on.

Voice 2: Is this about money, Baz? He's been generous.

Voice 1: I know. No, it's not about money.

Voice 2: We're all on good wickets here—

Voice 1: It's not about money.

Voice 2: What then? You growing a conscience or something?

Voice 1: Look, it's—

Voice 2: Because if Frank wasn't pulling strings then someone else would be pulling strings, you know that, right? And we'd be the dickheads making nothing out of it.

Voice 1: I've got a little kid, Turner. I can't be doing this forever.

Voice 2: Christ! Is this Baz King? *The* Baz King? When did you grow a vagina?

Voice 1: Fuck off.

Voice 2: You're having a moment, mate. Go do what you need to do. Put your dick in something. Go to Swan Street and buy a nice car.

Voice 1: I've got a nice car.

Voice 2: Buy yourself another one, I don't give a shit. But Frank doesn't like people leaving, you know that. It's upsetting. It worries him.

Voice 1: He doesn't need to worry.

Voice 2: You've been through it all with him, Baz. He trusts you. He doesn't trust everyone. You're important to him.

Voice 1: I appreciate that but—

Voice 2: The things you've made disappear . . . No one does spin like you do, Baz, and you know I hate making your big fat head even fatter than it already is. No one knows the people you do. You can make dead girls vanish.

Voice 1: Shit, Alex, that's not funny.

Voice 2: Where's your sense of humour? What's wrong with you? It was years ago. Frank didn't know the kid was there, did he?

Voice 1: But he made the place burn.

Voice 2: Old news, but yeah, so? What's happened to you?

Voice 1: I don't know. It's been a weird time.

Voice 2: Well, grow some goddamn balls, King. No one likes a sook.

Voice 1: So that's a no from Frank then, he won't be accepting the client termination.

Voice 2: Ha! No, he won't, you stand-up bloody comic. He'll be graciously pretending he never saw it, which is probably more than you deserve.

Voice 1: Right.

Voice 2: And you know what? We're lucky.

Voice 1: How do you figure that?

Voice 2: Because if Melbourne's going to have a Frank Agosti – and let's be honest, there's more than a handful of blokes who'd take his place in a heartbeat – then we're lucky we got this one. He's got good soldiers, Baz. He's a decent boss. Could have been a lot worse.

Voice 1: If you say so.

The audio file ends and Paloma looks over. Zita grips a golden chain around her neck with a small cross pendant, knuckles white. Her hand is quivering, her cheeks are flushed. Her gaze drills into Paloma's.

'Who did you get it from?'

'I'm sorry. Like I said – I can't say.'

'It's everything. All the corruption, the bullshit.'

Paloma nods.

Zita's fingers worry at the pendant at her throat, 'Is it enough? With everything else you've been sent.'

'I'd say so,' Paloma replies.

'Good.' Zita inhales deeply and sits straighter. Her eyes are hard and set. 'They need to rot in hell. The lot of them.'

THE FUNERAL

The air is cool and metallic-tasting, like a shiny coin. At the entrance to the church, Archie stands dressed in a small black suit with a white shirt and looks like a baby penguin. He scans the gathering crowd, eyes wide, until Jemima, in a fuchsia dress and black boots, swoops in and lifts him up in her arms.

The mothers greet one another.

'Hi Madison.'

'Birdie.'

It is a begrudging peace for the circumstances.

People stop by on their way in, paying their condolences to the two women and their children and kissing cheeks.

Paloma grabs Birdie's wrist gently when she greets her.

'Okay?' she asks her friend.

'Okay,' Birdie replies. She smiles at George by Paloma's side.

'We'll see you in there,' Paloma says softly, catching Jemima's eye.

•

Inside the church, a pianist is playing. Patti King occupies a pew at the very front, with Baz's sister, Rachel, sitting next to her. Patti is already weeping. When Madison and Birdie eventually walk in, flanked by Archie and Jem, Birdie slips into the row behind and Jem joins Patti, Madison, Archie and Rachel at the front. The coffin is covered in stylish white blossoms: fragrant lilies and roses and velvety flannel flowers.

Towards the back Paloma and George sit with Rose and Queenie and their nonna. Politicians and bureaucrats stream into the church alongside corporate clients, family friends, neighbours, cycling buddies and university mates. Paloma sees a deputy minister and lifts her hand in a subtle wave. George notices her other hand is shaking.

'Is this going to work?' she whispers.

George takes her hand and nods. 'Yes. It's going to work.'

Queenie points out Abigail Meyer and her daughters. 'They're sitting in the third row!' she says in an outraged whisper. A woman in the pew in front swivels around and eyeballs her to be quiet. Paloma spots Frank and Priscilla Agosti, Tamsin and Alex Turner nearby too. Frank is wearing tinted glasses and a crisp, brand-new shirt. Priscilla's hair is cut into a long bob that makes her look even younger than she is; Frank could be her father. Abigail Meyer leans towards Frank and whispers. He nods and smiles.

The priest at the front of the church clears his throat. He has large watery eyes and loose skin on his neck that wobbles when he speaks.

'Please stand,' he says eventually. 'Almighty God and Father, it is our certain faith that your son, who died on the cross, was raised from the dead . . .'

After the priest finishes his prayer there is a brief pause and the congregation replies together, 'Amen.'

When the priest pauses, Abigail turns to Tamsin. 'Where's Wyatt?' she asks. Camilla and Indigo sit near their mother. Their long shiny manes flow over the backs of their seats. Camilla is looking down at her phone.

'Surfing,' Tamsin replies.

'Oh, a shame,' Abigail says. 'And Charlie?'

Two hours before the funeral, Charlie told Tamsin that St Brigid's was a 'hostile environment' and that they wanted to switch to Victorian College of the Arts. Tamsin replied that Victorian College of the Arts is for dropouts and acrobats. Charlie had refused to get in the car with her after that.

'Headache,' Tamsin lies.

Abigail's seagull eyes slide over to Alex, who's already crying. He's got the tissues from Tamsin's handbag. Tamsin finds his snivelling shocking and unattractive; she hadn't expected it from him. But Abigail seems to light up. 'I didn't realise they were *so close*,' she says admiringly.

'Oh,' Tamsin says. 'Yeah. Really close. They spent a lot of time together.'

Abigail pats Tamsin's hand. 'We should catch up soon. Frank was talking about a day out on his boat. You'd come, wouldn't you?'

Tamsin nods.

'Priss gets seasick,' Abigail says, nodding towards her sister-in-law and rolling her eyes.

'I'm fine on boats,' Tamsin says quickly. She grips her husband's knee, feeling a rare surge of love for him and his sudden, pathetic tears.

Towards the end of the service, Jem recites a poem – 'In Blackwater Woods' by Mary Oliver. Rachel does a reading from Corinthians and Patti wails, leaning on Madison. Archie walks to the front to place one of his paintings from day care on the coffin. Any dry eyes left in the church are quickly filled with tears.

JEMIMA

After the service, the pallbearers – cousins and uncles mostly – with Archie and Jem walking out in front, carry their dad's coffin outside and slide it into the hearse.

Beside the hearse, Jemima listens to people make small talk about the weather and say, 'I haven't seen you for so long!' and 'He was a character wasn't he?' They make promises about catching up that they will not keep.

All the fakery makes Jem feel bleak. Any composure she had at the beginning of the day had unspooled when she read 'In Blackwater Woods'. Her dad would have liked her to read Banjo Paterson – he used to quote him a lot, but he'd had his time in charge. Jem found the poem online one night, along with bios of Mary Oliver and her partner, Molly. She'd stared at the black and white photograph of them sitting by the door to their house in Massachusetts. A house with wooden shingles and a doorframe painted white but worn and peeling. She knows it must be near the ocean, can practically feel it in her veins and smell the salt. She daydreams about it – swapping Mary and Molly for her and Toni, imagines them naked in the early summer mornings, rushing out to the water. She wants to run far, far away from all the so-called 'grown-ups' who are more messed up than anyone her age that she knows of. Grown-ups who lie by omission or sleep with the exes they hate or can't love properly. Who don't say goodbye properly.

An arm slides around her waist. It's Toni.

'Hey.'

'Hey,' Jemima replies, leaning into her. The hearse starts to move off. The crawling speed would have driven her dad to despair, Jem thinks, as Toni plants a light kiss in her hair.

For a moment Jemima thinks she might be imagining the police cars turning up. Four or five slide almost silently towards the church, lights on but no sirens. Paloma is suddenly close by.

'Aunty P?' she hears herself say, voice clotted with fear.

There are cops in uniform and cops in suits wearing bulletproof vests. One of them lifts his chin to someone and Jemima follows his gaze. It's George, standing close to her mother. Cops are striding up to Alex Turner and Frank Agosti. Alex's face blotchy and crumpled. Tamsin is silent and immobile, and instead of turning to her, Alex turns to Frank Agosti with a look like love.

She hears Toni murmur her name and feels her drawing her closer as police arrest another older man, who's yelling and swearing. They're putting Alex and Frank in handcuffs as Jemima is conscious of the fabric of Paloma's dress brushing against her arm, the warmth of her skin close by. Camilla and Indigo Meyer seem to be filming the whole thing on their phones while their mother is wailing, 'What the hell do you think you're doing? Do you know who he is?' Tamsin watches her husband disappear into the cop car like it's a bad dream she'll wake up from.

'It's okay,' Jemima hears Paloma murmuring, 'you're okay, Jem.'

'I'm scared.'

Paloma nods. 'You did the right thing.'

Jemima watches Madison, arms full of Archie and face full of contempt, lean forward and spit on the shoes of Frank Agosti as the cops manoeuvre him into a car.

JESS AND RICHARD

Jess holds Lizzie's hand in the waiting room at Kyneton Health. Lizzie is shaking. 'She was mucking around trying to do backflips!'

'It's okay,' Jess soothes, to no effect.

'I shouldn't have let her.'

'It's not your fault.'

The radiologist steps into the waiting room. 'Jasmin's mum?'

Lizzie springs to her feet.

'I've transferred Jasmin back to the doctor. You can go join her if you like. Jane will give you more information but it does look like a break, I'm afraid.'

Lizzie whimpers as Jess rubs her back. Even the radiologist joins in from the other side, both of them rubbing poor Lizzie's back as she weeps.

'Don't blame yourself,' the radiologist tells Lizzie briskly. 'These things happen. And they can be fixed!' The three of them lumber slowly towards the clinical rooms. 'You can have a big cry about it later tonight, okay? Have a big glass of wine and let it all out.'

Lizzie sobs and nods.

The radiologist points. 'She's just down there, third room.'

'Thank you,' Lizzie whispers, giving Jess a quick hug before turning to walk down the corridor.

'First time is the worst,' the radiologist says.

'Sure is.'

'When I saw you here I thought it must be one of your boys.'

'Not this time,' Jess replies.

She returns to the waiting room with its tables covered in old magazines and boxes of kids' toys. Jess takes the seat that offers a sliver of a view down the hallway so she can hear or see Lizzie if she needs her.

Richard drops into the seat beside her. 'Hey. How's it going?'

'Good. She's broken her arm by the sounds of it. Remember Amy?'

'The radiologist?'

'Says she's probably snapped it.'

Richard flinches. 'Poor Jasmin.'

'Poor Lizzie.'

'Did you tell her?' Richard asks.

'About the baby?' Jess is amused. 'Didn't really seem like the right time.'

'Do you think she'll be surprised? That we're keeping it?'

'It? *Her*,' Jess corrects him.

'Her,' Richard repeats, mesmerised. 'I keep forgetting.' He looks around the clinic. 'Been a while since we were here with a broken kiddo.'

'I was thinking that too. Didn't want to jinx it by saying it out loud. When was the last time?'

'Harry, maybe? When he slammed his finger in the door?'

Jess thinks about it.

'Or Monty?' suggests Richard. 'With the twisted . . .?'

He points towards his crotch and Jess claps a hand over her face. 'I think I blanked that out momentarily.'

'Really?' replies Richard. 'Even with Jack constantly repeating the words "testicular torsion" for the last two years?'

Jess laughs. It was awful at the time; Monty had required urgent surgery. Jack had needled him mercilessly and Jess learned more words for scrotum than she ever cared to know.

'What a dreadful mother,' Richard teases, 'laughing about your son's nuts.'

Jess gathers herself. 'Is it the kind of thing you expected, going into parenthood?'

'What? When we looked at the ultrasound scans and saw their perfect little lips and perfect little noses?' Richard sighs. 'Ah, no. Testicular torsion was not on my mind at the time.'

Jess leans against him. 'Perfect little lips and perfect little noses.'

'You know,' Richard takes Jess's hand in his, 'I've been thinking about work and wondering if it might be time for a change.'

'Get out of building?'

'Maybe.'

'The business is doing well. You've just hired Brooke . . .'

'Yeah, but—'

Jess lifts her head from his shoulder. 'I've been wondering if it's time we tried somewhere else altogether.'

'We've been here more than nine years,' Richard ponders.

'The kids could do with being in a bigger school with more sports or having more schools to choose from . . .'

'Bendigo?' Richard offers.

'Gold Coast?' Jess counters.

'Oh wow.' Richard laughs. 'I don't hate that idea.'

Only one of them remembers that it's Baz King's funeral today. Jess places her palm on her stomach, imagining the baby, currently the size of a pear. She is soft-spined, covered in fine hair and developing hearing. She is a salvation. She is a secret.

Her and Baz had scrambled away from the cafe to the hotel, one of the ones that Frank Agosti built and owned. They knew

Baz there; there was a room ready they could have. Jess wanted to tear off his shirt in the foyer, wanted to press him down on the huge velvet ottoman, leave the marks of the upholstery buttons against his bare skin.

Jess remembers the orgasm that left her breathless against the thick expensive hotel sheets she had squeezed between her fingers, her other hand pressing Baz against her, into her. The way the spring sunlight was pouring in because they hadn't bothered to close the curtains – they hadn't had time between getting into the room and getting into the bed. Baz's face, older now, more worn, but still so full of life and roguishness, almost unconquerable. Jess loved watching it succumb to her and succumb to the climax, a brief moment of owning him. A brief moment of being someone other than herself – Jess Dhillon, mum of boys, making ends meet.

'Don't get hung up on me,' Baz had told her afterwards, teasingly, sweat making a trail down his back. As though she hadn't been hung up on him for years. Close to a decade.

'Of course not,' she'd lied with as much nonchalance as she could muster.

Jess squeezes Richard's hand as a nurse walks by in scrubs, giving the couple a smile.

Sweet Richard.

Imperfectly, she loves him. She will never tell him about that afternoon or the possibility that their daughter – pear-perfect and beloved – may not be his.

BAZ

It's hard to know where to begin with my final story.

Perhaps it starts with Fred Sherman, who I met at the bar of the Auburn Hotel. Funny-looking guy – old but with lively eyes and sporting a loose blue linen shirt, the kind you expect on an architect or designer working in the city. It was clear Fred's wife wore the pants in their relationship; he spoke about Roma reverentially, as though she might walk in any minute and clip him around the ear.

Fred was the kind of person who made talking easy. He bought rounds of beer without hesitation and his eyes lit up whenever we stumbled across a connection. I liked him. He talked about his painting and his admiration for 'up and comers' like Vincent Namatjira. He told me about his dog, Lenny, and his daughters – it made him a bit weepy just thinking about them. I told him about Jem and Archie in return, but not Joe. I often left Joe out. It made things a bit simpler – I'm not saying I'm proud of that.

'Maybe one day you'll meet my Lenny,' Fred said. 'He's a fine dog. Though he's getting older now ... aren't we all? The years drop off him when I take him out to the country.'

I'd never heard of Whroo. Fred was besotted and poetic about the big chunk of dirt he'd bought despite his wife's misgivings. He was going to build a series of cabins the entire family could stay in, he explained. He would put a kiln up there and a studio, of course, maybe even do some teaching or host retreats. He had big plans. He got dreamy talking about that place. I couldn't have interrupted if I tried.

'And the land,' he said breathlessly, 'the land is something else.'

Fred described the shrubs and hunks of white rock, the birds that erupted out of treetops and the roos that watched warily from a distance. He spoke of the bark peeling from the gums like us, back in the day, when sunburn was allowed, he said. Fred made it sound like one of those old Banjo Paterson poems, the only poetry my father kept in our house. The kind of poems that made boys like me – white bread and city-bred – think that Australia was all ours.

Fred chatted on, he was that kind. He said there was a ravine on his property that Lenny liked to get lost in. Gave him a near heart attack every time the dog went in there, wondering if he'd fallen, wondering if he'd been bitten by a snake. But each time, Lenny reappeared and Fred would be jubilant and the world (and his heart) would be put to rights. I spotted his obituary a couple of years later; a tiny notice, like he'd made no real impression on the world. Father to Serafin and Katherine, husband to Roma – like he was an add-on. But Fred's time with me stuck. Especially later, when Kev told me what was going on inside my body.

He's a good doctor, Kev, but he didn't want to tell me. He was nervous. Which made me nervous. He talked about my clumsiness and twitching; the scrawling handwriting. He talked through the MRI and the reflex testing the neurologist had done with me; we both knew he was beating around the bush. When he listed some websites for me to look up, I asked, 'Is this what that Essendon player has?'

Kev's face said it all. I thought I might have to chunder in the little plastic bin beneath his desk.

I couldn't be that person. Trapped in bed, struggling to speak or feed myself. Madison having to look after me, having to wipe my hairy arsehole. My bike rusting in the garage. Archie growing up with a dad who couldn't toss a ball or blow up a balloon. Not making it to Jem's wedding day. Shrivelling away like an indoor plant in the corner of some room. I don't have the stomach for all that. Kev blathered on about Riluzole and Copper-ATSM, something new that had worked a treat on mice, and I laughed. The whole thing was so ridiculous. And bloody terrible.

Braver men, like Neale Daniher, deal with their diagnoses like raging bulls. They set up foundations and raise funds and have photos taken for newspapers and magazines. I would not be doing any of that.

No one, not even God, would get to write my ending.

And if anyone else wanted to kill me, they wouldn't get the chance.

I told Kev to hold off writing up our consultation until a week later, I'd come in and he could make his notes then, it would give me time to beef up the life insurance. I called Paul Mulqueen that afternoon and got the insurances in order so Madison and Archie and Jem would be more than sorted without me. I'm a strategist at heart; there was part of me invigorated by it all. It's amazing how quickly you can wrap up a life.

A few days later, I thought of Fred Sherman when I picked up Dad's Banjo Paterson book with its crumbling dust jacket and the smell of Dad — decay, Paco Rabanne and fury — still in its pages.

I gave away a few things that wouldn't cause alarm — a bike helmet, some books with my name written in the front posing as a loan, the landscape painting of Dad's that Rachel had always wanted, which I had never hung. I told her it didn't match our decor, which had always been true but I'd been a prick and kept it for years anyway. I slipped the Banjo Paterson book into Birdie's bag when she wasn't looking. I tried to be more patient with my mother. I wiped my computer clean as a whistle. I played with Archie but only when Madison went out, which wasn't often, in case she got suspicious. Some things happened that weren't planned — like sleeping with Birdie. And Jess. The body wants what the body wants. Even if it's a ticking time bomb.

I realised I had to be really careful if I wanted the things I'd arranged with Paul to hold. Pull my head in a bit. I thought I was going to lose it when I pushed the handprint and footprint cufflinks that Birdie had given me into Jem's top desk drawer, but I had to leave her something. I would miss her most of all.

•

On those days of getting things in order and the nights when I couldn't sleep, I found myself getting up out of bed and looking at that photo of Quinta Fernando online. She looked nothing like Jem but there she was, like my daughter, on the cusp of things – adulthood, career, love – smiling out through the camera with hope shining in her eyes. Frank hadn't meant for anyone to get hurt but Frank never means for anyone to get hurt, at least he didn't in the early days. That's the trouble with pushing at the parameters of your morals. A few little transgressions and they're like Swiss cheese, full of holes.

Things had got worse with Frank Agosti over the years. And Alex Turner. The two of them fed off one another like a couple of frat boys with a hunger for money, women and power. They had no trouble finding men to join their fraternity either – Judge Nigel Porter made proposals or dissents slide easily through the courts, Police Chief Tran vanished witness reports and complaints, and various hopefuls in state governments and councils lubricated Agosti's plans. The formula was simple – woo folks with power and possibility and keep them in line with their own secrets. The trick was controlling the whole web – it's difficult for a person to be corrupt all on their own. But manage to hold all the threads and you're laughing.

Quinta's face swam up at me in my feverish dreams. Her smile just below the surface of the water, water bubbling, popping and steaming. Her boyfriend, Benji, had been silenced and soon after, he had silenced himself. Early days, Frank talked of breaking a few eggs with a respectable amount of regret in his voice, now he makes any losses sound borderline noble. He calls the men who drive his slick black cars soldiers, calls Turner his lieutenant; makes it seem like a holy army. He's convinced them all that someone else would fill the void if it weren't him in it, and doesn't he do a good job, all things considered? Doesn't he look after his people?

The lot of them would have had me killed if the chance had been there. I took that pleasure away.

•

The worst part of filling those envelopes with the evidence Paloma would need to get the whole thing to come crashing down, was knowing that Jem would be reading and listening. My daughter would be able to see who I've been and what I've done. She's not stupid, that's how I could trust her to execute it. But because she's not stupid, she was always going to connect the dots.

It was a price I was willing to pay.

Jem will save Archie and Archie will save Jem – a pattern that will last them a lifetime.

Madison will find her way, as she always does, with Archie to love and help to become a better man than I ever was.

Birdie will have her heart full, finally, with someone who can love her properly.

And I will take my secrets and regrets with me.

Some mistakes can't be remedied. I can't fix or tidy everything; I've made peace with that. I made the choices I made, I've lived the life I was given.

When it came time for it, I pushed Jess's photo of my son into my pocket, wishing and praying I would see him next, despite it all.

I got to write my own ending and this is the one I chose. I don't care what you think of me.

I went out on wings of love.

BIRDIE

Albert finds Birdie in the front garden of Baz's sister's house. She's crouched behind a bottlebrush, heels stabbed into the dry ground. She's so startled by him that she swears and almost topples over. Albert holds out his hand for her cigarette.

'But you don't smoke.'

'Neither do you,' Albert replies.

Birdie passes him the cigarette, stands and brushes grass off her black silk dupion dress. Albert is wearing a new cobalt suit. He takes a drag of the cigarette and coughs.

'It's from one of Baz's cousins,' Birdie explains. 'God knows where he got it from – Indonesia maybe? He spends a lot of time there.'

Albert passes it back to her and nods at Rachel's house. 'How come you're not inside?'

'Too many Kings.'

Albert nods, understanding.

'Were you at the funeral?' Birdie asks. 'How come I didn't see you?'

'I was at the back.'

'Making room for the Meyers and Turners in the front?'

The corners of his mouth twitch. 'I did see them up there.'

'And the drama?'

Albert shrugs. 'Made me wish I'd brought popcorn.'

Birdie says, 'Baz would have been pleased. I don't understand it all but Paloma says she's going to explain. I'm not sure I want to know.' She hesitates. 'But maybe that's been my problem. Wanting to look the other way.'

'I'd guess it's been going on for a while.'

Birdie nods. 'You're probably right. And Baz will have been involved. Going out with a bang and front-page news, no doubt. He'd be thrilled.'

Jem comes to the front doorway of the house, her gaze moving from Albert to her mother and back again. 'Oh hey.'

Albert lifts his hand. 'I was coming inside to find you.'

'I wouldn't,' Jem replies. 'It's hell in there. I've never seen so many sensible flats or strings of pearls.'

'Sounds like my target audience,' he replies. 'The oldies love me.'

Jem plays with the silver ornaments on her wrist, tied on with a bit of pink ribbon. 'Each to their own. It's a hot frenzy inside. They're talking about the arrests. And pretending not to be talking about the arrests.'

'Are you okay, love?' Birdie asks.

'Yeah,' her daughter replies, seeming to chew it over. 'Yeah, I am.'

Birdie tips her head. 'What are those?' she asks, pointing to her daughter's wrist.

'I found them in my desk,' she explains.

'Are they your dad's cufflinks?'

'They are.' Jem looks at her mother meaningfully. 'Hey, Madison and Archie have left. Madison's brother is at their place – he's staying with them. So, I'm going to go soon with Toni. Back to her place,' she says. 'Is that okay?'

Birdie hesitates before nodding.

'Thanks, Mum.'

Birdie and Albert watch as Jem goes back inside.

'Baz loved those cufflinks,' Birdie says softly to Albert. 'I asked if I could give them to Jem a few years ago and he said no. It was the only present I ever gave him that he seemed to like or care about.'

Albert says, 'Not entirely true. You gave him those kids.'

Birdie tries not to cry. She looks away and stubs out the cigarette.

'Jem did a wonderful job with that poem,' Albert says.

'She did.'

'How do you really feel about her going home with Toni?'

Birdie sighs. 'Deeply hurt and desperate to be drunk.'

Albert laughs. Birdie crosses her arms to stop herself reaching out for him.

Albert pushes at the ground with the tip of his shiny shoe. He gently unfolds Birdie's arms and takes her hands in his. She's been cultivating numbness for so long that the sudden hope catches in her throat. 'Are you sure about us, Birdie?'

She knows that she wants to wake up to Albert every morning, his soft back and long feet, his kind face.

'Yes, I'm sure.'

'Okay then,' he says simply. 'Let's try.'

There is a warm breeze on their skin. The rumbling of small talk and gossip from inside the house barely reaches them as cicadas start up a steady chorus. Albert squeezes her hands and Birdie leans in, her forehead against his. She knows the risks of loving someone. The possibility of disappointment or disaster. The potential hurt and terror and urge to run, screaming, in the opposite direction. How easily love can be lost. Birdie chooses it anyway. When Albert kisses her, Birdie knows she is exactly where she is meant to be.

ACKNOWLEDGEMENTS

This book took a lot of corralling and cheerleading and I am so grateful for the crew of professionals, friends and family who helped do exactly that.

Huge thanks to the Ultimo Press champions who have been exceptional with their skills, flexibility, commitment and kindness, especially Brigid Mullane, Dianne Blacklock, Alisa Ahmed, Zoë Victoria and Andrea Johnson. Thanks too for the expertise and generous support of Thomas Coyle of Forensic Insight, Brianne Collins, Andrea McBeth, Sam Holford and Flynn Fletcher-Dobson. Importantly, this book wouldn't be in your hands now without the support of Alex Craig. Alex, thank you so much for your belief and guidance over the years.

A creative endeavour takes a village and mine is spread out across the globe. So much love and gratitude to those near and far including: Sarah Newman, Caroline Chapman-Smith, Monique Doy, Evie Kemp, Michelle Sokolich, Lucie Sayer, Thomas Swain, Brad Coles, Julia Batchelor-Smith, Katie Pocock, Celine Baber and Paul and Faith Town.

Book clubs are underrated sources of joy, stimulation and mind-broadening. Thank you to mine – Lou Powles, Anita Stewart,

Dani Gardiner, Greta Bertenshaw, Helen Oliver, Jane Christie, Jemma Glancy, Marcella Durban-Burgess, Ange Frazerhurst and, again, Julia Batchelor-Smith – who are particularly topnotch.

Who doesn't need a dazzlement of mermaids? I'd be lost without mine. Soul sisters, aquatic coven and for-life loves, thank you so much Tina Gibbes, Beth Beard, Ruth Johnson, Lisa Edreira Nicholas, Joelle Faulke and Anna Van Paddenberg for keeping this girl afloat in rocky seas.

Some people get lucky with the family they are born into or the family they make and I got extraordinarily fortunate with both. To Mum, Dad, Greg, Kendall, Matt, Wren, Noa and Bonnie – you are the best of the best. Thank you for always encouraging me, especially during some long, tough years.

Finally, this book is dedicated to my dear friend Liz Ireland. We have known each other since we were fourteen and have shared a lot of joy and heartache. We live on different sides of the planet but keep one another's secrets and have one another's backs. We want the best for one another and our sister-friendship is so precious to me. Thank you for everything, Lizzie, I love you.

Hannah Tunnicliffe is the author of several books for kids and adults including *The Colour of Tea, Season of Salt and Honey, A French Wedding* and the trilingual picture book *Marjory and the Mouse*. She is the co-creator of the Detective Stanley series published by Flying Eye Books. Her work has featured in the *New York Times Book Review* and she is the founder and host of the body acceptance podcast *Bod Almighty*. She is an eating disorder survivor, career and volunteer youth counsellor and holds a degree in social sciences and psychology.